The Pink Hotel

Anna Stothard

ALMA BOOKS

ALMA BOOKS LTD
London House
243-253 Lower Mortlake Road
Richmond
Surrey TW9 2LL
United Kingdom
www.almabooks.com

FT
Pbk

The Pink Hotel first published by Alma Books Ltd in 2011

© Anna Stothard, 2011

Cover design: Rose Cooper

Printedand bound in the UK by CPI Mackays, Chatham ME5 8TD

ISBN: 978-1-84688-131-2

To Sally

The Pink Hotel

1

Her bedroom reeked of cigarette ash and stale perfume. Two ashtrays were packed with lipstick-stained filters as if she'd just popped out for another pack. A suspender belt hung from a chest of drawers, a mink scarf was curled like roadkill at the floor next to her bed. A mirror opposite the bed reflected an image of me lying fully clothed and out of place on the crinkled sheets. My haircut and body could have been that of a boy, but my oversized eyes made me look like a Gothic Virgin Mary from a museum postcard. I wore a sweat-stained T-shirt and a pair of navy-blue tracksuit bottoms. My skin still smelt faintly of grease and coffee from Dad's café in London, but now the smell was mingled with dehydrated aeroplane air and smog from Los Angeles traffic.

Lily stared out at me from framed photographs around the room. In one photograph she was standing beside a motorcycle wearing a leather jacket. In another she was wearing a white T-shirt over a bikini and sitting cross-legged under a tree in the sunshine, laughing for the camera. In a third she was naked apart from vivid red lipstick and a floppy sunhat. Her skin in that last image was albino-white, as mine is, and also marked with four dark circles – heavy eyes and dark nipples. Her hair is black in the photograph, though, while mine is naturally blonde.

I got up from her bed and picked up a bottle of whiskey from a dresser near the door. There were no glasses, so I took a sip from the bottle and padded past her bed towards the bathroom. A pair of frilly knickers lay next to the toilet, and I tried not to let them touch my bare toes as I crouched to pee. Her bedroom was at the very top of a pink hotel in Venice Beach, Los Angeles. There'd been a funeral earlier in the day, but I hadn't made it to the crematorium. By the time I arrived in Venice Beach, Lily's wake had become a drunken vigil with over two hundred people dancing and talking and snorting and drinking all over the hotel. Nobody knew who I was, so I pulled my grubby baseball cap over my eyes and walked through the corridors as a child would walk through a cocktail party. I saw long fingernails and wet mouths; dilated eyes, bony shoulders and flashes of impossibly white teeth. I took a beer from an ice-packed bathtub and wandered uncomfortably around all five floors, examining people: an unshaven giant swigged vodka from a bottle and a skeletal middle-aged woman danced with her eyes closed in the middle of the room. There was a man with red hair who wore pointy snakeskin shoes and a half-open white shirt. People hovered around him and his freckled hands clenched into fists as he moved from guest to guest.

"I can't believe it," said a woman to the red-haired man.

"I keep thinking that she's just late," he replied, squeezing his freckled fists.

"Oh, sweetie," said the woman, "she was always late, wasn't she? She would have been late for her funeral."

"She was late for our wedding," the red-haired man continued. "Said she couldn't find matching underwear." A smile forced itself up through his frown, and others in the crowd laughed sadly. The red-haired man had a nasal twang like Bugs Bunny, which I guessed was a New York accent.

"You were a great team here," someone said to him.

I watched the sweaty red-haired man for a few moments longer. When he turned away from me I couldn't hear his conversation any more, so I continued through the carnival of mourners, eventually finding my way up towards the top of the hotel and a door marked "Private". Through the keyhole I could see a bicycle and a pair of Rollerblades. I expected this private door to be locked, but something was stuck, and it opened with a yawning creak onto the bare wooden floorboards of a cramped corridor that smelt of air freshener and closed windows. It was a relief when the door behind me clicked closed and muffled the sounds from downstairs. There was a dusty naked light bulb hanging from the ceiling above my head and sand in the cracks between the floorboards at my feet. The walls of the hallway were poached-salmon pink, much paler than the bright stucco façade of the beachside hotel. Through a door frame to my left the kitchen contained only a blue Formica table and two wooden chairs with padded seats. Dirty glasses and burnt-out scented candles cluttered the table, and unwashed dishes filled the sink. Doors were open on either side of the corridor – a living room with a flat-screen TV, a toilet, a small study with a desk covered in papers. The only door that wasn't open was the one at the end.

If it's possible to feel nostalgia for things you've never known, then it was a mixture of nostalgia and curiosity that made me lie down on her sheets and run a bath in a tub scattered with millimetre-long armpit hairs caught on a tide line of scum from the last time she or her husband took a bath. The party reverberated underneath, and I locked the bathroom door to take off my clothes as she must have done a million times, although she was likely more elegant about it. She wouldn't have nearly tripped as her ankles caught in the elastic of her sports trousers, and the various cuts and scrapes on her body probably didn't burn as they accepted the hot water. Her scabs didn't fray and dissolve in the heat as mine did. Her skin was probably flawless. I scooped bath water into my mouth and let it spill slowly down my bottom lip. Sitting on my haunches with my torso crouched over my knees and my nose just above the bubbles, all I could smell was steam. A moth watched from the window ledge above the tub, steaming her wings. Outside the window there was a bright-blue sky and palm trees. I flicked water at my mothy audience, and she scattered up towards the light bulb above the mirror.

I wondered what Dad was doing at that moment, and imagined him sitting at our greasy kitchen table biting his nails while his wife Daphne paced the room. Daphne would be trying not to shout about the stolen credit card, but every so often her voice would reach an almost inhuman pitch and then get cut off by its own aggression. Her bony fingers would be working their way repetitively through her mousy hair, while her shoes squeaked against the plastic tiles on our kitchen floor. Dad would be still and lost in thought, pretending to listen to Daphne repeat the same angry sentiments in slightly different ways until she was hoarse. Except this scene would have happened hours ago. It was midnight in Lily's bedroom, so it would be tomorrow in my flat at home. They would be encased in the morning hush after a night of screaming, putting on clothes and pouring water on instant coffee and unlocking the café. Daphne's lips would be pursed together, because she doesn't like working Saturdays, and Dad would be slamming things against metal surfaces.

Dad looked nothing like the red-haired man from downstairs. While the red-haired man had seemed to glide around the hotel lobby, serpentine as his shoes, Dad only moved if he had to. The red-haired man had gaunt cheeks and laughter lines. Dad had paunchy pink cheeks and deep frown lines.

I blinked away the image of Dad from my mind and sunk slightly deeper into the bathwater. I was just about to light one of Lily's cigarettes – kept in a jewelled box of razors and bath salts next to the bath – when a creak sounded in the corridor outside the bedroom. The bathroom was blurry with steam, and I only just managed to scramble out of the bath water to open the window above the toilet before the creak made its way into Lily's bedroom. The steam dissipated. I nearly slipped on the white tiles, tugged my tracksuit bottoms over wet legs, held my breath and then slowly descended to a crouch in front of the bathroom keyhole. I squinted and peered through it.

An extremely tall man was sitting on the end of Lily's bed, bang in front of the keyhole with his head in his hands. I'd noticed him earlier drinking from a bottle of vodka in the corner of the lobby downstairs, and had thought that he looked like something from a fairy tale about giants or ogres. He was in his mid-thirties and wearing a stripy shirt, a tattered black jumper and a pair of blue tailored trousers with holes like full stops and commas on his thighs. His black hair was only slightly longer than the stubble on his face, and he had a pair of stupid gold-rimmed sunglasses resting on his head. His trousers might have been expensive, but they were frayed at the hem as if he were dressed half in designer castoffs and half in items he bought on eBay when he was drunk. He sat still on Lily's bed, his shoulders slumped.

After a moment, the Giant looked around Lily's room and picked up a photograph from the bedside table. It was the one of Lily sitting cross-legged under a tree and laughing. The Giant fumbled trying to get the picture out of the frame with his big hands. He nicked his thumb and put the tip of it in his mouth like a child. I was glad the man was stealing the picture of Lily laughing in a big white T-shirt, not the one next to it, where she was naked. He eased the photograph out from under the glass and, just as he slipped it into his pocket, there was another noise from the hallway outside Lily's bedroom. For a moment the Giant seemed to consider making a jump for the bathroom. His green eyes flicked towards me and he put his hands on his knees as if about to haul his drunken body to a standing position. I held my breath and waited to be discovered inexcusably topless and sopping wet in a dead woman's bathroom, but the Giant's body was slow with alcohol and, before he got off the bed, Lily's bedroom door opened.

"What the fuck?" slurred the Bugs Bunny voice of the red-haired man. I couldn't see him through the keyhole, but could hear his heavy breathing.

"I'm sorry," said the Giant, who got off the bed and stepped towards the red-haired man, out of the keyhole's vision. There was a shuffle, and the muffled sound of skin hitting skin. The red-haired man swore, and the Giant made a noise that could have been a groan or the exertion of a punch. I couldn't see exactly what was going on, but the Giant stumbled backwards and nearly fell. Skin hit skin again, and then it was the red-haired man who collapsed onto Lily's bed. Everything paused, except the moth at the bathroom ceiling. The red-haired man didn't move from his horizontal position, but his blood-shot eyes were open, staring dumbly up at the Giant.

"Get the fuck out of here," slurred the red-haired man. He turned his cheek to the side on Lily's pillow.

"I'm so sorry," said the Giant.

"Then just fuck off out of my apartment. There's nothing here any more. You can all just fuck off."

"I'm so sorry," repeated the Giant. "I'm so sorry."

2

The red-haired man lay unconscious on the bed. He stirred briefly when I put a blanket over his body, but he didn't open his eyes or speak. There were granules of white powder tangled in his nose hair, and his skin was tacky like fresh paint. He had clearly dressed with precision earlier in the day. His snakeskin shoes were both tied in a careful bow, and his socks were the same colour as his suede belt. But now there was vomit on the trousers and his skin smelt of beer.

I quietly picked up a sequined dress from the floor of Lily's bedroom. I held it against my body, but it looked silly. I was nearly eighteen years old, and hadn't grown into dresses yet. They didn't suit me. I dropped the dress to the floor and put a man's bowler hat on my head. There was a messy jungle of silk, leather, cashmere and cotton on the floor along with a few man's shirts crumpled in puddles, a few ties and loafers and big trainers amongst the overpowering femininity. The wardrobe rail had fallen down while the men fought, so the room looked even more chaotic than before. Some patent red stilettos caught my eye, and a pair of grey ballet pumps. I picked up the mink scarf from the floor and wrapped it around my neck. It felt heavy and dead. At home in London I had a white melamine chest of drawers full of tracksuits, oversized jumpers and screwed-up T-shirts acquired from school lost-property boxes or locker rooms over the years. The drawers were decorated with the faded remains of red Arsenal football stickers, and on top were three football trophies and one swimming trophy. I'd been proud of these trophies at some point, but eventually they merged into the dark magenta of my bedroom walls.

Nothing in my flat at home was soft to touch. Dad liked to make use of "found" things, so all the bedspreads in the house were made of that faux-quilted polyester, stolen from bed-and-breakfasts over the years. Not that we went on holiday very much, but when we did we never went back to the same place twice. My bedspread was patterned with a faded bouquet in watery pastel colours, while Daphne and Dad had a mud-coloured bramble pattern. We still had two nice bath towels from the Hilton in Brighton, where Daphne and Dad spent their honeymoon, and five thin green towels from the gym where Daphne used to work as a receptionist. We didn't have too many problems with money, but still nothing made Dad happier than free stuff. One day Dad came home with a small city of discarded paint cans from outside the DIY store at the end of our road. They were colours that had been mixed wrong. Dad insisted that we spend my half-term holiday painting a rainbow of rejected colours onto the faded white walls. The "Canary Yellow" of our bathroom walls looked green in sunlight, the "Rum Caramel" of our kitchen cabinets was a watery-coloured varnish, the "Palace Velvet" of my bedroom walls was more swampy than palatial, and the "Ruby Fountain" of our living room was the colour of scabbed knees. He also insisted that we revarnish the living-room floor, even though the stolen varnish was granular with fat clumps of sand made to stop people slipping on factory floors.

I glanced at the red-haired man snoring now on his bed. A photo of his wedding day sat on the bedside table next to a glossy paperback novel. It was difficult to tell how old Lily was

11

in the wedding picture, but she was wearing a simple white dress with a veil covering big brown eyes. The red-haired man looked much more handsome in the photograph than he did lying on the bed. In the wedding photo he stood behind his new wife with a look of amused, baffled devotion, like he couldn't believe his luck. I noticed the actual wedding dress was in a dry-cleaner's zipped plastic bag curled on the wardrobe floor, where it had slid off the rail during the fight between the Giant and the Red-Head.

I owned just one photograph of Lily before she left us, which I found in Dad's desk drawer next to some spilt ink, old electricity bills and an ecosystem of dust. She left when she was seventeen, three years after I was born. In the picture she and Dad are sitting in a photo booth with me – three years old – in their laps. Dad has acne and Lily has pink hair. She was always dyeing it different colours. Dad is looking at Lily, who is already looking away from both of us up into the middle distance. I'm the only one who is looking at the camera. She must have left a few months after the photograph was taken. She looks as if she's already fading from the Tube-station photograph booth, like she's turning into a fairy child or a poltergeist as the camera flashes. I couldn't imagine her in the café, or helping me with my homework. She was always just an undefined thought in my head, or a shape that seemed sometimes about to appear in my peripheral vision and never did. Nobody heard a word from her after she left. We didn't even know she moved to America. The first time she ever felt remotely real to me was when I found out that she was dead, because at least that was physical. It wasn't the half-remembered smell of her or a story about how she stole money from Grandma's purse, or how she and Dad went on their first date to an aquarium. It was fact. She died. She was thirty-two. The accident happened on a road called Laguna Highway, somewhere outside Los Angeles, in the desert. She was riding a motorcycle too fast and not wearing a helmet. She never regained consciousness, and died in the ambulance twenty minutes later, the hospital administrator told me over the telephone while I stood motionless in our "Ruby Fountain"-coloured living room off the Finchley Road in London. The hospital administrator thought I ought to know that my mother was dead, since I was her only blood relative, but the hospital only knew I existed because of some information on an old healthcare document.

"It wasn't easy to locate your information, but I left a message on your machine four days ago," she said. I frowned. Dad hated talking about my mother, his first girlfriend. He'd mentioned her a countable number of times in my life, and all the small snippets of information came from my grandmother or family friends: Lily was a coward, a slut, a terrible mother.

"Are you still there?" the woman from the hospital said over the phone after I held my breath for a moment.

"I'm here," I said, exhaling. Downstairs, underneath the flat, Daphne and Dad were cleaning in the café kitchen. I knew every sound so well that I could almost see Daphne and Dad winding rhythmically around each other amongst wet metal and plastic.

"Well, I'm sorry to give you bad news," said the woman.

"I didn't know her," I said, picking at the skin around my nails and sucking little pockets of blood as they rose up. "Is there a funeral though?"

"She ran a hotel with her husband in Los Angeles. The funeral will be in Venice Beach, followed by a wake at the hotel nearby.

I'm afraid it's set up for Friday afternoon. I am really sorry: I left a message earlier in the week."

"Nobody passed it on," I said. "Do you think she'd want me to come? Did her friends know she had a daughter?"

"I just work at the hospital where she died. I never met your mother," the woman said.

"Did she have other kids?"

"No other children are mentioned on her documents," said the voice.

If Dad had sat me down and told me that Lily was dead, perhaps I would have shrugged and gone back to watching TV or reading my book: it's not like I knew her. But he hadn't told me, so instead of shrugging I packed my savings from the café and stole Daphne's credit card from her handbag, which was sitting on the sofa in front of the television. I knew the number, because Daphne had a terrible memory and had it written on an index card in the cutlery drawer along with Dad's mobile number. It took me ten minutes to book a ticket online, for early the next morning, and twenty-or-so hours later I was in my mother's bedroom at the top of a vast pink hotel in Venice beach, lifting a wedding dress up against my body. I glanced briefly at her unconscious husband and took off my own damp T-shirt to slip the dress over my head.

If the red-haired man had woken up at that second, he would have seen torn tracksuit bottoms sticking out from the milky froth of his dead wife's silk-and-lace wedding dress. For a moment I was caught inside the cloud of perfumed silk. The music was getting quieter in the layers of hotel underneath the bedroom, the party finally winding down. It must have been five or six in the morning by that point. I could have taken off the silly dress and snuck out. Nobody would even have known that I'd been there, but I couldn't take my eyes off the creature in the mirror. I didn't look anything like Lily. Nobody would recognize the connection. Who knows if her husband or anyone else even knew she had a daughter. I could have snuck out in the same invisible way I came. I could have gone home and worked at the café to help pay off the credit-card debt. I could have walked away from Lily's prostrate husband and snuck out of the party, but instead I picked up one of Lily's red stilettos. I wanted to take them, even though they wouldn't suit me and I'd probably never be able to walk in them. Then I figured maybe it wouldn't hurt to take a couple of dresses, a few pairs of shoes. Lily might even have wanted me to have some of her stuff.

I padded over to the wardrobe to look for a bag or suitcase or something, because all I had with me was my doodled-on school rucksack. Glancing at the red-haired man I got down on my knees to reach under the bed, which is where Dad and Daphne keep their suitcases at home. Sure enough, amongst old tissues, broken sunglasses and crumpled receipts I tugged out a beat-up red suitcase. It was about three feet by two and made out of material the colour of ancient red Play-Doh. It sort of smelt like Play-Doh too, chalky and dry, yet somehow comforting. Inside there were papers, postcards and photographs in some of the little pockets. "To My Darling Lily," I read from the first line of one of the typewritten notes, but then the red-haired man started to stir. He groaned on the bed, and a little bit of white saliva bubbled at the corner of his lips.

I began to put clothes quickly in the suitcase, on top of the letters, looking back to the red-haired man every two seconds to check he was still unconscious. I took a leather biker jacket, a pair of stonewash jeans, a silk fuchsia dress, a fitted black dress, a white cotton dress with black buttons down the front, four tops, some sunglasses, a little pair of silver teardrop earrings, some underwear, red lipstick, a suede tan handbag, two packs of cigarettes and a green plastic lighter. I picked up the shiny paperback novel from next to her bed and looked down on Lily's husband. The pointed tip of one snakeskin shoe was dangling off the side of the bed, and his chest hair was all matted around the gold chain at his neck. He might have been handsome once, but he was gaunt and pulpy now. He groaned again, rasping like his mouth was full of sand, but he didn't stir, and I went back to closing the suitcase over skirts, dresses, black boots, muddy red stilettos, and the pair of grey ballet pumps. There was a pile of twenty-dollar notes in Lily's underwear drawer, which I guiltily stuffed in a pocket of my rucksack too.

As I closed the suitcase clasp, the red-haired man made another noise, and this time the rasp turned into a cough that seemed to lift him out of unconsciousness and up onto his elbows, although his eyes remained closed. He coughed again, straining the buttons on his shirt and making the veins of his neck swell. As I stepped towards the bedroom door with Lily's suitcase in my hand, the red-haired man opened his eyes and stared at me.

"What the fuck," he said, quite slowly.

I didn't put down the suitcase when he spoke, but pulled the bedroom door closed with my free hand just as the red-haired man made an uncoordinated lunge towards me off the bed. The bedroom door slammed shut, and I didn't open it to check if he was all right, just legged it out of the apartment.

3

I'm usually very good at being invisible. Back home in London my friend Laurence taught me that the way to be a great petty thief is to switch off your personality while still being acutely aware of the world around you. He liked to shoplift, and I came with him sometimes, although before Lily's wake I hadn't actually stolen anything for years. Laurence used to preach that most of the million ghosts walking mindlessly from A to B in every city in the world are inconspicuous because they aren't noticing themselves, but an arrogant person or an anxious person is noticeable because they're so aware of their existence. Similarly, fine-pointed stilettos and push-up bras draw a woman's attention to herself, and so she exists visibly to the world. Laurence used to say that I had "kleptomaniac chic" down to a T, which apparently meant dressing as if unsure about my own existence. Even as a kid I was incognito. According to Dad I neither smiled nor talked until I was five, which caused everyone to think that I was either deaf and dumb or autistic or both. He said I was a "personified shrug", a kid on whose face fear, anger, amusement and love all looked the same – just a tilt of the head and a blank stare from inhumanly wide eyes.

I tried to be invisible as I rushed out of the private flat at the top of the Pink Hotel, but it's hard to pull off when you're scared. I dragged Lily's suitcase through the waning party, and at first I thought the red-haired man would clamber up from the floor and follow me. I kept looking back, but he wasn't there. Other people seemed to be looking at me though. There was a woman in a leather minidress, and a man with a gold stud in his nose who looked thuggish except for neatly parted black hair. I only noticed this man very fleetingly at the hotel that first night, but the mixture of schoolboy hairstyle and a thug face made me remember him later. The techno and electro music had stopped by now, so maybe someone had heard noises from upstairs. There were people asleep in different rooms, or still dancing to themselves in the hallway. Someone was vomiting in a toilet and I swear she looked up and smiled crookedly at me as I passed. Someone else was crying. I hurried downstairs and out of the hotel onto the boardwalk, where the light was just beginning to turn blue behind street lamps and palm trees. The suitcase wasn't heavy, just clumsy to carry. It kept banging against my leg, and I looked behind to check nobody was following me.

There were people smoking on the steps and two people kissing against the pink stucco walls, but nobody followed me. On one block of the road, homeless men slept in bundles of rags and corrugated cardboard. One of them looked at me with heavyset narcotic eyes, but the rest were curled up with their dusty eyelids closed. I gripped the suitcase tighter and kept walking until I couldn't see the homeless men or the pink walls of the hotel any more. Then I sat down on a bench in front of the blacked-out beach to open Lily's suitcase for a jumper or jacket to wear as the sun came up. From the chaos of my thievery I chose the leather motorcycle jacket that Lily had been wearing in the photo of her posing with her bike. I thought about phoning Dad to tell him I was OK, but decided to calm down before that battle. I zipped the leather jacket up to my neck.

At first it seemed unlikely that I'd be able to doze on a bench in front of a picture-postcard cliché of a beach, but soon the sun started to come up, and my adrenaline stopped pumping quite so hard. I lay down with the suitcase under my head on the bench. The light was beautiful, sort of frosty. I hadn't seen the sea since a caravan holiday in Cornwall six years ago. I don't love the sea in any cosmic sense, but I do like it. The Pacific looked like a different animal from the Atlantic. If the Atlantic was a foaming, snapping Rottweiler, the Pacific was a sleepy gecko in the sunlight. I had a recurring dream throughout that strange summer, which always began as a conscious thought while I was trying to lull myself to sleep and ended in dull panic. I'd begin with a deserted beach, all warm and wonderful. I would be naked in my dream, and for some reason pregnant, the thick water touching my white thighs and then my belly as I stepped further into the sea. The sky would always be full of blue seagulls in my dream, and I would find myself unable to ignore a red coin of colour that appeared on the horizon and grew. It looked like a sunset that had started in the sea before it hit the sky, and I wouldn't be able to stop looking and couldn't stop this feeling of panic, like someone was dying out there. I'd go and sit on the itchy beach and stare at this beginning of an upside-down sunset until I was actually giving birth, at which point I'd try to stop my thoughts. I'd wake myself up slightly, trying to go back to the feeling of damp sand between my toes, to imagine being blind, being asleep, but the thought-baby and thought-me wouldn't stop panting, painfully, giving birth on the beach. Then there would be an incredibly calm moment, like the exhalation of air after you come or lose your temper. I'd be in the water again and cleaning off all the blood from the baby. I'd put my fingers in the baby's mouth to scoop out the red coin of goo, and its mouth would be an echo of the blood on the horizon.

4

"Good morning," said a voice. I can't have been asleep for very long, because the light on the beach was still frosty when the flash of a camera woke me. I jumped, and my eyes focused on the Giant, who had fumbled to steal the laughing photograph from Lily's room earlier. He was standing above me now, silhouetted against the backdrop of the near-deserted beach and pointing a camera at me.

My fingers gripped Lily's suitcase. The Giant's irises looked very green in the rising daylight, and his lopsided mouth made one of his eyes seem smaller than the other. His lips were pursed, perhaps angrily. I didn't move.

"My name's David Reed," he said. Then he took another photograph. "I saw you leave the hotel with the suitcase," he added. "Thief," he slurred, drunk. "I wasn't going to do anything about it. Not my business. But then I'm walking over the beach minding my own business and – bang – there you are, looking photogenic. Right?"

"You should have kept minding your own business," I said, getting up off the bench with my hand wrapped around the suitcase handle. He took another snap of me.

These photographs reminded me of how a man once tossed off in front of me on the night bus in London, his face creasing as his hand worked faster, puckering his lips with concentration. I had thought the act mesmerizing, grotesque and humiliating all at once, as if he were trying to touch me without moving. There was a similar intensity in the way the Giant was looking at me, as if he was trying to memorize me for later. It's funny the way that men can possess women just by looking. They can take the woman home and merge her with other women in their head, change the length of her legs and the willingness of her mouth until there's a whole new version of the original girl dancing seductively in the head of a stranger. Like I say, my talents never lay in standing out from the crowd. I'm very sensitive to people looking at me, feeling it on my skin like physical contact even from a long way off. Luckily people very rarely looked at me in the way the Giant Man was looking at me on that early morning beach, or how the man had looked at me on the bus.

"No, no, no, sit down," said David. "I'm harmless. No worries."

He was clearly quite drunk, although maybe not as drunk as the red-haired man had been. The Giant stopped talking for a moment and took another picture. Then another.

"Did you take that from her room?" he said, nodding at the red suitcase.

"What are you talking about?" I replied. "This is my suitcase. I'm on holiday."

We could hear the sea licking up at the sand two hundred metres from the bench, and smell salty air. He also smelt of beer, nicotine and alcohol sweats. There were faded old scars on his face – one on his eyebrow, one under his right eye, and a thin scar down his nose. He had a spider web of wrinkles around his eyes, but they didn't make him look old, somehow. He looked boyish.

"I'm curious about what kind of person steals from a wake, though," he said, and shrugged his big shoulders.

"It didn't look like a wake," I mumbled. "It looked like some sort of rave."

"You didn't know her?" he asked, cocking his head to the side.

"I just thought it was a party," I lied.

"It was random opportunism?" he said.

"My boyfriend ran off with our rental car this morning. It had all my money, my clothes. Everything," I said. "You going to call the police on me or anything?"

He paused.

"No," he said, thoughtfully.

David pursed his lips and sat down on the bench next to me. The blond hairs on the back of my neck stood nervously to attention. Behind us the boardwalk was beginning to fill up with joggers and street vendors. I reached into Lily's suitcase and extracted a half-empty pack of cigarettes along with her green plastic lighter.

"Those hers or yours?" he said, nodding at the cigarettes.

"Hers," I said, then put one in my mouth and offered him the pack.

"That's audacious, stealing her cigarettes and then offering me one. I might be her husband, or her brother."

"Are you?" I said, glancing across at him.

"No," he replied, and lifted the whole pack to his mouth, removing one of the cigarettes with his lips. He looked at Lily's lighter for a moment, then flicked the tarnished silver roll to light mine before he lit his own. My heart jumped when he took a direct look at me under my red baseball cap, but he didn't seem to notice any similarity between my face and hers. I have a small, symmetrical face with big brown eyes. It's Dad's mouth, Dad's slightly pointed nose, Dad's pale skin and high forehead. I figured that on some unconscious level David noticed me because of an element of Lily in my eyes. He must have done, but he gave no indication of recognizing Lily in me. I looked nothing like my mother. We sat in silence for a moment.

"How do you know her, then?" I asked him.

"I used to be a fashion photographer," he said. "She – Lily – the dead woman – she used to be a model. We did a shoot together, years ago in LA."

"A model?" I said.

"Yeah, you got a model's clothes," he said.

"Did you love her?" I asked, thinking of that haunted way he picked up Lily's photograph in the bedroom. The words sounded childish even as they came out of my mouth, but he looked earnestly at me.

"She was one of a whole bunch of models," he said. "I took one awesome photo of her, though. She's walking some dogs. She looks beautiful in that photograph. Then I didn't see her again till years and years later."

"Are you still a fashion photographer?"

"Nah," he said. "I do paparazzi work now. How old are you?"

"Twenty-two," I said, and David yawned. His whole body arched with the yawn, his mouth stretching as if he were about to turn himself inside out.

My body has always felt divorced from my mind, but David's body seemed to belong to him. His smile was connected to his shoulders and his hands connected to his eyes. I wondered where his scars were from. He had an energy that made me think of fighting, and then of the football pitch in Swiss Cottage where I always hung out. The asphalt was surrounded by graffiti-smeared brick walls, and we'd hop over a large yellow skip to get foot holes in the bricks and then jump or tumble onto spiky grass. Most of the girls had flirtations with the boys. Some had sex, moved in and out of allegiances, dated and grimaced and sucked and grinned and fell in love, but I never once gave a blowjob behind the bike shed. I was friendly with a girl named Mary, and we would sit facing the walls as if we were having conversations with the graffiti and drag our thumbs down the bricks, seeing who could do it for the longest. It was always me, with a connect-the-dots of broken skin like a kiss that buzzed right down the inside of my knees.

It's difficult to explain the adrenalin I got from someone's trainer mashed into my shoulder or grazing my knee and smelling blood on shorn grass. I liked the relief of cold air forced sharply into my lungs and the respite of traceable pain on my skin rather than the fleeting and invisible map of pleasure that seems to happen with love or affection. Girls are meant to be subtler in their choice of violence, but it took me a long time to discover sex and charm. Instead I scraped my knees, spat on boys till they fought me in the football field, acquired black eyes and bitten lips and played chicken in the bramble bushes – running barefoot at friends in the middle of the night until our ankles were jagged with blood.

If you prick your skin with a needle, the pain signal will travel to the brain at ninety-eight feet per second, I learnt from my science teacher. Burning or aching travels at six and a half feet per second. Pain seemed so much less capricious than pleasure, and so much less terrifying than feeling nothing. By fifteen my body was a scarred map from which I could point out the fight or fall that caused each lasting Tick-Tack-Toe mark on my knees and elbows, the slash across my eyebrows and down my collarbone, the jumpy dotted lines on my knuckles. One scar on my bottom was from the time a boy threw me in a skip and metal cut through my jeans, the slice on my wrist was the time I fell on a shard of glass during a football scuffle and had to get stitches, another on my arm was from the time I was pushed off a skateboard. Although I pinch myself sometimes, and absently bite my lip, I've only really "self-harmed" once: a four-inch knife line inside my thigh. I sat on the edge of the bathtub to design it when I was twelve. It didn't even really hurt. I regretted it. It was interesting more than thrilling. It was harder to stop dragging the knife across than it was to continue with the movement. There was no thrill of connection in cutting myself; someone else had to do it in order to make me feel calm.

As David and I smoked Lily's cigarettes on the wooden bench, my nerves dissipated with the darkness. A skinny man slid past us on roller skates with a boom box on his shoulder. He put the music box down around a hundred metres from the bench and shouted "Here we go! Here we go!" – pirouetting on his glittery skates. It looked like something out of an urban, hip-hop *Fantasia* cartoon. Soon there were naked kids being pushed around the boardwalk in shopping trolleys, drinking milkshakes from buckets the size of their bodies. There were DJ decks set up on the street and toy trucks jumping around the legs of the bench, being attacked by tiny dogs wearing witty T-shirts.

"I'm sorry your friend died," I said to David.

"Me too," he said, shrugging, tipping his absurd neon-yellow sunglasses over his eyes. "That's fucked-up about your boyfriend stealing your car, though," he added. I had an urge to touch him. He looked perturbed and pale and drunk in the sunlight.

"What are you going to do?" he asked me, not smiling.

"I'll probably do some touristy stuff, then go home."

"England?"

"London."

"Your ex-boyfriend English?"

"Yeah," I said. I wondered if my nationality would make David think of Lily, but it didn't seem to.

"Did you have an argument with him before he stole your car?" David said.

"He ran off with a girl who works in some roadside diner. They exchanged numbers while I was in the toilet a couple of days ago. He gave me this guilty look when I came back. She served me pancakes without looking me in the eye, but she smiled secretively at him. You know the feeling?" I said, fingering the rim of my baseball cap and shivering. I'd never even set foot in a roadside diner, just seen them in movies and read about them in books.

"I need to go throw up," David said suddenly, nearly to himself. "I haven't slept for a while."

"Do you want me to get you anything?"

"I usually wait till I know a girl before I vomit and pass out on her," he said, standing up and trying to smile. He looked unsteady on his oversized feet.

"You sure you're all right? I could walk you somewhere?"

"You're very polite for a grave-robber," he said.

"Are you sure?" I said, wanting to help him.

"I'll be fine," he said. "Good to meet you."

"Sleep well," I frowned. He staggered away down the crowded street with a slight limp that made him look like some sort of poseur gangster, then turned and bent over to vomit in an alley off the main road.

5

I carried Lily's suitcase to a youth hostel away from the board-walk. The room I was given had two beds with squeaky springs and the mosquito screens had flies trapped on it. Every time a car came past the road underneath, the walls would light up yellow. It felt as if I were sitting inside a dying light bulb. It turned out that when I took Lily's shoulder bag I also stole her wallet, which had a further hundred dollars, some credit cards and her driving licence. The picture on the driving licence scowled at me. Presumably most people can conjure an image of their mother from childhood, but my memories are either from photographs or they're physical. I can't imagine what she used to look like, but remember fragments of her holding my hand too tight in a supermarket, the texture of her legs when I grabbed them, the extreme comfort of a silk blanket my dad's older sister gave me when I was born, which Lily used to wrap me in. Sometimes, when I'm anxious, the soft area between my fingers lifts up and tingles in memory of that silk blanket that I used to drag between my baby fingers. Odd things made me think of her, but I didn't think of her very often. For example there's a particular brand of cheap hair dye that used to make my stomach turn, only I couldn't possibly have remembered the smell of henna and peroxide from when I was under the age of three. Similarly I'm convinced that we were overrun by a plague of ladybirds around the time Lily left, but Dad doesn't remember anything of the sort.

"There weren't any ladybirds," Dad claims, but it would be just like him not to remember those leggy red shells gradually multiplying so they drowned in my bathwater and got stuck in the creases of my baby clothes. Ladybirds are meant to be lucky, which is strange considering the rhyme about flying away home your house is on fire and your children are gone. The ladybirds would fly at any available light source and then jump away from the heat, panicked, a little embarrassed, like a child touching an electric fence. A second later they would tuck their petticoat wings back under their shells and lift up for the light bulb again. I'm sure they formed mass graves in the bedside and kitchen light fixtures, all around the time Lily left.

I took off Lily's leather jacket and folded it over my arm, then placed it on the bed. I folded the three stolen dresses, smoothing away the creases and piling them up on the bed. They smelt of floral perfume. Then I took out the shoes – the red stilettos, black knee-highs, little grey ballet pumps – and put them to the side of the suitcase, under the metal legs of the little single bed. There were shadows of dirt on the inside of each shoe, like dislocated shadows. In a plastic cover under an elastic strap in the roof of the suitcase were typed papers full of legal jargon about the Pink Hotel – proxy, aforementioned, hereafter. Also under the strap were a "Certificate of Completion" and an "Evaluation Report" from a nurse's training college in a place called Glendale. It said she was "dedicated and enthusiastic". Tucked away near the report card was a photograph of Lily wearing pink scrubs, with her arm around a debonair-looking old man. It said "Teddy and Lily, Malibu Mansions" on the back. Then there was a pile of road maps, mostly of American states – Nevada, Alabama, California – but also of European cities – Florence, Berlin, London. The road maps had routes marked on them, the ink making funny patterns on the lattice of roads. Perhaps she travelled and never tried to find me. I tried to imagine Lily in London, sitting on an Underground platform or walking through the polluted circus of Finchley Road trying not to catch anyone's eye or step on the cracks. I wondered if she'd ever watched me from afar and not made contact: perhaps she'd seen me playing football, or at school, or waiting tables at the café.

I hoped to find a picture of Dad or of me among the rubble of memories tucked away in the suitcase, but the pictures were mostly of Lily herself. There were pictures of Lily and her husband swimming in a rooftop pool, Lily drinking red wine somewhere in the countryside, Lily wearing a diamanté cocktail dress and fur cape. I looked at a Polaroid of Lily standing with a motorcycle outside a blue concrete building under a sign saying "Eagle Motorcycles". This was the same bike that she was standing with in the photograph on her table at the Pink Hotel, which I supposed was her bike, perhaps the one she died on. The bike in the photo was slim and shiny, with a curved black-leather seat and silver handlebars.

In a side pocket of the suitcase were Christmas and birthday cards all bundled together along with postcards and letters. Some of the cards were from the man called Teddy from the debonair "Malibu Mansions" photo. The most arresting letters were the ones typed on thin paper and signed off "with love, for ever, for always" rather than with a name.

The typewriter had bruised the paper with long lines of indentations. I imagined Lily running her own fingers over the
words like they were Braille. "The sky is blood-red outside
my window tonight and I'm thinking of you," one of them
began. "The first time we met you were holding a small red
umbrella. Remember? And now the colour red makes me
think of you." There were no dates or names on the pretty
letters. "Later, I came to know your little red dresses," the
letters continued, "and the army of incendiary lipsticks on
your dresser." The letters made me feel like an eavesdrop-
ping child flummoxed by adult vocabulary and emotional
dynamics. I folded the letters along their original creases and
placed them back into the case. I figured they were from the
red-haired man, and felt guilty. Perhaps he'd report the theft
to the police, telling them to look for a girl with a baseball
cap and red suitcase. Of course, the pretty love letters could
have been from David. In any case I would have liked to have
found the magazine photo David mentioned, from when Lily
was a model and he met her for the first time.

I didn't dream about anything in the hours after Lily's wake.
It was the black-hole sort of sleep where you don't wake up
refreshed. I fell asleep in my clothes on the bed and eight jet-
lagged and dreamless daylight hours later I opened my eyes to
find my body thick with sweat from sun pouring in through
the hostel window. I took a deep breath and listened to funny
sounds in the corridor outside. In the next-door room, two
Australians were arguing about the merits of bamboo over
fibreglass in the surfboard-manufacturing process. Outside
the window a little girl was singing a pop song, a siren was
screaming, and there was an infomercial for laser-eye surgery

going on somewhere else. Lily's clothes were strewn accusingly over the floor. I dragged one of her halter-neck tops over my head. I'd been wearing the same T-shirt for ages, and it stank of skin and sleep. I put my own tracksuit bottoms on, my own scuffed trainers, and stuffed my Adidas zip-up hoodie in my rucksack.

6

The streets of Venice Beach were quieter than they'd been the day before, yet still strange. Elderly ladies in vast sunglasses were knitting on the bench where David and I had smoked Lily's cigarettes. There were Rollerbladers everywhere, zipping around pumped-up body builders and tourists wearing bum bags over big pastel T-shirts. I stopped to watch an old lady reading tarot cards and a woman in a tie-die dress making jewellery boxes out of shells. Eventually I arrived at the Pink Hotel, suitcase in hand. Everything looked different in the light. It was more ragged, with canned laughter from a sitcom jangling in the foyer and a couple of surfers drinking soda on broken sofas. There were still beer bottles and overflowing ashtrays scattered around, and the air was stale like nothing had really been cleaned properly yet. A concierge girl looked up at me over a pair of tortoise-shell Ray-Bans balanced on her freckled nose. Her skin looked a bit green.

"We've all got hangovers from hell, babe, sorry," the girl drawled. "I'm sure not going to be the one to disturb Mr Harris today. No way."

"He'll want to see me," I said. "I think he's probably looking for me, even."

"He's not looking for anyone, believe me," she said. "We had a big party last night, and now the cleaners have gone on strike and… you know? It's just not a good day."

"He was looking for me last night," I said.

"He doesn't want to see *anyone*," she said. "He's asleep."

I paused, thinking the girl was turning greener in front of me.

"But you've spoken to him today?" I said. The girl shrugged her bony shoulders.

"The TVs on up there and he's been clomping around. But he's asleep now, so call back later if you really need to speak to him."

Part of me considered leaving the suitcase there with the concierge girl, but I didn't want to abandon it before I'd spoken with Richard. I wanted to know why Lily became a nurse, for example, and when she was a model. I wanted to know if she mentioned me, and whether Richard had written her those love letters.

"Can I leave a note?" I said.

"Sure," she said, giving me a piece of paper and a pen, but when it came to writing something down I couldn't think of anything to say.

"Just tell him someone dropped by to give the suitcase back?" I said. "Tell him I'll come by again in a few days."

"Sure thing," said the girl, looking at the suitcase in my hand. "I'll tell him you'll come back later. What's your name?"

"He doesn't know me," I said. "Just say the girl who took the suitcase."

"Sure," said the girl, frowning for a second, then going back to her computer screen.

I smoked a couple of Lily's cigarettes in the car park outside a 7-Eleven near the Pink Hotel. Maybe Richard was so drugged that he wouldn't remember me stealing the suitcase at all. My thumbnail fondled the zip of the clasp, which seemed hot under the West Coast sunshine. I particularly wanted to touch the silk fuchsia sundress for some reason. My skin lifted at the idea like it used to lift when thinking about my silk blanket when I was a baby.

After a while I went into the 7-Eleven convenience store and bought a phone card from the teenage shop assistant. The buttons on the parking-lot payphone were all sticky, and it rang for ages before Daphne's irritated voice arrived at the receiver. I could imagine her oval face in the darkness, tumid with sleep and floral-smelling moisturizing lotion. Her cheek might have been momentarily scarred with the imprint of creases from the frilled edges of her special silk pillow that didn't make her hair frizz during the night. She always looked older in the morning, her skin a landslide that righted itself slowly throughout the day.

"Hello?" she gulped, and then coughed. "Who is this?"

"Me," I said quietly.

"Stupid girl," Daphne immediately snapped over the crackled phone line, "get the hell home, all right?" I imagined Dad, his hairy belly under the stolen bedspread, his hands reaching over to grab the phone from Daphne's fingers.

"You think I don't check our bank balance? I want you on the next plane home," said Dad sternly, and I could imagine him crossly putting on his glasses in the dark. "Right now. You hear? Get the next plane home or we'll be calling the police," he said.

"We absolutely will," Daphne said in the background. I couldn't think what to say: my mind went blank and my tongue felt twice the size of my mouth. I looked down at my scuffed trainers on the tarmac, and my hands holding a cigarette like a talisman. There wasn't anything to do except put down the phone on Dad. I often find it hard to say what I mean. It's like

34

the person who speaks isn't the person who thinks sometimes. My gut reaction was defensive, but they had every right to be angry. The little café Dad owned was off Finchley Road, an asthmatic motorway that runs from Swiss Cottage Tube station in London. It was part of a row of four shops – a shoe shop, a newsagents, a hair salon and us. We lived in the flat above the café, which faced a string of nice terraced houses with manicured front gardens on one side, and on the other South Hampstead railway station and a massive, sprawling, grey-brick estate. I used to go to school a stone's throw away from the estate, but when I was twelve I moved to a grammar school further away. The walls of the café were pastel-blue, with flowers stencilled along the edge, but the continual fizz of frying had turned the paint grey at the top. Every day after school I'd sit cross-legged on the industrial freezer in the back room and do my homework. Dad never made me waitress on weekdays, only Saturdays and Sundays, because Grandpa had made Dad work after school and he never got good grades. Dad dropped out when he was sixteen and didn't want that to happen to me. After finishing my homework I'd either help Dad with the accounts or I'd get my bike and go play among the grey stone walkways and interlocking tenements behind the café. The estate was a little town in itself, and shook every time a train passed underneath. It was a long, thin grey structure that curved along one side of the train tracks for maybe half a mile. Each flat had a balcony with dried-up plants dripping off them, or washing lines draped across, or beer-sponsored sun umbrellas that looked like they'd been stolen from a pub garden. The area around this was a labyrinth of pathways, stairways, playgrounds and hidden corners with flower beds everywhere. I suppose an enthusiastic architect assumed they'd be kept full of geraniums and daisies, but they were always full of dried dirt and ivy. There was one old lady in the estate who would potter around planting the odd solitary flower. She wore a wide-brimmed sun hat with tracksuit bottoms that were too small for her. The elastic caught at her calves, leaving her ankles bare. She'd plant a single purple chrysanthemum in a forest of nettles, but a week later the flower would be dead.

After putting down the phone on Dad, I sat down on the kerb with Lily's suitcase in front of me. A few moments later through the Californian heat and the rising chatter of car doors slamming in the increasingly busy 7-Eleven parking lot, the phone started to ring. It jangled anxiously, and a bony dog started to bark. A graceful man wearing lip gloss and a sailor's cap looked down at me, then looked at the phone. I thought for a second the sailor was going to answer it, but he just kept walking. It seemed to ring on for ages, but when it stopped I lit a cigarette with Lily's green lighter and tried to feel calm in the sunshine. I opened the suitcase on the tarmac and ran the cool hem of the fuchsia sundress between my fingers. I smoked with one hand and pulled at the silk with the other. After a moment the sun heated the silk, and it wasn't soothing any more. Everything felt sticky in the sunshine. There was a brown envelope at the bottom of the suitcase that I hadn't opened the day before. I thought it was sealed, but actually it was just tacky and old, and opened easily. Inside were a wedding licence and two photographs. The first photo was a faded Polaroid, labelled "Lily Dakin marries August Walters, in Jackpot, Idaho". In this photo Lily looked like she was playing dress-up in a stiff "party dress" that pinched her throat.

She wore her hair tied in a schoolgirl ponytail on top of her head, with a pair of rock-and-wire home-made earrings and two strands of limp hair dangling over her face. The boy had a thin shirt, two sizes too big for him, but he was even prettier than Lily. He had sandy hair, liquid blue eyes and a damp pink mouth like a bow that could be unravelled with a joke or a curse. They both stood hesitantly on the edge of adulthood. The photograph was fading, and had a sickly flash in the left-hand corner, where the colour had been sucked up. The groom looked as if he might still race toy cars when nobody was looking, and the bride looked like she might still collect furry stickers or play with dolls.

As for the second wedding photo, it was the same one I'd seen framed in Lily's bedroom, of her and the red-haired man. I wondered how Lily lost that indistinct and careful smile from the first wedding photo for the calm allure of the second. There was nothing written on the back, but there was a photocopied marriage licence folded in the envelope. The licence said that Lily Dakin, 23, married Richard Harris, 30, in Burbank, California. In this second photograph her hair was scraped off her face, and you could see the crow's feet around her eyes. I finished my cigarette on the kerbside, staring at these pictures, then walked into the 7-Eleven and asked the shop assistant whether he had a copy of the Yellow Pages I could borrow and a map of Los Angeles that I could buy.

7

There were twenty-two California listings for A. Walters. I sat with the sticky payphone up to my mouth and spoke to Abigail Walters in Napa, Abe Walters's son in Eureka, Anna Walters's boyfriend in Santa Maria, Ashley Walters in Orange County, Adam Walters's mother in San Francisco and then a woman named Candy Britannia in Los Angeles, who informed me that she was subletting from a man named August. She didn't know (or wouldn't give me) August's mobile number or new address, but she thought he worked in a Martini bar in LA – a place called Dragon Lounge or Dragon Bar or something to do with dragons, although she wasn't sure where exactly it was.

I tossed and turned in the Venice Beach youth hostel that night, and the next day found an Internet café to look up the addresses of all the "dragon" establishments in Los Angeles that might serve Martinis. There was The Dragon, a Red Dragon, a Dragon Bar, and a Twin Dragon Drinks. I knew that the August I found wouldn't be a boy my own age, but there was something about his Polaroid wedding photograph that made me want to find him anyway – perhaps it was because from the looks of things August must have been the person Lily called home in the years after she left me. While I was online I also typed the name "David Reed" and "photographer" into Google and got a bunch of results: a graphic designer from Texas, a professor of computer science in New Jersey, a Facebook page for a "freshman" in Northcentral University. Then there was a paparazzi website called "The List", which had the Giant's name connected to photographs of skeletal "It" girls stepping out of limousines, and small tanned men wearing sunglasses inside expensive restaurants. I figured that was the Giant, and pressed a "Contact us" button hidden at the bottom of the homepage, revealing the mailing address for their office in downtown Los Angeles. My return flight to London wasn't for three days, and if Lily's second husband wouldn't even come down and see me because he was too hung-over, I figured it couldn't hurt to keep the suitcase for a few days and learn something about my mother. I'd return the suitcase before going back to London.

It takes three hours to get anywhere on Los Angeles public transport. The same cooking channel was on the televisions at the front of every bus – men dressed as Zorro for some reason making omelettes on the beach. Out of the windows the city looked derelict and vast with crouched buildings on either side of thick tarmac highways. At the Internet café I'd Google-mapped the places I wanted to go and marked them all out on my 7-Eleven tourist map, but still found it nearly impossible to understand where I was. I even looked again at the pretty road maps in Lily's suitcase, but of course they weren't helpful at all. Each one was drawn over with lines that on second glance were not exactly routes, but patterns, pictures, shapes. The outline of an angular woman with vast breasts was created by tracing the lines of Wyoming and Colorado, then two closed eyes were drawn onto an aerial photograph of roads in South Africa. There was a map of Tuscany in Italy, where the city of Florence seemed to be the hole between a woman's legs; a version of New York where Central Park was clearly pubic hair, and a tourist map of Berlin where the Brandenburg

Gate was a woman's gnashing teeth in the middle of a cubist face. A badly photocopied map of Los Angeles had a woman's silhouette drawn in black pen using the western edges of different districts as the outline, and there was something very beautiful, very strange, about the detail.

On various complex bus routes I made my way from Venice Beach to Downtown LA, which equated to travelling from the elbow of the woman drawn on Lily's photocopied and doodled-on map to maybe the belly button.

I decided to go to David's office first, planning to move on to one of the possible dragon Martini bars in the evening. There's a flower called "bird of paradise" all over Los Angeles: it has orange leaves shaped like knives, although from a certain angle the flowers also look like gaggles of slim-necked tropical birds. There were clumps of these savage plants outside the office block in which the Giant, David Reed, apparently worked. It was a grainy building made of concrete and glass, the foundations surrounded by an array of wilting foliage. There were ferns, cacti, birds of paradise and strange, waxy bougainvillea that seemed to be sweating in the sunlight. On my second day alone in Los Angeles I sat sweating, too, on some dusty stairs opposite the office building, ready to disappear if I actually saw him coming in or out of the revolving doors. But it was Sunday, so I supposed he wouldn't come into the office at all. The stairs led up to a kind of raised mini-mall with a McDonald's, a Dunkin' Donuts and a Radio Shack. I'd peaked into the lobby and saw through the windows that there were lawyers and talent agencies and graphic designers listed on a board above the reception desk, along with "The List Photographic Agency". There was a receptionist working behind the desk, but she was reading a gossip magazine and hardly anyone came in or out of the doors that afternoon. I sat there for a few hours, hoping to see David's slouchy oversized body. Then when the sun started to go down I admitted defeat for the day and opened up my tourist map again to try and work out how to get to Chinatown, where one of the potential dragon Martini bars was.

I should have found somewhere to sleep and then gone to the bar, but it didn't occur to me. I'd never been alone in a strange city before, let alone a strange country. I'd been on camping holidays with friends once or twice, and the occasional weekend away with Daphne and Dad, but I'd never checked into a hotel alone or found my way around a new city by myself. The first dragon bar I found that evening was a Chinese dive where a bouncer with yellow teeth threatened to have me chucked out even though I was only showing the cook a photograph of my mother on her wedding day. I must have seemed nervous and strange standing there with my school rucksack in one hand and Lily's red suitcase in the other, baseball cap covering my boyish blonde hair. The Chinese bouncer didn't believe that I was old enough to drink. Instead of finding August that night, I slept in the first youth hostel I found, which was luckily only a few roads away from the Dragon Bar. It was a Chinatown youth hostel that smelt of burnt rice and incense. The bedroom was meant to be communal, with two sets of bunk beds, but I was the only one in the room. I slept with the suitcase in bed with me, between my body and the wall, my sweaty fist on the handle. Every few minutes a new noise woke me up. First there were toilets flushing and doors slamming, then the scream of two cats having sex on the rooftop, then junkies or insomniacs babbling on the street under the window. I wondered what David was doing while I was sleepless in Chinatown. He was probably fast asleep and dreaming. I imagined him on his back, snoring slightly, splayed out on a big bed like a starfish. Then I imagined that he couldn't sleep either and had his eyes open.

I left the Chinatown hostel as soon as it was light on Monday morning, and found another one in West Hollywood called the Serena Hostel, which was advertised on the back of the laminated tourist map from the 7-Eleven on Venice Beach. The Serena was next to a liquor store and opposite a depressing-looking ice-cream parlour that must have been a cover for something illegal, because nobody ever went in or out of it. It was a nice-enough place, though, with big rooms and messy communal areas full of candles stuffed in beer bottles, and notice boards offering bus tours of celebrity homes. Dust floated everywhere, and the plumbing creaked, but it wasn't expensive. The Serena was run by a gruff woman named Vanessa who wore long black dresses that made her look obese. She had three matted dreadlocks in her ashy hair and wore black lace-up boots even in ninety-degree heat. The co-manager, Tony, was an ex-bodybuilder who had a flattened nose and one finger missing on his left hand. They rented me a locker behind the reception desk so that I could keep the suitcase safe and not have to drag it around the city with me. The lockers were big and wooden, a bit like the ones in left-luggage offices at some train stations, except these ones had padlocks. You had to give Vanessa or Tony the key and ask one of them to open the locker every time you wanted to get something. Before I gave them Lily's suitcase to look after, I got dressed up slightly and took Lily's driving licence from the purse in her suede bag. I still wore my grubby baseball cap, but it looked sort of trendy with Lily's sunglasses and her slightly fitted black T-shirt in place of my hooded zip-up cardigan. I even wore a pair of her earrings: little silver-and-blue teardrops.

I crouched on the steps opposite David's office again in my baseball cap and Lily's sunglasses, not knowing what I'd say if he saw me. It would have been easier to speak with August than with David, since I had the wedding photograph to give to August. For David all I had to offer was a pile of letters that might not be from him at all. As I sat in the sunlight watching the revolving doors, I could tell who were paparazzi, because they came out with their eyes darting, a camera swinging like a poacher's gun across their shoulders. Many of them were bearded or thickly unshaven, and they'd slide sunglasses onto their noses as they walked away quickly, anxiously, like they were missing something; dirty-knuckled thumbs tapping away on mobile phones as they made for their cars or the coffee shop on the corner of the road. I ate a doughnut from the doughnut shop and felt sick, then flicked through the paperback novel that I'd taken from next to Lily's bed at the Pink Hotel. It was called *Enkidu*, and had a drawing of an animal-like man on the cover underneath the embossed title. She'd only got three-quarters of the way through, by the looks of the partially dog-eared pages. According to the back cover, the book was based on some old epic poem about a black-eyed man-beast named Enkidu who grew up among animals, but flicking through the pages suggested it was top-shelf stuff. Sitting on the steps opposite David's office, I read how Enkidu lolloped on all fours and suckled from the breasts of pigs until one day a hunter discovered him and sent a prostitute named Shamhat into the wilderness. There was a creepy sex scene in which Enkidu tried to suck milk out of Shamhat's breasts and then bit her nipples till she bled. I kept glancing up from the pages to scan the faces and bodies of people traipsing in and out of the office, but I didn't see anyone resembling David that day, and by the time I climbed on a bus to Boyle Heights with my annotated tourist map in my hands, my skin and clothes smelt of sweat and sunlight and doughnuts from the strip-mall shops.

At a bar called Twin Dragon Drinks, a disco ball hung on the ceiling of a room with sticky floors and fake-wood-panelled walls that you could hardly see behind the crowds of people palpitating to the music. I didn't look a thing like Lily's photo in her driving licence, but the bouncer ushered me in with a cursory glance. I shouted above the hip-hop music to ask all the barmen, doormen and waitresses whether they knew August. I showed them the photograph of Lily and August frowning solemnly on their wedding day, but everyone replied with shrugs and frowns.

"Nah, never met anyone named August…"

"Like, what, the season? No…"

"He looks cute. Don't know him…"

It was crowded in the bar, and people kept bumping into me, stepping on my toes and elbowing me as if I was invisible in the darkness. The drinkers and dancers seemed gigantically tall – white plastic platform shoes, hair extensions, muscular arms, tan girls and molasses-skinned men, baseball caps with the labels still on. Eventually I re-emerged into the warm Los Angeles evening and calmed down in the emptiness beyond the gaggle of smokers shifting from foot to foot in floodlights from the bar.

8

I decided to sit outside David's office for one more day. If he didn't appear I'd go to Venice Beach and give Richard back the suitcase as promised, but on the third day – when I was sick of smelling fried sugar and bland coffee from the doughnut shop – David stepped out of the revolving doors and into the sunshine. I hadn't noticed him go in, and I held my breath for a moment when I saw him. He was even taller than I remembered, but slightly thinner and gaunter. He had a broad chest and big shoulders. He wore massive sunglasses and shapeless grey flannel trousers. I turned my head towards him, but stayed firmly out of sight around the corner. Again it was like he'd fallen into a pile of laundry and squirmed until he had clothes on. He paused outside the office building for a moment, looked at his wristwatch, then limped towards a coffee house on the corner of the street. I stayed on the opposite side of the road and felt sick. After two days of kicking my heels with nobody to talk to except a mean Radio Shack employee and a prepubescent Vietnamese doughnut maker whose vocabulary was limited to snack-related necessities, you might think I'd have come up with a plan about how to approach David. I hadn't even thought about it, though, and on seeing him my mind went completely blank. I stayed crouched under my sunglasses and baseball cap on the steps. A few moments after going into the café, David came back out holding a paper cup in his hand. He walked back the way he came past the office and then four blocks down to his shiny black SUV. I watched from the other side of the road as he fumbled for his car keys and spilt hot coffee on his hand. He swore under his breath, or at least his lips moved, and he sucked his hand in a way that made me think of the half-animal Enkidu from Lily's book. His large hands seemed to be shaking. Eventually he put the cup on top of the car and managed to climb inside, bringing the coffee with him. Then he just sat at the wheel for at least ten minutes, staring straight in front of him without taking a sip.

The night after seeing David I chain-smoked out of my hostel window, and then got dressed from Lily's suitcase in her fuchsia silk dress and leather jacket. The sweat-stained ankles of her knee-high boots bit into the skin of my feet. There was even a little of Lily's blood, a dissipating flower of the stuff at the heel of the left boot, maybe from a blister. There was nothing I could do about finding David again until the next day, and I needed time to think what to say to him, so in the meantime I went to a tiny downtown dive called just The Dragon, not too far from David's office building. The Dragon was a long and thin room with an elaborate pastoral mural above the rows of vodka, gin and vermouth bottles behind the bar. Above the front door a beige stuffed cat bared his teeth and teetered on the wire spear that kept him upright, and along the walls were lots of different-sized mirrors. It was raining that evening. I could see in the mosaic of mirrors around the bar that Lily's fuchsia sundress didn't suit me. It was a beautiful thing with a high neck and a gold zip that traced my spine down the back, but it made me look pale and too skinny. I'd tried on some of Lily's lipstick earlier, but anxiously smudged it off again at the last minute before leaving the hostel. By the time I arrived, my dress was polka-dotted with polluted rain and my hair was frizzy.

At first I only saw one barman, a man with the word "nomad" tattooed in Gothic letters on his wrist. The bar was busy for such a small space, with three couples at tables around the sides and one group of students with beers and books in the corner. I was just rummaging in my rucksack for Lily and August's wedding photograph, planning on asking the nomad bartender if he knew August. Then August himself came backwards out of the kitchen with an armful of frosted Martini glasses. He wore a white cotton shirt with the sleeves rolled up to above the elbow. He must have been older than Dad, at least forty, but he looked quite similar to the youthful face in his wedding photograph. August's eyes were soft, his skin was thin, and he moved towards the bar with an aquatic elegance that belied his age. He walked like a teenage catwalk model, the complete opposite of the Giant's oversized and tipsy limp that had made me hold my breath earlier in the day. August had curly brown hair that was thinning slightly at the top of his head and cut much shorter than in the wedding photograph. He didn't look at me as I sat at the bar, but gruffly asked:

"What can I get you?" He wiped the smudge on a Martini glass with a chequered cloth.

"Whatever's good," I said. He stole a blank look at me, and then, without a word, filled a tumbler with ice. He poured a clear liquid over the ice, then filled the rest with vodka and stirred it all up before straining it into a Martini glass. He twisted a lemon slice into the liquid like he was wringing laundry, then spread the broken-fleshed lemon around the edge of the glass and dropped it into the vodka. He put it in front of me and gave me a quick, distracted smile.

"Enjoy," he said, and walked away. I put my fingers on the stem of the glass and was about to say something to make August come back, but my voice caught. I sipped vodka in silence and watched August's pretty face light up at the sight of a woman in a business skirt-suit talking about a new rock band she'd seen at a club the other night. Suddenly I felt exposed and wobbly on the barstool, so I climbed off and retreated to an empty table with a clear vantage point of the bar.

"They were just awesome," said the woman in the business suit, clasping her hands together and smiling. "Like, so cool. We danced for ages. It was fun."

"Yeah? Guess I'll check them out sometime," drawled August with his glossy brown eyes stuck on her.

"I'll burn you a copy of their album if you like?"

"That'd be cool," he said.

"No problem." She smiled and leant on the bar to continue flirting with him, while I sat and watched the back of his head bob up and down in the occasional burst of appreciative laughter. Occasionally she wound her shoulder-length hair around her painted fingers, or bobbed down to fiddle with the buckle of her heeled white sandals. I got Lily's book out of my bag and laid it out on the sticky table with the cover bent back to hide the drawing of a naked man on the front. I'd put the Polaroid wedding photograph in the paperback for safe-keeping and it peeked out of the side. I sat alone at the table for ages while more people turned up – a bearded man holding hands with a platinum-blonde, bottle-tanned woman, two men who read newspapers in silence. Eventually August looked in my direction and caught my eye for half a second, but by now I'd left it so long that I figured I might as well wait until he was closing up before giving him the photograph. Otherwise he'd wonder why I didn't just come out with the photo first thing. August slid back over to the other side of the bar while I went back to reading about Enkidu and Shamhat the whore. I read slowly, aware of August's shadow shimmying back and forth across the bar. At one point I think August and the nomad bartender whispered something about me, because when I glanced up they both looked quickly away.

It was around midnight when people started to leave. Most of the couples peeled off first, then the group of students with beers and books who'd been sitting in the corner, then the men with the newspapers and a group of businessmen I hadn't noticed come in, and the last to leave were the bearded man and his platinum-blonde girlfriend, who had been kissing him and giggling in the corner while August and the Nomad washed down the tables and turned all the lights on. I felt awkward still sitting there, but August smiled at me as the bar was flushed with phosphorescent light and the last people in the bar guffawed drunkenly out of the door. August's smile was a half-smile, really, sort of perturbed, like he couldn't second-guess the creature in an ill-fitting purple dress and knee-high boots reading in the corner. I thought he was going to say something to me or tell me they were closing, but he didn't. So I said, almost too quietly to be heard:

"Are you closing now?"

"Huh?" August said, leaning his elbows on the bar as if to help him hear me. Music was still playing in the bar, even though the lights were on.

"Are you closing now?" I said, slightly louder.

"You're English," he said. "Yeah?"

I nodded.

"I should be off I guess," I said without getting up.

"What you reading?" he said, smiling like he was laughing at me.

"It's not that good," I said, closing it and turning it on its back. "I borrowed it. It's not very good."

"You've been reading it all night, though," he said. "Must have been interesting enough. You want another drink before you go? We've been making bets on whether you were meant to be meeting someone or not."

"I wasn't meant to be meeting anyone," I said.

"No one stood you up?" August said. "Really? I mean, it's happened to the best of us. Nothing to be ashamed of."

"No," I said. "It just looked like a nice bar. Does that mean you lose the bet?"

"You looked like you were waiting for someone," said August, shrugging. "But I didn't realize you were English. The English are odd. Every English person I know has been fucked up," he said. "Strange people, you know?"

"I just felt like reading my book," I said. "I've been on holiday with friends, but they all left this morning and I'm leaving tomorrow."

"I can't hear you," he said. "Speak up." He turned back to where the nomad bartender was putting chairs on tables. "Rob! Turn the music down, will you?"

"It doesn't matter," I said. Rob rolled his eyes at August and obligingly turned the music down a few notches, then kept going with his tidying.

"I was wrong then, you weren't stood up, you're just a bit odd," August said, putting three Martini glasses on the bar. "I'm making Rob and myself a drink, I'll make you one too since you're here. It's Rob's birthday," said August.

"I don't want one," said Rob. "I'm going home."

"It's your birthday," said August. "You have to have one."

"It's my birthday and I want to go home to bed," Rob said, but August made three drinks anyway. When August walked over to my table and passed me my second Martini I moved my finger, just half an inch, so that our skin touched slightly.

"Enjoy," he said, and he smiled again. It was the smallest gesture, but my skin tingled. Maybe on some level his skin felt something of Lily in me, but what he probably recognized in this English girl wearing a rumpled sundress was her need to be touched. I should have taken out the photograph and given it to him at that point, right then before the other barman left, but I didn't. Instead I took a deep breath and smoothed Lily's dress over my legs. I thought of Laurence's words about being visible when you're aware of your body. My skin didn't smell of nervous sweat and LA smog any more. It smelt of vodka and the fading remnants of Lily's perfume.

"I'm beat," said Rob, downing most of his Martini in one and turning off the music from a box behind the bar, then walking to the door. He looked disapprovingly at August again. "Are you going to lock up, then?" said Rob.

"I'll lock up, dude, sure," said August. My heart started to beat quite fast, and it got faster as the door clicked close on August and me alone in the silent bar. I should have taken the photo from the book as soon as Rob left. That would have made sense, but my fingers didn't move. August gave me a puzzled look. He must have been wondering whether the potential result of this conversation had any chance of being worth the required effort, or whether he should just tell me to drink up and leave. August presumably thought I was some lonely tourist who'd been stood up and wouldn't admit it, or who didn't have anyone to spend time with in the first place. I took another sip of the Martini he made me. I touched the corner of the wedding Polaroid at the back of Lily's book, and thought that if anything got out of hand I could just show him the picture. I hadn't expected him to look at me like he was doing, so instead of showing him the photograph I smiled awkwardly at him across the bar. I'm not sure if I'm pretty – but I'm not ugly. Sitting in the empty bar with August, though, I felt small and anxious.

"So you've been on holiday with friends?" he said, not believing me.

"Yeah."

"From London?"

I nodded.

"Leaving tomorrow?"

"Yes," I said.

"Having fun in LA?"

"Uh-huh."

"Do you smoke?" he asked.

I nodded again.

"Let's go have a cigarette on the fire escape," he said.

And so I followed August through the overcrowded, damp-smelling back room of the bar, where he grabbed a pack of Marlboro reds and a Zippo from one of the many towers of boxes. The back door opened out into a little alley where deliveries were obviously made and the rubbish put out. August pulled down a ladder leading to a fire escape, and blood rushed to my skin as he took my hand to help me up the first few rungs of the ladder so I could sit just above him. I left my rucksack on the concrete floor amongst piles of cigarette butts under the ladder and climbed nearly to the first landing, then turned to sit down on the black-painted metal. August stood at the bottom, leaning on the brick wall with his face at the level of my knees. He lit my cigarette for me and passed it from his mouth, over my knees to my hand, then stood back a step and lit his own. We both inhaled.

"It's a nice bar," I said after a quiet moment.

"It's OK. It's fun."

"Do you own it?"

"I'm the manager. I live up there at the moment," he pointed to a window above the bar. "What have you been doing in LA? You had fun?"

"Just normal stuff. Tourist stuff," I said.

"Shopping on Melrose?"

"That sort of thing," I lied, not knowing what Melrose was. I sucked on my cigarette gratefully. I wasn't great at small talk.

"And you had fun?" he said.

"Sure," I said. "Are you from LA?"

"Nah, I'm from Nevada originally – the border between Nevada and Idaho. I've lived here a while now though."

"Do you have family in Nevada?"

"Brothers and sisters, sure," he said, but looked a bit bored with the conversation. He probably would rather have been talking to the girl in the business suit who wrapped her fingers around her hair and fiddled with the straps of high-heel sandals.

"You're shivering," he said, and put his hands on my knees even though I wasn't shivering at all. The air was damp from the rain, but not cold at all. He looked at my legs. Lily's black leather boots and purple dress only made my knees and thighs look more alabaster, more bruised and babyish clamped to-gether there on the fire escape. This sort of thing had never happened to me before, so I wasn't aware of the "cigarette outside, arm around shoulder, small talk, can we see each other again sometime" cliché of it all. We both finished our cigarettes, and he stamped them out on the damp floor.

"Shall we go back inside?" he said.

Perhaps that was it, I thought. He was bored and he'd like me to leave now, because I wasn't pretty or confident enough to be worth flirting with. He helped me down off the fire escape, though, and he didn't let go of my hand as I swung my rucksack over my shoulder and followed him back into the main bar, where he turned off the over-bright lights and plunged the room into half-darkness with two lamps on. He let go of my hand, and it fell down to the side of my hips. We looked at each other.

"Maybe we could see each other again," he said. He moved his face quite close to mine in the darkness. His breath smelt of olives, vodka and cigarette smoke.

"Sure," I said.

"I like you," he said. "I can't work you out. I'd like to take you to dinner sometime. Is that something that might happen?"

Of course he didn't mean this, because I'd already told him that I was leaving the next day, but it didn't seem to matter. He stood very close to me, then tucked my scraggly blond hair behind my ear and caressed my skin down from my ear lobe to my elbow. I suppose I must have tilted my head up slightly, because somehow we were kissing in the middle of the bar, and only a moment later he unzipped the back of Lily's purple dress and the silk fell to my feet. It happened very fast, and I didn't have time to think. I had a sense of a crowd inside of me while all this happened, like I was sitting in a triple-exposed photograph with partially opaque faces layered underneath my own. I wondered how many women he'd shared cigarettes with in that alleyway, how many he'd asked for dinner in order that they kissed him and let him slip their dresses from their bodies. He kissed me under my ear. He kissed my shoulder blade, breathing damp cigarette breath onto my skin. Soon I was naked apart from my knickers and boots, his hands cold on my skin, but I couldn't concentrate. I expect that Lily would have lived in the moment, but it was as if I could see the whole thing from the outside. Would she have moved in his arms like I was doing? How did her fingers feel against his body? Did he love her?

"Wait," I said to him.

"Shhh... huh," he mumbled into my skin, not really hearing me, and I let him continue for a moment, because the sensations were pleasant. I'd had sex a couple of times before, with Laurence, the shoplifting boy. The first time I had sex with him strange thoughts kept popping into my head. I had lain back and wondered who designed wallpaper and how it was made, then thought about whether it would be possible to melt tin in a saucepan. None of the feelings between my legs seemed half as interesting as the ache in my knees when I jumped off of a particularly high wall. This time, though, standing in the empty bar with August, I was trying to concentrate very hard on the present moment, the dots of bone snaking down August's naked back and the changing textures under my toes as he unzipped my boots and I stepped out onto the floorboards of the bar. But really my mind kept fading away. Although the feeling of his tongue and fingers on my skin was far from unpleasant, it was still as if I was watching the scene from elsewhere. Then he began to undo the clasp on his belt and I frowned, suddenly scared.

"Wait, stop. August, stop."

"How'd you know my name?" he said after an animal pause, his hand on the clasp of his belt. He pulled away and looked at me in the semi-darkness. "I've seen you before somewhere," he said again, wary now. "I thought I recognized you when you first walked in. I said to Rob: she's been here before, I recognize her. Have you been here before? Where do I know you from?"

The room felt draughty, and I felt naked, especially so because he was still wearing trousers and I was only wearing underwear. He took a step back and looked at me, prompting me to struggle Lily's dress off the floor and back over my pale body while he watched. My elbows got caught in the armholes, and a button bounced off the high-necked silk material onto the floor.

"Sorry, August, sorry. I'm Lily's daughter," I said under my breath, as I straightened the dress over my body.

He stopped.

"Where is she?" he said.

9

I sat guiltily on the table where I'd been reading all night, and he sat on a table way across the room. He had his head in his hands, and I could see the thinning hair on the crown of his head. It took me half an hour to persuade him that he couldn't under any circumstances be my father, and then he calmed down a little.

"That sounds like Lily," he said, when I explained how she died out on a desert highway because she wasn't wearing a helmet. "I wish someone had told me she was dead."

"When's the last time you saw Lily?" I asked tentatively.

"Ten years, I guess," August said. "She was twenty-two when we divorced. We weren't on great terms when she left though."

"You didn't see her again?"

"No."

"How old were you when you met?"

"Eighteen," he said. "Married when we were nineteen, divorce three years later."

"Were you happy?"

"In a way."

"What sort of way?"

"I'm not sure I feel comfortable talking to you about this," he said. "I don't believe I just tried to fuck Lily's kid," he laughed nervously, then frowned again and laughed again to himself. He wouldn't look at me.

"I'm sorry I didn't tell you before," I said. "That's why I came tonight. Then I thought I'd wait till everyone left before I brought it up and then…"

"And then. Yeah," he said.

We were silent for a few moments.

"You really didn't know Lily at all?" he said eventually, tilting his head and glancing thoughtfully up at me. He seemed a very long way away, across the bar. "She never wrote or came to visit?"

I shook my head.

"Well," he said, taking a deep breath. Suddenly he looked like a different person, much more grown-up. "She was up and down. She was an adrenaline rush. Like in one moment she could make me extraordinarily happy and then extraordinarily unhappy. So yeah, we were happy a lot of the time. But we were unhappy a lot, too."

"Did you meet in Los Angeles?" I asked.

"Nevada actually," he said. "She was sitting on the kerb outside my Dad's grocery store in Jackpot, this little town on the edge of Idaho and Nevada. She had her hair in two French braids." August grinned, relaxing more. "One resting on her shoulder and one down her back. She was wearing this shit-hot blue miniskirt, right, kind of tacky, but childish-tacky, you know? Like it was from a school uniform. She was only eighteen. And a white tank top with blue birds embroidered around the neckline."

"What was she doing in Jackpot?" I asked August. I imagined him strolling over the hot tarmac motorway in the middle of a nondescript town, towards my teenage mother. I imagined Lily's bare feet resting in the dust and her arms around her stomach. With neatly painted fingers she shaded her face from a sun that was so clean it almost made the dry grass around the grocery store look as if it was about to bubble or go up in flames – and in my imagination August smiled at her.

"She didn't *mean* to be in Jackpot," August said. "Nobody ever means to be in Jackpot. She was on her way from New York to LA, getting Greyhounds and hitching. Some trucker was giving her hassle, so she got out."

"Did she have an English accent?"

"She'd only been in the States a few months when I met her. It was when we moved to LA that she started pretending she was from Nevada. She could do the accent, and she liked pretending. Pretending was her hobby. Every day was theatrical, you know? If she was sad, she'd dress entirely in black, if she was excited she'd sing show tunes in the shower till the neighbours complained. She wore high heels to the supermarket and fake fur to the cinema. We used to have 'character nights', where we'd go out bar-crawling pretending to be aristocrats, or invisible superheroes, or ninjas. She was never boring, but she was exhausting."

"Did you love her?" I asked.

August nodded.

"Sure," he said. "Of course I did. I married her."

August let me stay at his flat above the bar that night, because it was late and the West Hollywood hostel was a while away. He looked nervous when I asked to stay, but he couldn't really say no at that point. He relaxed once we were at his place, though, him sitting on the mattress, me on the sofa. It was just one room with a beat-up-looking sofa, a mattress, and a tiny kitchen table. He gave me pyjamas trousers to wear with a

T-shirt. He still tried not to look at me, although his eyes kept flickering over to tiptoe across my skin and then jump away again. It felt strange, almost powerful, that I was making him nervous, even if it was only by association.

"Are you sure I don't look like her?" I said to August. I glanced up at him and tried not to bite my nails or tear up loose skin on my fingers and draw blood.

"Not really," he said. "I don't know, you seem like more of a… tomboy than she was. Right? You walk different. You seem quieter than her, too."

I shrugged.

"Why did you divorce, then?" I asked. "If you loved her?"

"Life isn't that simple. We grew apart, I guess," he said.

"You said she left you," I said.

"We grew apart, *then* she left me," he grinned. He had a nice smile. "For most of the time we were married she had this awesome enthusiasm, you know? She would suck you into her moods, her whirlwinds, but at some point she started spinning too fast. She worked at a bar downtown called Julie's Place and started having an affair. I'd met the guy a few times at parties and stuff. He was some slime ball who lived above Julie's bar, the sort of guy who'd sell his grandma for cigarettes."

"What was his name?" I said.

"Richard, I think?"

"She married him," I frowned. "Richard Harris?"

"That's him."

"But – you know – he can't have been *that* bad. I mean, as an influence. Lily did nurse's training a year after they got married, you know? I found her report card from a nurses training college, and it said she was 'dedicated and enthusiastic'."

"Well, she was enthusiastic," August said. "But never for the right things, at least when I knew her. But you're right, it's not like I saw Richard's good side. He just wanted me out of the picture."

"Did you put up a fight?"

"Not much. Like I say, we weren't on cloud nine any more by that point."

"Do you know when she was a model?" I said.

"She was in a few things while we were together, toothpaste and stuff, but she was always missing auditions and forgetting to turn up to shoots. She wasn't the most reliable girl, your mother, but you know that."

"She must have got better, to be a nurse," I said hopefully.

"Maybe she changed, who knows," said August.

We were quiet for a moment. The late-night air went silent. If you listened you could hear cars buzzing like insects down the road underneath his apartment and the click of a woman's high heels on the damp streets. I turned my head to look out of the window and caught that 6 a.m. city moment where the workaholics and alcoholics, early birds and insomniacs fleetingly collide. There were spotty teenagers walking back from the night shift at some garage, dragging their oversized limbs and not talking to each other. One of them almost bumped into a smart businessman getting into his Mercedes, and the businessman swore, already hating the day.

"She wanted an abortion. My Grandpa talked her out of it," I said to August. He sat down on the sofa next to me and I turned my face towards him slightly. The beige linen sofa was uncomfortable, and it had a rip in the back, like he got it off the corner of a road and never fixed it up.

"Well, sounds like she was just a baby herself; you can't blame her for that," he said.

"Dad says Lily wasn't the nurturing type – that's why she left me, I suppose. My Grandma, my Dad's mother, she gave Lily two goldfish to look after when Lily first let slip she was pregnant. Lily named one of them Satan, one Guinevere, and they were both dead within a week."

August laughed.

"She vomited the only time they tried to make her breast-feed," I continued. "She didn't touch me if she could help it. She even left me in the supermarket once."

"On purpose?"

I shrugged and put the tips of my fingers lightly on August's brown skin, tracing the muscle of his shoulders, pressing my finger into the space like a button behind his ear lobe. I paused for some sort of reaction, but he didn't stop me. I kissed his ribs and tasted bone. August held my hips and hesitated for a second, then lifted my spine to place his body inside mine. He left his blue T-shirt on my torso and heat crackled bitingly at our cool skin. He did it with his eyes closed, as if the sight of me was peculiar, like I was a wet dream from his teenage days.

10

I hated sleeping in the same bed as anyone else, let alone in someone's arms. Even the thought of sleeping while in physical contact with another human being used to make me so conscious of breathing that inhaling became as complex as keeping a drum rhythm. Even if comfortable, I'd itch to turn over into another position, my knuckles would ache to be cracked and I wouldn't fall asleep until I'd excavated myself. I'm better with sleep now. That night, though, August fell immediately asleep a few moments after he came, while I lay awake and wished that I wasn't sober. Sleeping in the same bed as someone seems more intimate than sex. Sleep has been a kind of demon in my life – seductive and spiteful. I used to talk in my sleep, throw things even. I'd wake up backwards on the bed with my pillows on the floor and my alarm clock in my sock drawer. In other centuries or other countries they might have called me possessed. I used to keep bottles of night-time cough syrup packed side by side in my bedside drawer, too, and took spoonfuls of codeine so that I'd fall asleep without having to invent stories that I had no control over, which, if I wasn't careful, could sink into terrifying dreams that I had even less control over. I hated my imagination. I hated my lack of control over it. Then at the age of twelve I decided that the stories in my head were better than reality, and so I slept as much as possible for nearly a year and a half of my life without a drop of cherry-flavoured syrup.

Lying next to pretty August in the small bed in Los Angeles, though, I didn't sleep at all. I studied the shadows and tried not to move much or wake him up. I did a lot of thinking that night with my face against the wall and my back strategically making a barrier between our bodies. I wondered how much Richard wanted the suitcase back, and if David was still drunk. It sometimes seems that men and women are born to be a particular age. David was meant to be in his twenties. I'm meant to be fifteen, maybe. Children are allowed to be perplexed, but adults are judged on how well they mould to the world around them and how well they connect. If you're no good at connecting then you're a failure. There were some girls back in London with slicked-back ponytails and low-slung jeans who seemed only to be biding time until they were thirty-five. Their eyes were ahead of their sharp mouths as they sat on the railings, smoking dope and waiting for something that never happened. Often their skin was bracing itself for wrinkles while they blew smoke out with a flurry of guttural swearwords. These girls occasionally came to the football field to find boys, but they didn't speak to me. There were chubby little boys with greased hair, pin eyes and oversized football shirts who ought to be nineteen and ever after would be faintly absurd. Occasionally a slump-shouldered woman would walk past the football field on her way back from the all-night supermarket, and it would be obvious that she was born seventy-two: her body only needed to catch up, and she might be considered beautiful.

In the same way, August had the ephemeral expressions of an enthusiastic child still brimming on his face, and it made the laughter lines around his mouth stand out. He must have been unapproachably pretty at seventeen, but his forehead had contours now and his nose was broken in the middle with a jagged bump. I wanted to draw a map of his body while he slept – like the maps in Lily's suitcase of memories – especially the sheet wrapped around his right thigh, and how what must once have been a perfect washboard stomach now inched out, just a little, towards gravity. For a moment there was nothing else in the world but that yawning breeze in the white curtains and the gurgling dripping of a tap in the kitchen. There was nothing more than stretching naked next to a sleeping boy and running my fingers over a cool patch of material at the top of the bed, feeling the nerves down my spine awaken inch by inch. I rolled over onto my back and took in my surroundings, which for a moment did not make sense. Martini bars and cityscapes, dusty roads and blue miniskirts, everything came back to me simultaneously and with equal luridness.

I turned onto my side and closed my eyes on the darkness. I lay there for hours trying to regulate my breathing. I thought about David again, then about August. I swallowed, and the body next to me stirred. It was a peculiar feeling, almost like I could still feel his touch on my skin, like I was indented. I told myself to calm down, be normal, fall asleep, but it felt as if ants were crawling between my muscles, my sweating skin kinetic with them. The air in the room didn't have enough oxygen in it. I was breathing August's carbon-dioxide, and my breathing sounded so loud I was surprised it didn't wake him up. It wasn't dark enough in his flat, either, and I could hear the day beginning outside. I couldn't stand the proximity, the weight of his presence on the bed, his breathing near my ear, the feeling that he was full of dreams. He seemed to be smiling in the darkness. Eventually I pushed August's bed covers slowly off my legs, peeling my anxious limbs from the mattress inch by inch, heavily, escaping. I stuffed Lily's purple dress into my rucksack and zipped Lily's knee-high boots on underneath August's tracksuit bottoms. I took the Polaroid wedding photograph from the Enkidu book, placing it carefully on the pillow next to August's sleeping body.

Outside his block of flats I lit a cigarette and felt giddy with relief. Emptiness and air hit my skin. Skyscrapers flanked the busy road. Sucking happily on my cigarette I started to walk in the direction of a bus stop at the top corner of the street, Lily's boots clicking on the pavement as I hugged her leather jacket over the T-shirt August had leant me to sleep in. The morning air was cold in the shadows of the Los Angeles skyscrapers and hot inside the pockets of light that snuck through between and above the buildings. My plane back to London was meant to leave that afternoon.

11

When I was eleven, all gangly-boned and scrawny with large gaps in my mouth that hadn't yet been filled with second teeth, Grandpa (Dad's father) bought me a box of magic tricks and a dictionary. Who knows what made him buy that particular pair of presents, but I'll always like him for it. In the magic box there were red plastic thimbles, coloured marbles, little sponge bunny rabbits and playing cards with prank corners. At home the only full-scale mirror was in the tan-tiled bathroom on the back of the door. I would spend hours and hours sitting on the edge of the bathtub practising sleights of hand in the mirror, but if anyone except my own reflection watched me perform, I'd mess up. Similarly with the dictionary, I almost never used my favourite words out loud. I hoarded them and used them to communicate only with myself. "Beguiling," I'd say before I fell asleep, thinking of cunning bumblebees. "Ecclesiastical," I'd mumble in the bath. "Exacerbate. Nebulous. Redemption."

Grandma and Grandpa owned the café and the flat then. They slept in the main room, Dad slept in what became my room, and I slept on a collapsible bed in the living room. Grandpa died of prostate cancer during my Christmas school holidays when I was eleven, a month after he gave me the box of magic tricks and the dictionary. Grandpa had one lazy eye, which was a putrid yellow like the yolk of an old egg. The iris bled out into the white area, which was grey with age. It was difficult to know where he was looking, and I used to think that he did it on purpose. "Just keep practising, kiddo," he'd say when he saw me, cross-eyed and dizzy, trying to look at two things simultaneously. I still don't understand whether he was blind in one eye, or whether his eyes could focus on separate objects at the same time.

Dad and I were with Grandpa in the hospice room when he died, but Grandma was in the cafeteria buying coffee. It was a white room with beige furniture, a framed seascape on the wall above the bed, and an itchy blue armchair near the little window where I was curled when Grandpa stopped breathing. It was like the hospice was trying to make death as banal as possible. I was reading a yachting magazine that I'd picked up downstairs, *Yachting Digest* or something, and was flicking through dull photographs of boats when I felt the air in the room congeal slightly. I knew that he was dead before I looked up, and my most coherent memory is of the shiny magazine page resting on my knee. The light from the frosted windows was hitting the curl of the page in such a way that the photo was almost obscured by a pillar of white glaze, but underneath there was a small white boat, photographed from above, ploughing through water. My throat tightened with the atmosphere, and I glanced up. "Desiderium," I thought to myself, "a yearning for something that you once had, but is now lost." It was a lovely word, like "desire" and "delirious" and "dearest" all smudged into one.

Grandpa's lazy eye was looking right at me, although his "real" eye was pointing in Dad's direction. There was a puddle of gunk in the corner of both his eyes and a line of fluffy saliva on his frowning lips. Why hadn't Dad wiped it off? The strange thing was, it didn't feel like a very big moment. It didn't feel like his "soul" left his body at that particular moment. He used to be a handsome man, he used to be charming, and he used to tell really dumb jokes all the time, mostly about politicians I hadn't heard of. He used to wear colourful bow ties and he used to give me pound coins when Grandma or Dad weren't looking, but in my self-obsessed and childish opinion at the time, if he wasn't doing any of these things then he wasn't my Grandpa. Lying grey-skinned and vacant on the thin hospital sheets he didn't look like anyone I knew. He looked like a painting or a sculpture before he died, and he looked like a painting or a sculpture after he died. When I glanced up from my yachting magazine, all I did was blink.

"Dad?" I said eventually, when my father didn't take his eyes off my Grandpa. "Dad?" I repeated.

"I think he's dead," he said slowly, measuring the situation.

"Shall I call a nurse?" I said calmly.

"No," Dad said.

"He's looking at me," I said.

"No," Dad said again. My right leg, curled underneath my body, was welling up with pins and needles, but I didn't move a muscle.

"Dad?" I said again.

"No," he repeated.

After that, Grandma had a number of strokes. She'd always been peculiar, though. For example nobody ever saw her eat. Ever. She was the talent behind the café, and a wonderful cook. She was the reason she and Grandpa started it in the first place, and the menu Dad cooked is still from Grandma's recipes. She made fish pies and lamb stews and even fiddly, suburban middle-class dishes like cheese soufflé, but she never set a place for herself at the dinner table. Nothing made her happier than seeing Dad or Grandpa eat her cheesy mash potatoes or minced-chicken lasagna, but only water and instant coffee touched her lips in public. One time, when I was eight or nine, I came to get a drink in the middle of the night and saw her stuffing Ritz crackers in her mouth, the crumbs tumbling into the sink. I held my breath and stood still in the shadows while she tore open the wax paper and crushed the salty yellow biscuits into her mouth. She was wearing a cotton nightdress with teddy bears on it, and her hair was loose around her face. The crumbs stuck to her chin, and I could see the lumps struggling down her long, thin neck, like a mouse swallowed whole by a snake. The next morning the rubbish had been taken out before I woke up, and there wasn't a crumb to be seen.

She adored Dad. She was quiet about it, as she was about everything, but he was her whole world. Although before she had the strokes she fed me and corrected my homework and drove me to football tournaments and was almost always kind to me, she did all that for him. She didn't really approve of me, because of how I came into existence. Years later I questioned Dad about her eating habits, and he didn't believe me, never having noticed that she didn't eat. Dad didn't notice the way Grandma watched us all devouring the food she made or the pleasure she took in every fat chip and slab of crumbly quiche she made in the café kitchen. Perhaps it was to do with rationing during the war, or some confused remnant of her Irish Catholic upbringing. The way she buttered bread for chip butties was like a man putting suntan lotion on his new bride, or a priest at the rosary. It's funny what Dad never noticed.

He didn't even notice that she occasionally spoke to herself in a nervous, heated whisper, especially while she was cooking.

A few months after Grandpa died, Grandma had the first stroke. I was practising my magic tricks in the bathroom when she collapsed onto the shop floor. As she screamed a gurgling, broken scream, Dad and I rushed out into the hallway and down the stairs. I was eleven and barefoot as I stumbled helter-skelter down the cramped staircase. She was sitting on the floor, half her face and body sort of melting, muscles sunken. I grabbed the phone and called an ambulance while Dad struggled to stop her thrashing out at him. She never really recovered, especially because the nurses kept making her eat. She had other strokes and died in a hospice six months later. Again I worried about when "souls" left bodies, and whether they could leave before a person really died. Our neighbours, and people at the hospital, kept saying that Grandma "wasn't herself", but I wanted to know what that meant. She was strange before the first stroke. Was that strangeness part of her "self" or a deviation? When did she stop being herself? If she didn't know she was different, was she unhappy? What happened to her "self"? How did she lose it?

After Grandma and Grandpa were both dead, I slept an awful lot. I'd wake up in cold sweats imagining that I'd lost my mind. My brain would be empty, bombed out, wordless. My most extreme panics are the wordless ones. It isn't quite terror, then, but a glimpse into that amorphous baby time before language, when terror couldn't be tamed by words. So my panics are also hallucinations of death, because Grandpa didn't have language in the weeks before he died, and neither did Grandma. With Grandma it was horribly gradual. She got her pronouns muddled, and then she lost her nouns, until she spoke a sort of jabberwocky language.

"I'd really rather fall off now. I'm just dafting today," she'd say. "When I was then I knew everything and now I know nothing." But soon it disintegrated into "horrorgroves" and "nickelush", "logeytongues" and the "dollish dead". She'd speak this nonsense incessantly though, which I assume is because a silence without words to bind your thoughts was even more terrible.

12

The summer I was in Los Angeles was one of the hottest on record for California. "Drought Forecasted for Los Angeles Summer," announced news broadcasts on the little televisions at the front of the public buses as I travelled from August's flat back to the youth hostel. "Heatwave Threatens California Power Grid!" "Fire warnings!" The Serena Hostel's air-conditioning machines groaned and dripped into foamy puddles on the wooden floors, while pigeons huddled for shade on the window ledge next to my bunk bed. There were swarms of seagulls on Sunset Boulevard, pecking at the steam from loosened dustbin bags. Perhaps the heat upset them, and they got lost on stray currents of boiled air, landing in a panic on hot concrete instead of sand.

The café near David's office was a self-conscious space with multicoloured tables and bad art on the walls. Mostly people put earphones on and worked while drinking their soy lattes and black coffees. I saw the same faces, the same Apple Macs and graduate-law textbooks each day, so it didn't seem particularly strange for me to arrive in the morning and stay until closing. People wearing suits held meetings there, too, and I eavesdropped on scared-looking producers stuttering with coffee-induced confidence about their ideas for quiz shows or sitcoms. Los Angeles must be the only city in the world where you sit in a café and hear one guy say, "No, no, you don't understand – the radioactive monkeys have escaped" – and then hear another person analyze their own lives in movie-writing language. "Consciously I'm in love with my wife," one man said to his friend, "but unconsciously I'd rather do my secretary. It feels like this is a real first-act turning point for our marriage, though, you know?" The men nodded solemnly at each other.

A friend of mine at school used to complain about how irritating it was that a woman couldn't sit alone at a café without men thinking that she wanted company, but nobody came to talk to me, and I didn't catch anyone's eye. I happily read Lily's racy paperback, studying how Shamhat the whore begged Enkidu the animal to fight a demigod called Gilgamesh in her hometown of Uruk. I pawed avidly over these warlords and their love lives until finally, nearly three days of café-living later, David swung in again and ordered a double shot of espresso.

I lifted my chin to watch him pay for his coffee. While waiting for his espresso he glanced around the room and half-smiled at two paparazzi boys on a far table, who waved back at him. A blonde girl glanced up at David and then went back to reading a book called *Building a Character* by Stanislavski. David noticed the blonde, then took the coffee off the counter and poured a vast amount of sugar into it at the sideboard. He looked in my direction as he did this, but didn't see me: he looked straight past me into the wall. Instead of going over to him or saying his name to get his attention, my elbow carefully knocked my mug to the floor. It smashed into three little pieces, and tea splashed all over the place causing everyone in the café to turn and look at me. I pretended not to know that David was there while I apologized and helped the waitress pick up wet ceramic from my feet. Only when she was mopping up the tea did I glance around the room and see that David was finally frowning in my direction. Perhaps he wouldn't remember me at all. My heart started to beat too fast. At first he certainly couldn't seem to place me, but I raised my eyebrows in feigned surprise at the sight of him. I smiled hesitantly and waved at him.

"No way," David smiled in disbelief, and then paused for a long time, as if making sure. "It's the grave-robber, right? You're the girl from the beach?"

I didn't really know what to say, so I pulled my knees up to my torso and then immediately put them back down again. I closed Lily's book and put it away. My mouth was dry.

"Guess so," is all I could think of.

"You look different. Remember me?" he said.

I was wearing Lily's stonewash skinny jeans, her grey ballet pumps and her black T-shirt. I wasn't wearing my baseball cap.

"You threw up on the road," I said. "Of course I remember. It's weird to see you again."

"Been to any productive funerals recently?" he said.

"I tried to give the clothes back the next day, only Lily's husband had a hangover and wouldn't see me. I felt bad about it," I said. "Did you know Richard?"

"No," he shrugged. "Not really. So what did you do with the clothes if you didn't give them back?" David said.

"Kept some. Sold most of them," I said.

"So lunch is on you," he grinned. I glanced up, and when I didn't reply he said: "What brings you to this part of town, though, anyway? I always thought coincidences hardly ever occur in Los Angeles, but recently I keep being proved wrong."

"I'm just hanging around in LA for a while," I said. "You?"

"Work. You should try it sometime: it beats grave-robbery."

"Stop it," I said. David and I remained silent, watching each other. Perhaps he was remembering the exhaustion of that morning, or how the taste of Lily's cigarettes mixed with salty morning air.

"You look different," he said. "A little less feral."

"You look worse, if that's possible," I said.

"Thank you," he replied, sarcastic. He did look worse. There were swollen pockets under his eyes, and his skin was sallow with several broken veins on his cheeks, like tiny fireworks. It looked as if he'd lost a lot of weight quickly, all in the week since Lily's wake.

"You know, I felt sort of guilty after I left. Like, I harassed you and hit on you and then left kind of abruptly. I was crazy blind drunk, and to be honest it'd been a rough couple of weeks."

"You were chatting me up?" I said.

"Don't pat yourself on the back, I have awful taste in women."

"And a terrible sense of timing," I said.

"Says the girl who stole from a funeral," he smiled, then paused. "Have you had lunch?" he asked.

"No," I replied.

"Would you like to?"

"I'm not buying," I said.

Lunch was a sort of picnic in his SUV, which had that new-car leather smell. He parked in the derelict parking lot of a bar called Platinum. It had tinted windows and a metal door with a small grate at eye level. It was either a strip club or a casino, but there was no music or noises coming from inside. There were one or two cars outside the little building, and lots of graffiti around the edges. David and I listened to basement remixed hip-hop from his iPod and shared his homemade sandwiches – each one had its crusts cut off and was wrapped in silver foil. There was something paradoxical about David from the start. He was disdainful, yet anxious. He was too old for basement hip-hop remixes. He had a brand-new SUV with DVD players built into the big leather seats and satellite navigation, but in the back seat there were turrets of girly gossip magazines. He lurked in the parking lots of z-grade strip joints to catch celebrities or politicians at compromising moments, but he cut the crusts off his own sandwiches and kept emergency Oreo cookies in his glove compartment.

"I'm not strobe-lighting," he told me, when I picked up one of the gossip magazines he worked for and asked how he decided to join the paparazzi. "If there are thirty cameras waiting for Britney outside the Roosevelt, I'm not one of them," he insisted. He had an ironic smile and mischievous eyes that goaded me to ask where he would be – up a tree in her back garden? Skulking in the gas station where she bought her cigarettes? Waiting in the parking lot of a bar with blacked-out windows in the middle of the day? Where? But I didn't ask. The photo David took that afternoon in the parking lot was of a film star I didn't recognize. The stout and balding middle-aged man came out of the heavy metal doors of the Platinum Club looking bedraggled, his shirt limp across his shoulders from sweat and his bald head glowing. I didn't even feel very sorry for the man. He already had gallows in his eyes as he walked straight to his car, like some haunted storybook villain transplanted awkwardly into the Los Angeles sunlight. The villain didn't even know he had his photograph taken. The *Los Angeles Times* ran an article about the famous actor's crippling gambling addiction the next day. I wondered why David had asked me to share his sandwiches. Was he being nice, or had he recognized me as a relation of Lily? Did he really believe the coincidence of me turning up at the café?

"Where'd you get your scars?" I said to David after a long silence between us. The car now smelt of crumbled Oreos mixed with new leather. His scars, like mine, weren't immediately obvious, except in certain lights, when they flashed for a second.

"Accident-prone," he smiled. "You?"

"Mostly fighting," I said, crossing my arms and touching my face with the tips of my fingers.

"Fighting?" he smiled.

"Playing football. I don't know," I shrugged. "Not proper fighting. Where you from?"

"Coney Island. You ever been?"

"No. It's a fairground near New York, right?"

David laughed.

"There are fairground rides on it, sure," he said. "But people live there." I blushed and felt stupid.

"Were you a 'carnie' at the fair, then?" I pushed on, even putting on an American accent to say the word "carnie", which I'd heard from some American sitcom. I didn't really know what a carnie was, and my accent was awful.

"You know, I kinda was," he laughed. "My dad was a mechanic – he worked for the Astroland Amusement Park. Not quite a carnival, but near enough. My mother died when I was twelve, but she used to work there at a popcorn stand. My first girlfriend was a mermaid named Emma. She worked at the Coney Island Freak Show."

"A mermaid? How'd that work out?" I laughed. I was happy at that moment, hearing about mermaids and freak shows,

I almost wanted to tell Dad. He wouldn't even have been interested, though. He lived in a world where you got by. You didn't live, but you kept going. Maybe that was why Lily left him. He'd have been expecting me home three days ago, and I hadn't called to explain yet. He'd be very angry by now, but I knew he wouldn't actually call the police.

"It's caused a lot of confusion, the problem of how mermaids make love," David said, "but in my experience they unzip their Lycra fins and unknot their plastic glitter-coated shells from around their adolescent breasts and fumble around in the gritty back room of a Coney Island theatre." I laughed, and he continued: "She dumped me for a realtor three times her age."

"You really do have bad taste in women," I said.

"Ah, there are plenty more fish in the sea," he laughed.

"You've used that joke before," I said smiling, and he might have blushed. He looked straight out into the windscreen, and I remembered the desolate look in his eyes when I watched him sit in the car a few days ago.

"Couple of summers after Emma dumped me," he continued thoughtfully, "a friend of mine got a job at Disney. He was Donald Duck for two months, and he started dating Sleeping Beauty – who, somewhat ironically, was a methamphetamine addict. One weekend I went up to visit him and ended up sleeping with the girl who played the Little Mermaid at the underwater grotto. I don't remember her name."

"Ariel," I said.

"Lucy to her friends," he said.

We paused.

"You have little lines around your eyes," he said to me.

"Yeah, so do you," I said and closed my eyes briefly, touching the thin skin around them.

"But I'm old, I'm thirty-two next Wednesday," he said, and then paused. "You said you're, what, twenty-two? I think you've either had your heart broken one too many times, or nobody ever told you to moisturize."

"What a weird thing to say," I frowned, looking away.

"Just observing."

"My mum died when I was three," I said.

"Yeah? That's hard."

"You can't miss what you don't know," I said.

"Bullshit," replied David. "Course you can."

I shrugged.

"Would you like to have a birthday drink with me next Tuesday?" he said.

"Dunno," I said, trying not to smile. "Maybe."

"I'll pick you up from your hostel if you give me the address, say 6 p.m.?" he said.

13

Lily and Dad had their first date at the London Zoo Aquarium. They'd met two weeks before during a table-tennis tournament at the local community centre. It was Grandpa who gave Dad the money to take Lily out, not knowing how much trouble their relationship would cause. I heard Grandpa and Grandma arguing about this once, which makes me think maybe she got pregnant on that first date, perhaps even at the Aquarium. Certainly she got pregnant somewhere during the first few weeks of knowing Dad. I like to think it was the Aquarium rather than some cupboard in the community centre or a bed in whatever foster-home council flat Lily was staying at.

"What was your first date with Lily like, though?" I asked Dad, following him from the TV room to the kitchen one morning when I was ten or eleven. "Was it fun?" I called her Lily, not ever Mum. Actually I didn't speak about her much at all, because Dad didn't like it, and those conversations always ended with him being bad-tempered. That Saturday morning Dad put the kettle to boil and slid Pop-Tarts out of their silver packaging into the toaster. I was still in my pyjamas, which were bright-red and covered with Arsenal logos. I stared up at Dad from the opposite side of the kitchen counter.

"We looked at the sharks, I guess," he mumbled. "It was all right. Quite fun." He pushed down the toaster racks.

"Why did you look at the sharks?" I said.

"Cos I like sharks."

"Did she like sharks?" I said. This was before Dad and I had painted the walls of the flat weird colours, so everything was dirty-white or brown back then.

"Aren't you late for school or something?" he replied.

"It's Saturday," I reminded him. "When you went on that date, with Lily, did you look at the jellyfish?"

I'd just watched a National Geographic documentary about jellyfish at school. I'd been fascinated by their jellied tendrils and throbbing bodies. I liked the names, too: "moon jellies", swarming together in astonishing numbers. "Gelatinous plankton", "sea nettles". I'd written a story about them in English class. A jellyfish fell in love with a wave in the middle of the ocean. The jellyfish chased the wave all the way to a beach, where the wave broke into a million pieces. The lovesick jellyfish was so distraught that she, too, climbed up onto the sand and died there.

"I only remember the sharks," Dad said about the Aquarium date, intently watching his Pop-Tarts.

"Did you know jellyfish aren't really fish? They don't have brains and they don't breathe."

"Oh?" he said.

"And they're made of ninety per cent water," I said.

"Huh," he said.

"They look sort of like aliens, right?" I said.

"I don't know what aliens look like," he said.

"That's true," I said. "Do you think Lily liked the jellyfish? Did she see them? Or did she like the sharks?"

"I don't know what she fucking liked," Dad snapped, and then his Pop-Tart popped, which made us both jump. I took a step away from the counter and looked away from Dad, out the living-room window, where there was a blue helium balloon floating up in the sky. There had been a jellyfish called Man-of-War in the documentary, which floated like a bubble above the water, but had fifty metres of bulbous blue tentacles underneath the surface. The beaded tendrils throb with the water currents, twisting up and down in blue curls. There's another type called Nomura jellyfish, which can weigh up to 450 pounds and looks like some big chunk of melting coffee ice cream.

"Sea horses mate for life when they're in the wild, but in tanks they're promiscuous," I said, hoping to continue talking to Dad, although he was already preparing to take the Pop-Tarts into his bedroom.

"Where'd you learn that word?" he said.

"Promiscuous?" I said.

"That's not a nice word," he said.

"It means to love a lot of people," I said. "Is that bad?"

Dad laughed, then grinned at me, splitting the Pop-Tart in two parts and blowing on the molten jam inside. He chuckled.

"That's a good one," he said.

"What's a good one?"

"Nothing, nothing. You're a hoot."

"Why am I a hoot?" I said, frowning. "What's a hoot?"

But he didn't answer, and walked resolutely back into his bedroom with his plate of cooling Pop-Tarts. The door clicked closed, and I turned on the television. It was never really clear how Lily and Dad ended up with me. I do wonder why nobody let Lily have an abortion. Perhaps Lily and Dad left it too long before telling Grandma and Grandpa, or perhaps it was to do with Grandma's Catholic childhood, even though she hadn't believed in God or been to church for years. Sometimes, when I feel low, even now, I think about how easy it would have been for me to not have existed at all, and everything seems better.

14

After my lunch with David I went back to the hostel and asked Vanessa, the manager, to get my suitcase out of the locker. I knew the next thing to do was phone Dad and tell him I wasn't coming home just yet, but the thought made me feel lonely. Anyway, it was too late to do it that evening. It would be early morning in the café. I'd do it first thing the next day. So I procrastinated, sitting on the floor of the dormitory room and flipping through Lily's letters and photographs again. There was a zipped plastic side pocket I hadn't noticed before, like where you'd keep cosmetics or something if you were actually going on holiday. In this compartment was a graph entitled "contact sheet" listing names and phone numbers, one of which was Teddy Fink, the same name as on the Christmas cards I'd already flicked through and the photograph of Lily wearing scrubs. There were also a couple of matchboxes from Julie's Place, which I assumed was the place August had mentioned where Lily used to work, and where she met Richard. There were a couple of shiny magazine pages folded up in the corner of the zipped compartment. One of these was an advert for toothpaste, just like August had said. It was all creased and mangled. The maps and letters and legal documents were all kept carefully, but these magazine pages were just folded haphazardly and shoved in the side pocket. The colour had worn away from the creases, and the pages were stuck together slightly in parts. The second page was an ad for a lingerie shop where Lily was one of a crowd of girls standing around in white-lace bras and silky knickers. Both of those photos were sort of ridiculous, but it was the third photo that caught my eye. Lily must have been in her early twenties, and the caption said "Photography David Reed" at the bottom. It was the photo David had mentioned on the beach the morning after Lily's wake. In this photo she looked like she knew everything there was to know about the world, and as if it was under her thumb. She was walking nearly naked down a vacant suburban street wearing knickers and a little waistcoat, holding two leather dog leashes that were attached to two savage pit-bull terriers. The scarlet of the leashes matched Lily's flamboyant cherry lips as she laughed. "I came to know your little red dresses and the army of lipsticks on your dresser," I remembered reading from the anonymous letters. The photograph of Lily was a beautiful composition. You could almost tell that David loved her just from the way he made her look in the photograph. It made me want to experience things she'd known. She looked more alive in that photograph than I felt, actually alive, sitting on the floor of the creaking West Hollywood hostel.

The next morning I sat perched on the edge of a crumbling wall next to a public telephone outside a Thai hot-dog stand on Hollywood Boulevard. There was a huge plywood sign in the shape of a hot dog above the bamboo door, but the pink sausage had a smiling face with slanting eyes. There was a homeless man who shuffled back and forth down this stretch of the street every day, endlessly. He passed by in a noxious cloud of odour while I put my phonecard in and dialled London.

"Yup?" came the reply on the other end of the telephone. I could hear the television on in the background, BBC Ten

O'Clock News. I'd been in LA over a week by this point, and my plane home was supposed to have left three days ago. I could see it all: the gaudy walls around him, the little vein that rises in his forehead when he's tired or angry, the ink marks on his fingers from doing the café accounts.

"Dad?" I said.

"Where are you?" he said, slowly, after a pause.

"Still in Los Angeles," I said.

"Are you all right? You weren't on the flight."

"I'm fine," I said. I tore some skin off my nails.

"I spoke to Lily's husband, you know," Dad said.

"Richard?" I said, and frowned. "Why?"

"He called the flat and said he was looking for you," Dad said. "And he was pretty fucking irritated when I didn't know where you were staying. I knew nothing good would come of you going to the funeral," he said.

"I'm fine," I said. "Everything's good."

"Not according to Lily's husband. He says you stole a suitcase from his bedroom during Lily's wake. He said you've been hanging out with Lily's first husband, dragging this suitcase all over Los Angeles."

"How did he know I'd met her first husband?"

"I don't know how he knew, but he wasn't happy."

"When did he call?"

"Two days ago, on Thursday," Dad said. "I told him you were meant to be on a plane Wednesday evening, but you hadn't turned up."

"I didn't steal from Lily's husband, I borrowed some things that used to belong to my mother," I said. "And then I tried to give the stuff back, but he wouldn't see me."

"Well, he didn't sound happy. He wants you to call him. Do you have a pen? He gave me the number."

"His wife just died. Of course he's not happy."

"Do you have a fucking pen?" Dad said.

"Wait a second then," I said, and rooted around in my rucksack for a pen and something to write on. I scrawled down the number, although I was starting to lose any intention of giving the suitcase back. I didn't like the sound of Richard, and I liked the suitcase now. I liked the clothes. I liked reading the letters.

"What was in the suitcase you took?" Dad asked after he'd read me the number.

"She ought to have been paying you alimony or whatever you call it," I said to him, slipping Richard's phone number into the pocket of Lily's jeans and thinking of some way to get Dad on side. "They had this huge hotel on Venice Beach, and she had tons of clothes and jewellery and stuff. She was rich, Dad. Loaded."

"You stole jewellery?" Dad asked hesitantly. "I can't believe even you would be stupid enough to steal jewellery from a wake. Tell me that's not what happened."

"Just shoes and stuff, not really jewellery," I said.

"He was livid."

"They were nice shoes?" I said, kidding. He didn't laugh, and nor did I.

"How about you just come home?" Dad said slowly, weighing up the situation. "Forget it all and get on a plane. Don't call him even, he didn't sound like a nice guy. Don't meet him. Just leave the suitcase wherever you're staying, or throw it away."

"You mean not give the suitcase back?"

"The man sounded angry, and he didn't sound nice. You stole a dead woman's clothes from her wake and expect her husband to be understanding? I'm not saying that's OK, just that you didn't know what you were doing. I think you should just cut your losses and come home. We don't know what sort of a person she was."

I imagined the fuzzy bits on Dad's jumper, the fluff that always happened if you washed anything in our broken washing machine. Daphne could spend hours watching TV and tugging off the fluff from Dad's jumpers, like a monkey couple pulling ticks off each other. The television flicked off in the background, and Dad sighed into the telephone. The room would have gone dark except for a side lamp on the dining table behind.

"I need to give the stuff back," I said. "Don't I? He'll understand once I explain."

"She wasn't your mother," he said. "A few hours of labour and a chromosome doesn't qualify her as that. She was a manipulative, dangerous little girl who showed every sign of growing up into a manipulative and dangerous woman who we were lucky not to have in our lives. I don't know much about Richard, but I know I don't want my daughter to have anything to do with him." Dad enunciated his words with such precision that I could almost hear spit land on the phone mouthpiece.

"Why? What do you know about him? Did she ever make contact with us, and you never told me or something?"

"Never even a postcard," said Dad.

"You would have told me, right? If she'd wanted to get hold of me?"

"She wasn't chomping at the bit, she was a selfish cow."

"I don't exactly trust your telephone messages," I said.

"I genuinely didn't think you'd care that she was dead," he said.

"Well I did care," I said.

We paused for a moment.

"I just know the man on the phone – Richard or whatever – sounded angry," Dad said. "You know I gave up a lot for you. I'm the one who looked after you."

"I'm really sorry about what she did to you," I said.

"To us," Dad said.

"OK."

"I want you home," Dad replied. "I don't want you to get in any more trouble than you're already in. I need you to come home now."

"Bye, Dad," I said.

I stood next to the phone feeling deflated. Traffic fled past behind me, scattering fumes and dirty pigeons into the air. I have a little scar on the bottom right of my lip, created because when I'm nervous or concentrating I fold my bottom lip up into my mouth and bite down – just slightly. Maybe the canine tooth on the right side of my mouth is sharper than the left, because it's only ever the right hand side of my lips that break. I've been breaking the same space for so long that the skin opens easily now, shrugging up a little blood to the surface.

15

August stared straight up at me as I walked into The Dragon, but then he looked immediately away. It had been four days since I left him sleeping, and I felt uncomfortable at the sight of him. He took his time serving drinks to a group of men in thin silk ties before he came up to where I was perched at the bar. It was a Sunday, and not too busy. There were the men in thin silk ties drinking Martinis, two women on their second bottle of white wine in a corner, a group of tourists with sunburnt noses, and a man with a gold stud in his nose drinking beer on his own at the window. The man sitting near the window had a thick neck with greasy black hair parted at the side like a schoolboy. I stared at this man for slightly longer than I should have done, trying to think why he looked familiar.

August poured out a round of five tequila shots with slices of lime and a little bowl of salt for the businessmen with thin ties. He watched the men down the liquid and suck salt off their wrists then he slid over to my side of the bar and put down a glass of Coca Cola in front of me. He tilted his pretty head to the side and didn't say anything. His face was much thinner than David's face. August was pretty, while David might not even have been good-looking, not traditionally at least, with his oversized limbs and eccentrically ugly clothes. At the sight of August I felt more anxious than I had done before arriving. I was wearing Lily's tight black knee-length dress and a smudge of her red lipstick over my mouth this time.

Her earrings framed my pale oval face, and her sunglasses kept the hair out of my eyes.

A few years after this night I actually decided to try and find August again, but it turned out that The Dragon Bar had been bulldozed into a vacant lot surrounded by walls of graffiti, and nobody knew anything about him. I like to think that he got married and had his own kids, maybe moved to the suburbs. I like to think he got a golden retriever that looked a little bit like him, and that his second wife buries her perfectly painted toes in the sand sometimes just like I imagined Lily doing outside the grocery store in Jackpot when they were kids themselves.

"Sorry about leaving the other day," I said to August.

"No problem," he said calmly, and smiled stiffly at me.

"I'm sorry, though," I said again.

"Not even digits on the pillow?" He smiled then, and raised his eyebrows slightly awkwardly, self-consciously amused by the situation as it had turned out. "It's like something I might do. Or Lily might do."

"Really?" I said. I twisted Lily's teardrop earrings and fiddled with her sunglasses.

"Cut and run," he said, and then laughed. "You even stole my T-shirt and sweatpants."

"Sorry," I said, taking the tracksuit bottoms and T-shirt out of my rucksack and passing them over the bar in a plastic bag. I noticed the nomad bartender, Rob, roll his eyes as August took the clothes and put them underneath his side of the bar.

"You remember we talked about Richard, Lily's husband?" I said. August flinched.

"Be careful," August said. "I don't think Lily was hanging out with a nice crowd."

"That's what my Dad just told me. Richard called my Dad, looking for me," I said.

"Richard turned up at the bar on Wednesday evening, the day after you came to find me. I guess he figured out that you might be trying to talk with people who knew Lily," August said. "So he thought of me."

"And you told him I'd been here, then?"

"I told him you'd come by. I didn't know you'd stolen from him, did I? I thought he was concerned about you or something."

"I took some things Lily would have wanted me to have," I said.

"Not according to Richard. That man wants his stuff back. He left a phone number for me to give you if you came by again."

"I already have his phone number," I said.

I moved my glass of Coca Cola around in its own little puddle of condensation. Light from the ceiling caught in the glass at the bottom of the tumbler. The bar smelt of peanuts, popcorn and sugar. I felt a rush of focused dislike for Richard, and maybe a little bit of fear creeping on the surface of my thoughts.

"Do you know a guy called David Reed?" I asked August. I locked my hands together on the bar and squeezed my skin. "He's a photographer who took Lily's photo? I think they were having an affair."

"His name doesn't ring any bells."

"But she kept modelling after you guys were divorced?"

"Can I give you some advice?" he said.

"All right," I said.

"It's none of my business, but Richard isn't a man to fuck with. If she was having an affair, keep it to yourself. If you stole something from him, give it back. I didn't want to get on the wrong side of him ten years ago, and I don't want to now."

"What's so scary about him?" I said. "I saw him at the wake, and he just seemed like a fuck-up. He looked more like a wedding singer than someone to be scared of. He passed out in front of me and snored. I put a blanket over him. There was nothing scary about him."

"He asked me to get in contact with him if I saw you again."

"So tell him you saw me," I shrugged, but something stopped me from mentioning the hostel I was staying at.

"I don't want to tell Richard that I saw you. I told him you wouldn't be coming back here, but I'd rather that wasn't a lie, all right?" August furrowed his brow.

"OK, if that's what you want," I said, and counted the erupting bubbles in my half-finished glass of Coca Cola. August smiled a regretful smile and looked away from me. The women drinking wine were giggling. The man with the nose stud looked up from his beer at me, then stared out of the window.

"Do you think I should call Richard?"

"I don't want anything to do with any of it," he said.

"But you already have something to do with it," I said.

"I don't want to see you here again," said August. "Thanks for the photo you left. It means a lot to have that. But I don't want to see you again."

"Sure," I said, feeling cheap and strange.

It wasn't late when I left The Dragon Bar, maybe eleven o'clock, but I felt anxious as I stood at the bus stop. There was a middle-aged woman in a white beautician's uniform and denim jacket playing Tetris on her mobile phone. She kept looking up at me, and at a group of boys wearing baggy trousers and basketball jumpers who seemed to be staring at me rather than at her. Palm trees swayed up against the flat blue sky, and my body hardened with being watched. I felt ready to run or kick or spit, but nothing happened, and I assumed it was just paranoia.

There was a noise around a corner on the other side of a locked-up dry-cleaner's shop, then nothing except the beautician's fingers on the phone keypad and the shuffle of oversized teenage trainers on the concrete. For a second I thought I saw the man from the bar with the nose stud and the schoolboy tidy hair, but when I blinked he was gone again. There was a shadow of a man standing in the darkness on a nearby corner, though, who got into a beat-up-looking old green car, and the green car followed behind the bus for a while after we drove off. I sat at the back and looked through the murky rear window into the traffic underneath, but I couldn't see the driver's features, and once we got off the freeway we seemed to lose the green car. For the last ten or fifteen minutes of the journey I was sure that the green car had been a figment of my imagination, and that nobody was actually following me. I calmed down, but the panic reminded me of walking home from the football pitch to the café sometimes late at night, when I'd imagine creatures in the shadows. I've always been prone to irrational panic. It heats up inside me, under my armpits, behind my eyeballs. I'm not scared of pain or even sadness, only panic. I don't struggle with depression and don't think about death a whole lot. Even when I feel unhappy, tiny things still seem shatteringly beautiful, like the exact range of colours in a brick wall, or someone smiling to themselves while they're alone. But panic caused me trouble, along with the occasional inability to control the movements of my thoughts. The panics came on when I'd been alone for a long time in a crowded place like a department store or library. It also happened when I hadn't touched or made contact with anyone in a while. It was to do with either a very strong sensation of being watched, or suddenly being convinced that I had actually ceased to exist, that all I did was observe, and that I wasn't connected to anything or anyone.

Both panics began slowly with shallow breathing and an ache behind my eyeballs. My thoughts would then become exaggerated, full of exclamation marks and italics. There were two scenarios: either I hadn't looked anyone in the eye or had a conversation for so long that a kaleidoscopic feeling came over me. I'd be terrified that I was no longer attached to the world around me, so I'd need to touch someone in order to reconnect.

Then the other panic was the opposite. I've always been sensitive to people looking at me. If someone stares at me while my back is to them I can feel their eyes touching me. It heats up, and the little blond hairs at the back of my neck quiver. In these panics it would often be like everyone was looking at me suddenly from every angle, even when there weren't people looking at me at all. My mouth would fill with saliva and my skin would tingle too much. This sort of panic was more difficult to relieve, because the more you thought about it the worse it got, and really there wasn't any relief except being alone. Often there would be words in my head, too. I'd tell myself everything was all right and there was no reason to be scared, but these thoughts would be exaggerated, italicized, just like the other sort of panic. Soon the words would be pushing me straight into a panic attack, which was wordless and thoughtless and felt like my heart was exploding.

16

The next morning I called Richard's mobile number from the public phone near the Serena Hostel. My hands were shaking, and my plan was to say I'd thrown the entire suitcase in a downtown skip and didn't want anything to do with it or Lily any more. I'd say sorry for stealing from him and sorry for throwing Lily's clothes away, but if he asked to meet me I'd insist I was about to get on a plane and go home to London. My skin tingled as I dialled the number off the scraggy bit of paper in my pocket, but all I got was a dialling tone like his phone was turned off. I stood around in the heat for a few more minutes and then dialled the number one more time – carefully, checking each digit – and again I got a dialling tone like the phone wasn't switched on.

After that moment of bathos, I didn't feel like going back to the youth hostel, so I walked down Hollywood Boulevard and pottered aimlessly around the Waxwork Museum by myself, wondering why a waxwork panorama of the Crucifixion was included in an exhibition devoted to a cocktail party of Hollywood stars. The faces seemed to be dripping and melting in front of me. There was Charlie Chaplin with thin cotton trousers, Marilyn Monroe with matted tufts of beige hair and American pop stars I didn't recognize wearing moth-eaten miniskirts. In the near-empty gift shop I palmed a miniature Marilyn Monroe from a shelf into my rucksack and realized it was the first time I'd shoplifted anything since I was thirteen.

The miniature Marilyn was also a scented candle, and it had a limp wick sticking out from the crown of her melting head. Her face was squashed and distorted. I dropped her into the pocket of my rucksack without blinking, and then continued around the shop. I smiled at the cashier as she looked up from her mobile phone to smile dumbly at me with blue eyes. There were books about famous people and Los Angeles history around the room, well-thumbed and unsold, then posters of tourist attractions pinned to the walls. I bought a postcard of the Hollywood sign for fifty cents.

I'd never stolen anything serious before the evening of Lily's wake. In the past I'd only ever stolen stupid stuff, like gum and magazines, although I did use to keep watch sometimes for Laurence when he stole CDs. The first thing I ever stole was a two-centimetre-wide mottled gobstopper from a supermarket near school when I was ten years old. I saw the nugget of smooth sugar wrapped in some sort of crinkly cling film opposite the cash register, and I wanted it to fill up my mouth. I remember reaching very calmly over to the shelves of sweets and putting the candy up the sleeve of my jumper. None of the supermarket shop assistants looked my way, and I felt a rush of power. I marched out through the doors and skipped down the busy street with a smile, turning into an Underground station where my lips forced themselves over the edge of the massive globe of chemical sweetness. I wiped leaking saliva away from the corner of my lips and turned away from the crowds flowing into the station.

After that I continued to steal little things occasionally until I was thirteen and got caught stealing cheap earrings. As I said before, there was something bland about me that often stopped people from noticing my presence, especially as a kid. Teachers never called on me for the answer at school, and I never raised my hand, even though I often knew the answer. I could skip class and nobody realized. Nobody bullied me. I was always naughty, but I very rarely got into trouble. Grandma cooked and cleaned for me, of course, but she always talked over me and never with or to me. I was there, around and about, with stolen gum in my pocket and filched biros in my bag, but nobody saw me. Even when I got a scholarship and moved from the state school to the grammar school, aged twelve, I somehow managed to remain relatively inconspicuous. I got into trouble more than I used to at the state school, but still had a knack of being incognito when it suited me.

When I was caught shoplifting a year after moving schools, I mostly just felt relieved at being noticed. I'd tried to steal some earrings worth £1.99, and the manager of Woolworths marched me into a little room full of cameras and showed me a video of myself palming some ugly fake-silver hoop earrings into my pocket. I don't think I even meant to do it – I certainly don't remember being conscious of the action. Seeing myself on the video was like seeing a doppelgänger or a ghost. The grey creature in the video hardly looked at the earrings, just slipped them off the rack and into her pocket without stopping. Her nose was greasy and her skin as pale as her hair. She could have been a boy except for a softness around the jaw and a curve of the mouth. Her face betrayed nothing of the action her hand was making, just like a trained magician. Standing in the little back room and seeing the CCTV footage of my ghost, I was sort of scared. It's amazing the manager even noticed, that's how close I was to being invisible back then. The video made me think that if I blinked I might exit the world altogether. The manager called Dad into the shop, and we filled in paperwork and wrote a statement and I was banned from Woolworths for a year, which was hardly a big deal. Dad seemed a bit irritated at how much fuss the manager was making over some ugly earrings. I said sorry, and Dad made me do unpaid shifts at the café in penance.

Seven years after sucking the gobstopper, four years after being caught stealing ugly hoop earrings, a week and a bit after my mother's funeral, and one day before the birthday of a man who loved my mother, I found myself walking around auto-repair and mechanics shops in Los Angeles asking people if they knew Lily or recognized her distinctive-looking motorbike. The bike from Lily's photo looked different from other motorcycles you saw in the street, so it made sense that someone who knew about bikes might recognize it or even Lily. Although I've never had any interest in cars or bikes or engines, Dad liked cars and talked about them quite a bit, so I knew something about them. I enjoyed trawling the LA mechanics shops asking whether any of them had heard of Eagle Motorcycles or knew where I might find the shop from the photograph in my mother's suitcase. In the photo she was standing with the Eagle Motorcycle sign hoisted above her and her painted fingers on the pretty silver motorbike.

I'd typed "Eagle Motorcycles" into Google, but nothing came up except a Hell's Angel-type motorcycle club in South Carolina, which didn't square with the photo of Lily and her slim, vintage-looking motorcycle. In the photo you can't see much except for powder-blue walls, a door and the dusty sign. Ever since I stole the suitcase, a thought had been growing that maybe at some point I'd go visit Laguna Highway, the road where she had the motorbike accident. I could put down a flower or something and say goodbye to her. There are more auto-repair shops in Los Angeles than there are Starbucks coffee franchises and Mexican restaurants. There was one on every other corner: the flat, warehouse-type façades set back beyond railings and moats of tarmac or concrete.

All day I kept getting on buses, whatever bus came first, and getting out again when I saw a mechanics shop. They were usually on the corners of big roads, advertising "front suspension", "mufflers" and "electrical work". I was hoping I'd stumble across a sign saying Eagle Motorcycles, but of course I didn't, and it turned out that nobody had even heard of the name.

"Looks custom-made," said a smart man wearing blue overalls looking at the photo of Lily. Massive bikes were lined up like a robot army in the window, their Cyclops eyes winking in the sunlight. These animals didn't look like the motorcycle Lily was standing next to in the photo. These bikes were much bigger, with engines like swollen tummies. These were sci-fi creatures, time machines, tanks. The smartly dressed motorcycle salesman in the blue overalls adjusted his thin-rimmed glasses and squinted at the photo of my mother standing with her bike.

"I'd say it's made out of used parts, you know?" he said. "Beautifully done, though. For sure. That's a frame, I think, from an Ariel motorcycle? Maybe the engine too? But the wheels are from something else, maybe a Harley, I can't tell. The photo's too small." He gave it back to me.

"You don't know where I could find another one like it? Or where this one might have been from?" I said.

"Uh-uh," he said, and shook his head. "Like I say, looks handmade."

"And you've never met the woman in the photo?"

"Uh-uh," he said.

The other mechanics and salesmen in other auto-repair shops all said the same, squinting at the photo and shrugging over its heritage. Never heard of it. Nice thing. No clue.

"Beautiful bike, though," said one mechanic. He seemed to be studying Lily's legs more than he was studying the bike. She was wearing a short suede skirt and beige high-heeled sandals in the photo, her legs and shoes the same colour as the sand at her feet. You couldn't see the sky in the composition, or the surrounding buildings.

"Can't help you," he said, and went to serve another customer, leaving me to absorb the smell of oil and singed metal in the shop, browsing shelves covered in handlebars, oil and mosaics of wing mirrors. I went to five auto-repair shops that morning, but none knew anything about the bike except to say it wasn't a brand they knew. Then the idea – a sudden thought, not quite an image – of crushed metal came into my head. I blinked away the idea of Lily's accident.

Sitting on the stone bus-stop bench an hour later, I studied one of Lily's tourist maps with my knees dragged up to under my chin for a while, thinking, letting red-and-yellow buses fly by through the low-slung layers of smog. I took the waxwork Marilyn Monroe out of my rucksack and put her out on the pavement. A young woman walked past the bus stop wearing a bikini, and I took another look at my map, figuring I couldn't be too far from the sea. The waxwork Marilyn looked sad in my sweaty hand, smelling of wax and chemically created

lavender. I didn't have the suitcase with me, and I had no
intention of giving it back to Richard now if I could help it,
but I was curious about him and the hotel. If I was careful,
Richard wouldn't need to see me. Even if he did see me, he
probably wouldn't recognize me from the split-second moment
we'd locked eyes in their bedroom during the wake. I left the
stolen Marilyn Monroe on the kerb of the road, a tiny little
wax hitch-hiker, and hailed the next bus I saw that was bound
for Venice Beach.

The boardwalk was fairly empty that weekday afternoon, with
only a few surfers and sunbathers dotted around the beach. It
was a Monday, ten days since the wake. From a distance, the
hotel looked just how I remembered it – with stucco pink walls
and pale-green window frames. The fire escape snaked down
the beach side of the hotel, and the words "The Pink Hotel"
were stencilled on the side in faded mint-green paint. There was
some graffiti at the bottom of the building that I hadn't noticed
before, and as I edged slowly closer it was obvious that all the
lights were off in the windows. Even closer, right up to walls
near the door, I saw there was cardboard on the insides of the
bottom-floor windows and pieces of wood nailed over the front
door. "Do Not Enter," ordered a rusty metal sign nailed onto
the door. I had been bracing myself to sneak a look through
the doors or the windows and see Richard in the lobby, or to
jump out of the way and hold my breath if he were to bump
into me rushing out of the front door. I tried to look through
the bottom-floor windows, but you couldn't see anything
except shadows. After a moment I noticed that a waitress in
the opposite café was staring at me, so I backed away from the
now derelict hotel. I touched the stucco walls of the hotel and

stepped away from them. There were cigarette butts around the edge of the door, broken glass in one of the windows. I remembered sneaking out of the front door ten days ago with Lily's suitcase heavy in my hand. I lit a cigarette with Lily's green lighter and smoked it slowly in the road while feeling the waitress watching me from the window behind. Eventually I stamped the cigarette out amongst the others on the concrete outside the nailed door and walked over the road to the café. It seemed strange that only ten days ago this had been entirely alien and now it seemed much more normal: the smell of salt and hot tarmac, the unsteady palm trees down the beach front, the homeless people blowing their noses on rags and leaning on their shopping trolleys full of plastic bags, the sea.

A bell rang as I pushed through the doors of the Alchemy Café opposite the Pink Hotel. The café was around the same size as Dad's café at home, and it was laid out in a similar way, with the sandwich counter at the end and mismatched tables dotted around in a way that's meant to suggest bohemian chaos, but in fact is carefully orchestrated. The waitress who smiled at me wore her brown hair in pigtails and had black bushy eyebrows. She wore a little silver crucifix around her neck.

"Hi," I said, sitting down in front of the window and not taking my eyes off the abandoned hotel across the road. "Can I have a vanilla milkshake?"

"Milkshake coming right up," said the girl with the pigtails and bushy black eyebrows who'd been staring at me. The café was clearly a family-run place because there was a second woman with big bushy eyebrows and a crucifix, the waitress's mother or aunt maybe, counting receipts by the till. A familiar smell of fried bread and ground coffee beans filled up the air, and the walls were stained with greasy fumes just like Dad's café at home. While the younger waitress was in the back making the milkshake, I caught the older woman's eye and smiled at her.

"Can I get you anything else?" she asked.

"Do you know why the hotel opposite is closed?" I tried.

"Management problems," said the older woman. "One of the managers died the other week and a few days later they boarded up the windows."

"How long after she died did they close the hotel?"

"Maybe three or four days after the wake?"

"Did you know the managers?"

"We didn't socialize with them, if that's what you mean. Have you stayed at the hotel before?"

I shook my head.

"It had quite a reputation," she said.

"A reputation for what?" I asked, just as the younger waitress came out of the back with my milkshake.

"Awesome parties," said the young waitress with a smile. "I saw you looking through the windows. Didn't you know it was closed?"

"I was just wondering why it was closed," I said. "It looks like a nice place."

"Not really," said the older woman. "It used to be a nice place, before the new managers came five years or so ago."

"What was wrong with them?"

"They didn't bring a nice crowd. Not a nice clientele, you know? Trashy types. Drugs and motorcycles and dirty-looking people. I'm sad she's dead of course, it's awful, but I'm not sad her husband has shut the hotel."

"Did you ever go to one of the parties?" I asked the waitress with the pigtails.

"No, but my friend Daria was a cleaner there. She said some of the things you saw in the morning were *nasty*, if you know what I mean."

"She's eating, Missy, don't talk like that when someone's eating," said the girl's mother as I sipped the cold froth of my milkshake. "Fact is the hotel wasn't good for the image of the café: we got all sorts in here for breakfast on a Sunday morning, and most of them hadn't been to bed."

"Not to sleep," Missy grinned, and her mother looked mock-shocked, turning away. "I heard a customer say that the guy – Mr Harris – is just closing down for the season while he sorts himself out. He was devastated after his wife died, that's all. Poor guy. She was gorgeous."

"Who closes a beachside hotel during peak season?" said Missy's mother with a huffy voice, tidying up the sandwich counter. "I heard there are serious money issues."

"What sort of money issues?" I asked.

"I think they were quite extravagant. People stayed for free, they threw a lot of parties," said Missy.

"They didn't *look* like the sort of people who kept clean accounts, if you know what I mean," said her mum.

"You don't happen to know where the manager went away to, do you?" I asked. From the café window you could see a skateboarding ramp with kids leaping up over the edges like grease spitting from a wok.

"We didn't really know him personally or anything," said Missy. "We just saw him around sometimes. They came to the café occasionally, but not much. We'd just see them holding hands on the beach, or sometimes I'd look out of the café window in the morning and see them arguing on the fire escape or the roof or something, still dressed up from the night before. If I were going to guess, I'd say he was devastated when Lily died – I'd guess he just wanted to be any place except the Pink Hotel."

17

On Tuesday evening, just before 6 p.m., I lit a cigarette outside the Serena Hostel, waiting for David to pick me up. It was getting hotter in Los Angeles as the days ticked on. I was wearing Lily's red stilettos and had my school rucksack slung over my shoulder. I wore Lily's white halter-neck top and her silver earrings. I scanned the street to see if David's car was there already. One black SUV in the traffic looked a bit like David's, but inside was a petulant blond man talking into a Bluetooth earpiece. "You asked me how I'm doing," he whined, his windows rolled down so that everyone could hear his vocal argument, "and I tell you – and then you bring it back to yourself. You always do that." Then the traffic moved, and the petulant blond drove off, so my eyes jumped over to another passing car, with a young woman singing along to the radio, then another car, with a backseat full of scrambling children.

There were some cars parked on the kerb just to the right of the youth hostel, and I glanced at an old green car that looked nothing like David's snazzy SUV. Fast-food packaging was strewn on its passenger chair, and pine-tree air fresheners hung on the dashboard in front of a man with a thick neck and sharply parted black hair. I stared at the driver for less than half a second before he glanced up from a magazine he was reading and stared me straight in the eye. He revealed a squat face, stuck on a neck as big as my waist, and a gold stud in his nose. I caught my breath – feeling that calm white heat that comes from a sudden rush of adrenalin. I slowly turned away from the green car – a Volvo, I think – and started walking in the opposite direction, past the entrance of the Serena Hostel and then towards the liquor store on the corner, but the green Volvo driver with the schoolboy haircut was already stepping out of the car in my direction.

The next few seconds moved quickly. I'd got around the corner by the time the man caught up with me. We were outside a blue apartment complex crawling with bougainvillea when he put his hand on my bare shoulder to stop me walking any further.

I stopped walking. Fighting always felt intimate to me. Lily had avoided making physical contact with me if she could help it, but after she left Dad and Grandma didn't touch me much either. My friend Mary and I used to spend a lot of time scuffling with friends on the football fields instead.

"Richard just wants to see you, kid," said the man with the nose stud. The skin of his hand felt colder than I expected, I guess because his car was air-conditioned and he'd been waiting in it for hours before he saw me. I could have broken into a run, but I wouldn't have got very far in Lily's stupid red stilettos, and he probably would have grabbed me. So I stayed put and tried not to bite my lip.

"Did you follow me back here from that bar the other night?" I said over my shoulder. The man's cold hand ran down from its resting place on my shoulder to curl itself around my wrist, which he twisted slightly behind my back. It didn't hurt, but my muscles strained, and we both stood quite still. I shivered.

"Where's the suitcase, then?" he said.

"I dumped it in a skip downtown last week," I said. "I don't want Lily's shit. Where's Richard? I looked for him at the hotel yesterday and the hotel was all boarded up. He doesn't answer his phone or anything."

"I'll take you to see him," the man said, and turned me around so I was facing towards the hostel entrance and his car. He still had my wrist twisted behind my back.

"I'm not going to hurt you," he said, and nudged me forwards with his shoulder. I leant back to stop moving, but he twisted my wrist so sharply that I found myself doing what his body was telling me to do, and walked forwards in the direction of the hostel and the car.

Even though it was only early evening and still bright, nobody on the streets did anything. It was like everyone was in a different movie from me or something. A middle-aged woman with shopping bags walked past without stopping. She had very blue eyes, which looked directly at me, then escaped towards the street in front of her. When we got to the corner outside the liquor store I started to struggle, because people were always going in and out of that shop. I wriggled in the man's arms, and he twisted my arm back further, but it didn't hurt enough to stop my struggling.

"Get off me," I said, fighting under his grip now, twisting so he had to force my other arm behind my back and hold me. I was beginning to panic. I could see the man's green car parked twenty metres away on the kerb, and however much I squirmed he just kept squeezing harder. Nobody from inside the liquor store looked my way, and no one came out.

"Get the fuck off," I said, and kicked backwards at him like a horse. I missed his knee, but caught his toes under Lily's high-heel shoes and the man loosened his grip for just long enough for me to break away.

He only lost contact with my arm for maybe half a second, enough time for me to take three steps in the opposite direction from his car. Just as he grabbed me again, jarring my shoulder, David appeared around the opposite corner of the block two hundred metres in front of us.

"David!" I shouted. David had appeared, staring at the floor, but he looked up when I shouted his name. His lolloping gangster walk broke immediately into a lolloping run like a lazy giraffe. "David!" I shouted out again, and without warning the man with the nose stud wrenched my rucksack off my shoulder and dropped his grip on my arm. The sudden release of pressure made me stumble in Lily's shoes. The thief only caught my eye for half a second, then immediately started to walk away down the street with my rucksack in his hand. Perhaps he was scared of David for some reason, or perhaps the reason was merely David's looming size. I took a few steps after the thief, but I was so disorientated and unsteady on Lily's heels that I tripped over a broken piece of pavement, and when I scrambled up to my feet again David was there next to me.

The streets kept flowing forwards. Across the road on the right was the empty ice-cream shop with a rare customer licking a chocolate ice-cream cone. The customer's tongue seemed very long, lapping in and out like a gecko in the heat, and she raised her eyes to gawk at me. An elderly man was smoking a pipe at a bus stop. He stared at me through the bubble of his pipe smoke. Even a bag lady was ogling at me. She was wearing torn leggings and a felt hat, clutching a shopping trolley full of blankets, empty bottles and recyclable cans.

"What just happened?" David said, anxiously glancing around the street. I could smell myself, particularly my own underarm sweat and the slight spattering of blood at my knees. The man with the nose piercing was getting in his car, and I didn't try to stop him or scream. The man even caught my eye as he closed the car door, but David was there now, and I didn't know what to say. Words stuck in my mouth, and it was almost a relief to see there was a little bit of blood on my knees, articulating some pain for me.

"My bag just got stolen," I said shakily to David.

"By who?" David said.

"He's gone. It doesn't matter. There was nothing in my bag really." And in a second the man really was gone, driving off down the street in his dirty green car.

"Did he hurt you?" David said.

"No," I said. "It's fine, there wasn't even anything worth having in the bag."

"Shall we call the police? What did he take?" David said.

"Nothing valuable," I said. There was maybe twenty dollars in the bag. The letters, photos and clothes were all in the locker at the hostel, but the key to the locker was in the bag, which I suppose was what the man wanted. I guess he'd been watching, and knew I kept the suitcase in there. I guessed the man would go through the bag and watch me from somewhere, waiting to see whether I went into the hostel or went away with David. I didn't want anyone to have the suitcase. I wanted it myself. Richard had known Lily for years, he didn't need the evidence of her existence in the way that I needed it. I wriggled my toes in Lily's shoes.

"Can I borrow your phone for a second?" I said to David, and when he presented it, I turned away from him to get the number of the Serena from directory enquiries. The hostel was two seconds away, but I didn't want to risk the man being there, standing in the foyer.

"He's an ugly guy with a thick neck and a nose stud," I said over the phone to Vanessa. "He'll come in with my locker key, but please don't give him the suitcase, OK? Tell him there is no suitcase in that locker and you don't know what he means. It means a lot to me. It belongs to my mother. Will you tell Tony and whoever else is working?"

"Have you called the police?" Vanessa said.

"I don't want to call the police right now, but please don't give him anything from the locker, OK? Please?"

"I'll make sure no one takes your suitcase," she said soothingly, as if this was a daily occurrence. "If the little shit comes, I'll get Tony to have a chat with him."

"Thank you so much," I said. "It means so much to me."

"No problem," said Vanessa.

I thought about what was in the rucksack. The Enkidu book was in there, still unfinished, along with half a sandwich I'd eaten for breakfast and a pack of cigarettes I'd bought that morning. The only important thing apart from the locker key was my wallet, which Dad had bought me for my sixteenth birthday. Dad had been so sweet, giving me that present. He usually gave me things to do with football. Every Christmas, a new football shirt. Every birthday, a brand new football. Not that I'm complaining, I liked footballs and used to wear a lot of football shirts, but the wallet had been a remarkable change from the norm. It was a man's wallet, made of real leather with a green silk lining. Green is my favourite colour. It also had the passport photo of Lily, Dad and me, from when Lily was a kid, which obviously I put in there, not Dad.

David put his huge hands on my little shoulders and smiled down at me. I had to tilt my head in order to look at him.

"My wallet was in there," I said, very aware of how close my lips were to his neck, and very aware of his smell. I paused and realized that my hands were shaking. He took his hands off my shoulders and I felt embarrassingly warm, weirdly and unexpectedly girlish. He took his sunglasses up from his eyes. He still looked unwell, with puffy eyes, but he smiled at me. He was wearing a cotton T-shirt, and I have never wanted to touch anything so much as I wanted to reach up and touch him just then.

"Your hands are shaking," he said to me.

"They'll stop in a minute. Happy birthday," I smiled.

"I'm so sorry I was late," he said. "This wouldn't have happened if I'd been on time."

"Don't worry," I said, feeling bashful.

Bashful wasn't something I did. Before LA, like I said, Laurence was the only boy I'd ever slept with, but I'd also never kissed anyone except for him. Kissing always made me feel squeamish. I would be as likely to let someone's tongue inside me as any other body part. Laurence was skinny and tall, with pale hair and pale eyes. He smoked a lot of dope and had a messiah complex, always coming out with platitudes such as "people who fight fire with fire usually end up burnt" or "we come to love not by finding a perfect person, but by learning to see them". We'd been friends since we were ten, when I tricked him into jumping off a wall. He broke his leg, and I was forced to go visit him every day for a fortnight. There was never anything romantic between him and me. Part of my punishment for tricking him into jumping off the wall was that every time Dad made me visit him, Laurence persuaded me to show him my knickers or my nipples until I'd earned his forgiveness. He never touched, just looked. At the time I didn't have a clue why he wanted to see my underwear so often. Years later we did have sex a couple of times when we were bored or high, but I found it about as interesting as showing him my nipples when I was ten.

Unlike Laurence's precocious serenity, David seemed strangely unsure of his surroundings half the time. He was turning thirty-two, but in a way seemed younger than me, like he wasn't sure how to behave. We spent his birthday sharing a coconut curry in an over-lit Thai restaurant near his flat. Thai pop music whispered from televisions in the corners of the room, where distraught Thai pin-up boys tore off their T-shirts and sung about love.

After I cleaned my bloody knees up in a toilet cubicle, David and I sat at a window table looking out through bamboo blinds and a dusty window onto a big empty car park. Bored valets in ragged clothes read porn magazines on the kerb. David and I talked about how he started taking photographs on Coney Island and how he moved to Los Angeles when he was twenty.

"Did you meet Lily in New York?" I said.

"Who?" he said, then realized. "No, I met her in Los Angeles," he said, looking a bit distracted and perturbed at the mention of her. "I moved to Los Angeles and did fashion work, lived the high-life for a while before I got into paparazzi stuff. I worked on movie sets, in art departments, too, cos I like taking behind-the-scenes photographs. Paparazzi work is a kind of backstage photography, only on a grander scale, and guerrilla-style." He smiled, and told me he enjoyed it more than fashion photography, although it was less glamorous.

"I'd love to be a screenwriter," I said. "I want to write horror or sci-fi movies, the B-rate stuff that goes straight to video."

"Like *The Astounding She Monster*?" he said.

"You've seen that?" I said, amazed. It was this 1950s gangster flick about a gorgeous alien whose touch was deadly, which I'd seen with Dad. "Have you seen *The Butchers*?" I said. "I used to watch these movies all the time as a kid. They're amazing. How come you watched them?" I whispered at him, laughing.

"My Dad liked them," he said.

"Mine too," I smiled.

"You get on with your Dad?" he asked.

"Sort of. We fell out when I was seventeen because I got expelled from school, and he never really got over it. He doesn't really care that much, but that's all right in the grand scheme of things, you know. I'm fine without him. You get on with your Dad?"

"He's still in New York. Lives in a nursing home on Coney Island, right near the tenement building he was born in. He's a hit with the ladies there, he still takes women on dates to get cotton candy and sugar popcorn like he did when he still had teeth."

"Probably why he doesn't have teeth any more," I said, smiling.

There was a Thai quiz show on the television. The contestants had to invent acronyms out of random words. David and I watched the show during a pause in our conversation.

"This is fun," David said, and half-smiled at me. "You're making my birthday nearly bearable."

"What would you be doing if I wasn't here?" I asked.

"I'd be watching this Thai game show and eating curry on my own," he said.

"No you wouldn't," I laughed, wondering. "Do your friends know it's your birthday? Are you seeing them later?"

"Nah, I don't shout about my birthday from the rooftops any more," David shrugged.

"I'm glad you're having fun," I smiled.

"Fun: Fanatical Urban Nuns," he replied, with a nod to the game show on the television flashing with static above us.

"Fanatical: Four Ambidextrous Nymphs Attacked The Igloo Causing… Atrocious Laughter," I said, taking a while to think of each word.

"Nymph: Not Your Mouth Please Honey," he said.

"Honey: Happiness… Offers No Escape Yet," I said.

He laughed.

"True," he said.

It was late by the time our conversation stalled a little and we both looked out of the window at the car park and the scraggly valets. I was worried about going back to the hostel that night. Richard or the man with the nose stud might still be waiting for me, or the hostel might have called the police if someone had come in to claim the suitcase. Or the suitcase might be gone, which I didn't want to think about either. I certainly didn't want to talk to the police, but I was most scared of Richard and the man who'd stolen my bag.

"Hey David," I said.

"Yeah?"

"Don't think I'm weird or anything, but I don't suppose I could sleep on your sofa? Just for tonight. I don't mean…"

I said. "You know. I really mean the sofa, like not in a euphemistic coffee way, in an actual sofa way."

And I really did mean it in an "actual sofa" sort of way, not in the confused way I'd let August light my cigarette on the fire escape outside the Dragon Bar. I didn't want to have to go back to the Serena that night, but I didn't want to ruin things by sleeping in David's bed. I wanted to sleep on David's sofa.

"Of course," David said simply. "No worries."

"It's not that I'm scared of that jerk from before, it's just that it's late and they sometimes rent your bed to someone else if you're not there by eleven," I said. "But not if it's any trouble or anything."

"No worries," he smiled. "I'm actually working tonight, though. There's some stuff happening around and about, so I won't be in the apartment."

"Are you sure you don't mind?"

"Positive," he said.

"Sure?"

"Sure," he said.

"What sort of stuff is going on? Celebrities?"

"People are more interesting at night. You get to see what you're not meant to see if you go out at night."

"Are you an insomniac?" I asked.

"Recently," he said. "A bit."

David's flat was within walking distance from the restaurant. He had an amazing collection of bad horror films, just like Dad did, but his walls were also covered with bookshelves. Obviously he was a lot older than me, but it didn't necessarily show until I realized how much more information might be in his head than was in mine. English was my best subject at school, but I hadn't really read much. I later discovered that the most beat-up and scribbled-on of David's books were by Hemingway and Capote, but two entire walls of his small flat were covered in bookshelves. There was Fitzgerald, Aldous Huxley, Mark Twain, Joseph Heller, J.D. Salinger and loads of beautiful books on photography that he kept in a mysterious order based on merit rather than alphabetized by title or artist. There were no personal photographs on his walls, none of his toothless father or dead mother or Lily, but there was a whole set of prints in which random people were seen from behind. There was an old lady with her back to the camera, a little girl running away from the camera, a skinny woman in a miniskirt putting her middle finger up to the camera and a photograph of a busy shopping street in which everyone's face was in some way hidden by hats, other heads or pillars. The photographs were all framed, yet they were somehow desolate. There were no close-ups or faces.

The rest of David's flat was excruciatingly tidy. There wasn't even any food in the fridge, and his IKEA sofa bed folded neatly out in front of his flat-screen television.

"Here's a glass of water," he said, handing one to me and then looking a little confused about the situation. "Do you want anything else? I don't have people over much." He'd already piled sheets and pillows and a blanket on the sofa for me.

"That's great, thank you," I said. "It's really nice of you."

"I'll be back early tomorrow morning. If you want to leave before that," he said. "Just lock the door from the inside. There's a bus stop on the corner. I know where you're staying and everything, so..." He paused. "And don't steal anything," he said. "Please. OK?"

"OK," I smiled. "I'll try my best not to steal anything."

"Thanks," he said, and smiled.

"I only steal from funerals," I said.

"Phew," he said. "Good to know." There was an awkward moment, and then we both looked away from each other.

18

The next morning I woke up early, before David came home. I showered in his spotless bathroom and snooped around the flat. His bedroom was very tidy. He had a huge wardrobe across one wall, sectioned off by a broken sliding door. It made me smile that he managed to look so chaotic, so mismatching, when everything around him was so well ordered. I checked the pockets of a couple of trousers in his wardrobe, but didn't find much. There was a biro, a broken bit of camera, a cigarette butt wrapped in tissue and a telephone number written on a napkin. Face down in one of his drawers, among folded boxer shorts and balled-up socks, there were a couple of photographs. I was hoping to find the one of Lily that he stole from her bedside table at the wake, the one of her sitting cross-legged in her bikini and white T-shirt, but instead they were of David and friends. One was of David and a group of glamorous, bedraggled-looking friends all holding beers outside a bar and grinning. Another was the same group of people sitting in a beat-up gold car with David in the driving seat.

The car seats in the second photograph were made of tan leather, which matched the honey-gold glitter of the paintwork outside. It reminded me of old American movies. The car had a curved nose like the snout of a bear, and the "bling" paint job seemed exactly right for the stubble-cheeked and green-eyed man in the driving seat. It was haphazardly outlandish, but without self-consciousness, more like an oversized pet than a mechanical object.

There was also a lovely photograph, really beautiful, of David sitting on the hood of the dented old car with a camera held up to his face. In this photo you could see that the car was a Buick, and David looked forlorn, staring blankly at the camera. I put the three photographs back face down in the drawer. The walls of the flat were beige, the carpets were beige, and the curtains were covered in those geometric patterns you see on public-transport upholstery. Even his kitchen cupboards were nearly empty. He seemed to live off ham sandwiches with the crusts cut off and Oreos.

I flicked my eyes over the books, which did have personality. On the bottom shelf were the art photography and fashion books, those big coffee-table things that cost a fortune. Each book had one or two Post-it notes sticking out, which corresponded to where David's photos were. The first photo that I saw of David's was in a coffee-table book called *Suburban Circus*, which was full of strange-looking people doing domestic things. I was struck by a triple-jointed woman cleaning her bathroom in a tutu, and an albino teenager standing on a staircase wearing the most amazing green-silk ball gown, as if about to go the prom. David's photo was on page thirty, and it involved a dwarf woman giving head to an enormous man in the middle of a well-manicured rose garden. The photograph was taken from a distance. For some reason, as I looked at the photograph I thought of being taken by Dad to Gulliver's Village off the M40 in England when I was little, all of those tiny houses scattered around, when I thought the village would be super-human size. Dad and I ran around through the streets

– him pretending to be King Kong and me pretending to be the woman in *Attack of the 50-Foot Woman*, seeking revenge on everyone who had crossed me. In David's blowjob photograph there were car headlights hitting the sexual ensemble through what must have been a rose or bramble bush, because the light was all broken in places. It made the bodies molten, as if they were made of sweating plastic. It also looked so fake that the small woman could have been blowing up a massive doll and soon the man would shudder out of her mouth and up into the sky.

Other examples of David's photography were more traditional. In one fashion magazine there was a perfume campaign earmarked, although it didn't have his name on it. The photo was of a naked woman covered in sand, lounging on the beach with her back arched. In another magazine there was a fashion spread of models in bikinis on a Los Angeles rooftop, and in another a spread of men and women walking their dogs in city streets. One of the dog-walking photographs was the same photo of Lily that I found in the zipped plastic compartment of her suitcase. I pressed my finger to Lily's pretty face and tried to imagine how she felt, teetering down that road with David looking at her. I put the magazine back on the dustless shelf and noticed a newspaper page folded up tight there between two magazines. It was flattened and faded, like an awkwardly pressed flower. The corners bristled when I opened them out, revealing a page of Death Notices from the *Los Angeles Times* two and a half weeks ago. It was half a page long, and looked like a group of personal ads or classifieds, but each little inky box was selling a memory rather than a raffle ticket or a kiss. There was Mavis Miller, who passed away peacefully in

Pasadena, aged 92. And there was Linda Barretto Tengco, 42, of Porter Ranch, CA, who was survived by husband Vergel. I learnt that Walter, 81, was a beloved husband, father and grandfather, but he passed away November 13, 2009 at Los Angeles, California due to complications following surgery. And Dan Silverman wanted donations to be made to Cancer Research in lieu of flowers. There was a strange and succinct poetry to these memorial boxes, all of which seemed curiously impersonal. Only two of the death notices had pictures, and one of them was a photograph of Lily. It was a small picture, half the size of a credit card. Her hair was long and dark in the photo, her big eyes outlined thickly like a Manga cartoon character or a wide-eyed animal. The page smelt of chalk, the way old newspapers usually do.

"Lily lived life to the fullest to the very last moment," the death notice said underneath the smiling photograph. "She is survived by Richard, and many friends who will never forget her. A wake, but the way she would have liked it, will be held at the hotel." I stared at the newspaper page for a moment longer, touching the photograph with my thumb, then folded it along David's crease lines and slotted it back between the two fashion magazines on his shelf. I put everything back exactly where I found it and left David a Post-it on his pale-wood kitchen table, thanking him for letting me stay and saying I'd like to do it again some time.

19

The morning after I left David's flat, I called the Serena from a payphone to ask if the man with the gold nose stud had approached them about Lily's suitcase.

"We didn't give it to him, of course," said Vanessa. "Tony took the key from him and told him to fuck off or we'd call the police."

"What did he do?"

"He argued for a bit and then left," said Vanessa.

"What if he comes again?" I said.

"We'll do the same. He just seemed a bit stupid as far as I could see. Nothing to worry about, sweetness. He just kept saying that the suitcase didn't belong to you and I kept saying I didn't know what he meant."

"It belonged to my mother," I said.

"You should call the police yourself if you're worried," she said. "Can't say he seemed like a wholesome sort of man."

"Have you seen him around today?" I asked.

"No, but I'll keep an eye out," she said.

"Thanks, Vanessa," I said, knowing I wouldn't call the police.

I didn't go back to the Serena that morning, but changed buses at the corner of Hollywood and Gower, opposite a cut-price furniture shop and in front of a converted theatre that was now offering a course in "How to Succeed in Life". At the bus stop everything was two-dimensional in the afternoon heat with the smoggy sunlight flattening the palm trees to the concrete buildings and the glassy yellow sky. Everything was stuck flat to everything else, like the cardboard cut-out background of a child's puppet theatre.

"Too hot, huh?" said a woman in a hat and a man's oversized T-shirt. She was carrying a plastic bag from the 99-cent store and a suitcase on wheels. I nodded and turned away from her to watch two girl guides or scouts or something on their knees shining the star of a TV actor that I hadn't heard of. One of them was scrubbing the bronze crevices with a toothbrush; the other was buffing the marble. They didn't talk to each other, but both frowned and sucked their tongues. The woman with the hat shuffled onto the bus ahead of me, and pigeons flung themselves sideways as the vehicle pulled out into the road. I sat down right at the back. At the next stop, a clique of small Mexican women sat in the seats surrounding mine. They were discussing something uproariously funny, which meant little bits of their sweat kept rolling through the air and landing on my bare shoulders or knees. A bald white man with a golf hat kept telling the gaggle of women that they had no manners, that they were offending his eardrums and that the next time he saw them he would blow a whistle loudly into their ears. They laughed and ignored him, all of the women smiling with kind eyes and pinched leathery skin.

I took a bus downtown to look for Julie's Place, the bar August had mentioned where Lily met Richard. I got the address from the matchbox packet in the zipped pocket of Lily's suitcase. The bar was a dark-brick building with hedges outside and a flat roof on top. It had heavy doors that were closed in the early-afternoon sunlight, but had the words "Julie's Place" written over the top. I smoked cigarettes outside on the kerb next to a lamp-post for ten minutes before deciding to walk around the side and under a brick arch to a large car park at the back, where I found two camp men chatting at the mouth of an open door. Los Angeles is backwards – people come in through the car parks, and the front doors are just for show, because no one but hobos and idiots ever walks around the town. Beyond this car park was a graffiti-covered brick wall and a retro Coca Cola advert that was sliding from its hinges. The two men were both dressed solidly in black. They had the high cheekbones and expressively earnest eyes of actors. Neither of them looked at me. They were talking about scripts. I stood just around the corner and listened for a moment. One was writing a thriller about cocaine-smuggling snake worshippers in Texas, the other a teen romance about foreign-exchange students who turn into werewolves.

"Excuse me," I said after a moment, stepping forwards. They looked over at me with their nearly matching big eyes and per-fect molasses tans. I felt nervous, but asked: "Is Julie around?"

"Inside," said one of the actors. I stepped through out of the sunlight into a hallway with black-painted walls. "So anyway, like, it's meant to be like better than taking ex, being bitten by a snake," I heard behind me. The hallway curved into a sweat-smelling bar. The lights were all off, and some of the chairs had been unpacked already, but most were still upside down on shiny wooden tables scattered around the room. There was a pinball machine in the corner, and an American football game playing on the flat-screen TV above the bar. The walls were made of peeling veneer, and there wasn't any air-conditioning, just two black-painted fans stir-ring the sweaty air.

"Hello?" I said. There didn't seem to be anyone around. "Hello?" I said again, then went over to one of the pinball machines and slipped a quarter in. A sports commentator on the TV was talking about the history of American football, and I pulled back the pinball spring. Just as I was about to start playing, thinking of the Trocadero Arcade in Leicester Square where I used to hang out playing video games sometimes when I was little, a voice said:

"We're closed."

I jumped and turned around, losing the silver ball down the pipes of the machine. Behind the shiny chrome bar was the same skeletal woman with cropped black curly hair that I'd noticed dancing with her eyes closed at Lily's wake. She was wiping down the bar with fingers covered in costume jewellery plastic rings. She was a tiny woman with bones that were visible under thin, pale skin. She seemed held together by hair and clothes rather than skin and bone, as if her fingers might crumble to dust if you removed all the plastic rings. She must have been in her forties, but looked older. She didn't smile at me.

"Are you Julie?" I said.

"Did the boys let you in?" she said sharply, ignoring my question. "Can I see your ID? You look about ten, no offence."

"I'm looking for Richard Harris?" I said.

"He hasn't lived here for years. I'm afraid you're going to have to leave. I can't have underage people in my bar. I haven't seen that man in years."

"Were you at Lily's wake?" I said.

Julie paused. She stopped cleaning the bar and looked at me. She had cavernous eye sockets with the skin stretched and swollen like blisters underneath. Even in the dark you could see the red veins under the skin of her eyelids. Her eyebrows were painted on above her eyes in pale-brown pen, and they gave her an expression of perpetual surprise even when the rest of her features seemed sunken in sadness. Everything about her was tense, from the corners of her mouth to the sinews in her skinny neck.

"Did you know Lily?" she said quietly.

I considered the question for a moment. I didn't feel like confiding in this anxious woman about anything, but there was something shifty about the way her eyes flickered at the mention of Richard and how she'd lied about not having seen him in years. I didn't like her, but decided to tell her anyway. I still felt high from my evening with David, like nothing could touch me.

"I'm Lily's daughter," I said.

"Lily's *daughter*?" Julie said, incredulous, and smiled for the first time since I'd seen her. She had sharp little teeth, and flashing them didn't suit her.

"Technically," I pointed out. "I mean, biologically. She didn't bring me up or anything."

"Lily's *daughter*?" Julie said again, with the same intonation. "Are you serious? I've known Lily since she was twenty-one. I think she would have mentioned a daughter."

"She doesn't seem to have been particularly vocal about my existence."

There was a long pause.

"I don't believe you're her daughter," Julie said. She took a long look at me, then disappeared into the back and didn't reappear again for ten minutes. At first I thought that was Julie's last word on the matter and she expected me to leave while she was gone, but then I imagined she might come back with something of Lily's – another photograph, perhaps. For a second I even thought she'd come back with Richard trailing behind her.

Instead Julie came back into the bar with an infinitely more relaxed expression on her sharp face. She didn't offer any explanation for her odd behaviour. The tight curve of her lips had melted into a mercurial smile, and her bony shoulders had dropped an inch. I guessed she took a pill or smoked something, but later it turned out that she was quite a serious heroin addict. She never gave any explanation for her moods, which moved in waves from relaxed pleasure to nervous horror every few hours, and then back again once she'd disappeared into the back room and remerged.

"You're not kidding me about Lily, right?" Julie said, looking at me with consumed eyes. "Tell me now if you're fucking with me, OK?" she said.

"I'm not fucking with you," I said. "Could you tell me about her? I didn't know her, and I'd love to hear about her, if you didn't mind."

"You don't look like her, you know?" Julie said.

"Yeah, I know," I shrugged. "You can ask Richard, though. Richard knows she had a daughter. I'm definitely her kid."

"No, no, you don't have her profile at all. You don't have her nose: she had a better nose. You don't have her hair. Of course she had black hair when we knew her, but she *was* a natural blonde at some point I suppose."

Julie tried to touch my face across the bar, but I moved away, and she looked genuinely hurt by my reluctance to have her bony fingers on my skin.

"You're not like her at all," Julie said sharply. "She was sensual. She was full of love." Then it was my turn to be hurt for a moment, and I flinched, looking away.

"Sorry. That was a mean thing to say," Julie mumbled. "Fuck. I'm all weirded out now. She never mentioned you at all. You're pretty in a different way."

"It's fine, don't worry. I know I don't look like her. I don't want to look like her."

It turned out that Julie hadn't seen Richard since Lily's wake, and she didn't know where he'd disappeared to.

"Fucker owes me money, though," said Julie.

"How come?"

"He always had some scheme on the go."

"Like what?"

"They had creative minds, those two, but straight things got bent in their presence. Nothing was ever what they said it was going to be."

"I don't understand," I said.

"Property development became insurance fraud – that sort of thing." She laughed gleefully, then continued: "After dabbling in property development they set up a motorcycle company. They got plenty of interest, cos his bikes are beautiful things, and she was one of those people who could charm a pig into a butcher's shop if she tried. A year later he'd filed for bankruptcy, and they'd only finished three bikes…"

"So he made the motorcycle Lily died on?"

"Sure, I guess. It just makes you want to cry, doesn't it?" she said with dry eyes. She blinked a few times and looked exhausted. "I don't know. She was reckless. It wasn't his fault. His bikes were beautiful things."

"Why did you lend them money recently?" I said.

"Supplies," Julie said, then giggled a little manically. "Cos I'm stupid."

"Supplies for what?"

"They organized some of the best parties in LA. Everyone wanted to be there," she smiled. "Like the wake, but better. Good parties. Everyone loved them."

"So drink and drugs and stuff?"

"That sort of thing," she said.

"Did he love Lily?"

"Everyone loved Lily," she said.

"And you really don't know where he might have gone?" I said.

"His phone's not working," she said.

"I know," I said. "He's looking for me, and he left a number, but it doesn't work. He made a big deal about me phoning him, and then his phone doesn't even work."

"He owes people money, that's why his phone doesn't work," said Julie. "I'm sure he'll find another way to get hold of you if he wants to. He usually gets what he wants." I looked at Julie's fingers, crawling over themselves at the bar. Her lips were dry, and the skin was peeling off around her sharp little nose. She poured vodka over some ice and sipped it slowly. Without us noticing the bar had filled up. There were lots of hipsters wearing trucker caps and geeky tortoise-shell glasses. I ended up staying there for a few more hours watching Julie get wrecked behind the bar. All the customers knew who she was and seemed to enjoy her unreliable company. Every hour or so she'd disappear and return refreshed, but by the end of the night she was cadaver-pale with blue lips and bloodshot eyes. She moved as if walking through sludge, and smiled at me occasionally across the overheated room. The lazy ceiling fans couldn't keep the place cool, but people didn't seem to mind sweating. Triangles of sweat expanded on the backs of T-shirts and between girls' breasts. Eye make-up melted into inky tears and lipstick disappeared altogether. Nobody else really spoke to me, but I eavesdropped on actors and music journalists and cameramen for a while. In the crowds I kept watch for Richard or the man with the nose stud, but they didn't turn up at Julie's place, and they didn't turn up during my bus ride back to the Serena Hostel. I checked that the green Volvo wasn't parked anywhere near the hostel before I got too near, and I glanced around the front door before stepping inside. I didn't get back to the hostel till late, long after I figured Vanessa and Tony would be asleep.

The woman who often worked the night shift for the Serena was an Australian girl called Miranda, who drank a lot of Diet Coke. The cans would be lined up on the counter while she played on the computer all night.

"Hi, troublemaker," she said briskly. "You OK?"

"Are Tony and Vanessa annoyed at me for making trouble?" I said. "Do you think they want me to leave?"

"They run a youth hostel in West Hollywood. They're used to trouble. Someone left a note for you, though," she said. "I don't know if it has anything to do with anything from before." She handed me a bit of paper, and I looked at it nervously. "It wasn't the ugly Spanish guy," she said. "It was some big guy with weird clothes?"

I smiled at Miranda and padded upstairs, where nearly all the beds were occupied with a Japanese package holiday, but Vanessa had made sure my bed was kept free. The tourists were all asleep or whispering with each other in the darkness. I climbed under the covers of my little single bed in the corner and opened David's message under a night light.

"Hey," I read, squinting. It was handwritten, unlike the anonymous letters, which were typed. David's message was written in nearly illegible, boyish handwriting. He pressed hard on the paper with the nib of his pen, and the resulting note was messy and compact. "While you're in Los Angeles you can sleep at my apartment sometimes if you like," the letter said. "Someone might as well. I'm certainly not doing much of it. Anyway, this hostel is a total dump. Did you know that someone was chopped into little pieces on this block last month? Did you know that? A third of the victim's pieces were found in the dumpster outside Rite Aid, a third outside the booze store, and a third in a blender with a box of blueberries and some super-strength protein powder. I'll be in tomorrow evening if you come over. I'm not asking you to move in or anything ridiculous. The sofa is free, and I'm just saying that I'm never there, you know? Plus it would assuage my guilt about being late to meet you the other day and allowing you to get mugged. So I'll see you tomorrow evening if you like. Best, David."

20

I had a bad dream that night. It was about not being able to move. Every time I breathed, I'd faint and wake up exactly where I'd started. This dream was a recurring one. It started in London two weeks before Lily died, the day I was expelled from school and Dad stopped talking to me properly. One of the most popular places to sit during good weather at school was on the fire escape outside the bathrooms on the ninth floor. The walls were covered in green gangrenous tiles that gave every face a horror-movie glow. There was a row of sinks, a single long mirror pockmarked with rust, and then a frosted-glass window that you could climb out of to huddle on the fire escape. You could smoke out there, and the teachers wouldn't be able to see you unless they were round the side of the school, which they never were because it was overgrown and dirty. Plus you could spy on the lonely fat woman watching daytime TV in the building opposite and the bodybuilder doing press-ups endlessly in the window directly above her. Everyone thought they ought to fall in love. You could always hear the edgy, watery sound of teenage girls laughing from beyond that window.

When my friend Mary and I were younger, we used to play a game with some other kids in my old school from time to time where we'd squeeze pressure points in each other's necks so that we'd become dizzy and pass out. If you put your index and middle finger on both sides of your neck and press the big blood vessels that run up and down there, you end up fainting for around twenty seconds. It feels sort of funny, like a head rush, but we never did it more than a few times, and it never caused any trouble.

Then one lunch break there were some kids putting on make-up in the bathroom of my new school, talking about how to make themselves faint. They asked me if I knew how to do it, and all I did was tell them how it was done. I obviously told one of the popular girls, because within a week all the younger girls at school were busy making each other faint in classrooms, bathrooms, music rooms, locker rooms and hallways. They were crouching down in frog positions against walls and pushing desks together to make beds to lie down on. It became much bigger than it ever was in my old school when I was that age, with five girls fainting during a maths lesson and one of them not waking up for twenty minutes. The teacher thought she was asleep. It's something I noticed about all girls' schools – crazes spread like fire. Another girl started to bleed out of her ear during P.E. The worst was the group who decided to make each other faint on the fire escape. As far as I understood when people explained it to me later, the game was to faint while looking down a sheer nine-floor drop, but have friends there to stop you from falling.

The obese television addict from the flat opposite said that three girls were laughing hysterically, and when the middle girl came back to consciousness, she vomited over the rail into the overgrown alley underneath. Then she seemed to faint again, only this time she slumped forwards and her friends somehow didn't catch her as her weight shifted the wrong way, the axis of her hips tipping her forwards. She was only eleven years old, and she died immediately on impact, flat out in the shrubs. Somehow all of this was traced back to the fainting lesson I'd given earlier in the week.

"I got a call from your headmistress," Dad said when I got home from football practice that freezing cold evening. "They're finally chucking you out of school. Congratulations. I knew it was too good to be true, you going to that school."

"Huh?" I said dumbly, out of breath from kicking the football all the way home and then running up the stairs. I'd skipped school that afternoon to play football, and I didn't even know that the little girl had fallen off the fire escape. I'd been hanging out with some friends from my old school, oblivious to the paramedics and ambulances that had been swarming around my new school all afternoon.

"Do you know how lucky you were to get to go to that school? Do you know what most people would do for that opportunity? I thought you might do something with your life," he said.

He was wearing a lime-green sweater, and looked old that evening. He was only thirty-five, but he could have been fifty. The strange thing is that once Dad had decided – or been told – that I was reasonably smart, he seemed genuinely proud of the fact. I once heard him boasting to his friends about me getting a scholarship, and another time boasting about how he always had his daughter check his accounts at the café, because she had "a real head for business". I was, apparently, going places. But still, he didn't stick up for me when they threw me out of school. He just accepted it.

"You're smart, but you're a fucking idiot," he spat at me across the kitchen.

"What did I do?" I said, baffled. Were they throwing me out for bunking off school sometimes? That was the only thing I could think of.

"You taught the fourth-year girls to get high by cutting off their blood supplies, that's what the headmistress said you did. What do you have to say about that?"

"No I didn't," I stuttered, adrenaline hitting me.

"I'm bored of your excuses," he said, and turned away from me. "I can't be bothered with all your crap. They've expelled you. Some little girl died because of you, so they don't want you at their school."

"Who died?"

"She fell off the fire escape attached to the ninth-floor toilets."

"When?"

"This afternoon."

I closed my eyes for half a second and saw it: her head sinking forwards suddenly, pressing the pivot of her bony hips onto the railings while her friends were in hysterical giggles around her. Perhaps the friends thought she was laughing, too, but instead her limp arms swung as the body weight shifted and her little eleven-year-old feet came off the ground. She was probably wearing high-heeled pumps, that's what all the younger girls were wearing. How could her friends not notice? Maybe they were laughing so hard in that uncontrollable adolescent way that they didn't see their friend's weight shift. I bet the friends grabbed at her legs as she fell, the laughter stopping.

"I'm sorry," I said. I imagined the girl falling to the ground.

"Tell that to her mother and her father. Tell that to her friends," Dad said.

"I'm sorry," I said again. He didn't look at me. "I told one girl how Mary and I used to do it. That's all. I wasn't there when they did it."

"You're a bad influence," Dad said. "They regret letting you into the school. You know how much trouble it was getting you into a good school?"

"You didn't go to any trouble, Dad. My old teachers went to trouble: you didn't even know I was doing well at school till they called and told you."

"Well, there's gratitude," he said. "If I'd known you were going to fuck it all up anyway, I would have let you do more shifts at the café."

"She made herself faint on a ninth-floor fire escape when I wasn't even at school and it's my fault? I'm so sorry she died, but I didn't do it. I have AS exams in a week. They can't throw me out of school now, can they?"

"I'm not going to argue with you about the rights and wrongs of the shit you get up to any more," he said.

"You never argue with me about the rights and wrongs of anything I do. The only rights and wrongs I get from you are if I put too much salt on the chips or over-fry the fucking burgers," I said, although that wasn't entirely true. Since I moved to the grammar school he did get irritated if I got bad grades or if he found me skipping lessons. It still baffles me that he let me get expelled from school so easily. It took me a long time to forgive him for giving up on me that day. Even when I did a night course to finish my A-levels, years later, I couldn't bring myself to tell him that I did well.

"The fact is the school has asked you not to come back and take your AS exams at the end of next week. You have to do the exams somewhere else. You're out," he said.

"So stick up for me," I said. "Tell them that it's not fair. I didn't do anything wrong. Those exams are important."

"Life's not fair, right?" he said. "Sometimes you have to take the consequences."

"You're just going to accept it, then?" I said.

"Why should I believe you?"

"Because I'm your daughter and you love me," I said, and he turned away from me. He started to unload the dishwasher, and I watched his balding head dip and rise behind the kitchen counter. He looked blasé, almost bored.

21

It was a warm day when I took a deep breath and rang David's doorbell. There was a long pause when I didn't breathe at all, but then he answered the door in orange tracksuit bottoms and no T-shirt. He smelt of shampoo.

"Hey there," he said.

"Hi."

"I'm glad you came," he said. "You got my note, then?"

"How do I know you're not the protein-powder killer?" I replied with a smile, not coming in through his door.

"Because I don't like blueberries," he said.

"The murderer would say that," I smiled.

"I'm the one inviting a known thief into my apartment."

"You're *very* brave," I said sarcastically, putting on a sweet voice for a second and then snapping out of it.

"No suitcase?" he said, looking me over. I'd swapped lockers at the Serena. Vanessa and Tony seemed to have taken a shine to me, and they let me rent a locker. I was wearing Lily's fitted white cotton dress with black buttons up the front, which I hadn't worn before, plus her grey ballet shoes. I had the strap of Lily's tan suede shoulder bag in my fist, and a plastic bag full of her clothes. In the plastic bag I had Lily's jeans and T-shirts, and ballet shoes and sunglasses – even the stilettos, but I left the leather jacket, knee-high boots, silk fuchsia dress and black minidress.

"Sold it, remember?" I lied. I was careful not to have any of her letters and photographs on me when I was in David's flat, or at least not when he was around. Having gone this far without telling him, I didn't want him to guess who I was just yet.

David was out most of the time. His block of flats looked like an army barracks from the outside and a Spanish motel from the inside. The four floors all had balconied corridors outside them, which looked down on a fetid swimming pool where nobody ever swam, but people socialized around and used to cool their feet in the crazy sunshine. It was only if I knew he was going to be out for a while that I'd bring Lily's letters to his flat and spend my days smoking his cigarettes on the hot steps while reading Lily's love letters. It was a relief not to have to sleep in the Serena Hostel any more, and although I was still always looking over my shoulder, I felt safer than before.

"To my darling," wrote the anonymous writer of the typed love letters, which I read while sitting by the swimming pool in the sun. "Do you remember the lunar eclipse?" the letter said. "You asked me why it happened, and when I explained it to you, lovely you, there was this thoughtful sweet look in your eyes and you said, 'So, it's a coincidence of geometry.' What a beautiful phrase, I thought. You liked words. Another time I explained 'non-locality' to you – a phenomenon I hardly understood, about when two particles remain synchronized over vast distances? Again, you liked the word. You whispered 'non-locality' repeatedly into my ear, in dulcet tones, as if it was a sweet nothing.

"I was showing off, trying to explain quantum physics to you, but now I can't help thinking that the same idea might seem proof of a kind of magical correspondence between far-away structures which, even across massive reaches of space, are communicating far faster than the speed of light. It's called 'entanglement'. You laughed at the word 'entanglement' as you began to say it over and over and over again in different ways – in a low voice, in a high voice, in a happy voice, a sad voice – all the while staring at your hands making drunken patterns in the air.

"You looked beautiful, but it scares me that I can't remember the exact patterns your hands made in the air, or exactly how you were wearing your hair. Even when you're nearby, I feel sometimes as if I'm fictionalizing you, as if you're a figment of my imagination. Sometimes, I see you in the corner of my eye when you can't possibly be there. God, you know, I love you, but sometimes my memories turn briefly to vitriol.

"Do you remember the first time we made love? I was lying face up on the bed. You turned your back to me and sunk my body inside yours, while all I could see was your thrusting bottom and your shoulders. Your haunches flexed like an animal's, the soles of your feet curling, and I felt entirely disconnected from the orgasm that eventually shuddered down your back. I just remember your hair bouncing in the half-light, and how you put your hands to your head like a rodeo girl before you finished.

"After you were finished, that first time, there was an awkward quiet, because where do you go from that position? It doesn't bode well for affectionate nuzzling or restful conversation. My hands were resting lightly on your hips, and your body was limp. You removed me from inside you without turning around: you just held the condom between your fingers and lifted up your bottom slightly. Then you padded off to the bathroom to wash me off your body, and I was left bemused at how such a beautiful creature could be quite so base.

"Sometimes I think of you not as the beautiful one dancing the mamba or talking to me about her dreams, but as a slut with her back to me on that first night when you hardly even kissed me. I am writing in anger. I'm sorry. I don't mean it. I love you too much, sometimes. With love, for ever, for always."

I thought the letter was beautiful. But at the same time it made me nervous. I folded it up along its original creases and put it away. The letters implied something unstable and unfinished.

Often David didn't even come home all night, but he seemed to like having me in the flat when he did. I was always relieved when he came home. I'd catch him smiling at me, but he also complained that I was taking up space, that he was too hospitable for his own good, wondering why he'd invited a stranger to sleep on his sofa. He was moody, like a child. I ignored him when he was in a bad mood, but even then he was fascinating. Was he so lonely that he let a stranger with kleptomaniac tendencies lodge in his house? He was gregarious and charming, if a little awkward, so why didn't he seem to have friends? Nobody came to the house, and he didn't speak about meeting friends when he went out. Where were the glamorous and bedraggled-looking friends from the hidden photographs in his underwear drawer? Often we ate dinner together in those first two weeks, before we started sharing a bed. He told me that he used to get terrible seizures as a child, so he had thick white pills to counteract that. In return I told him strange and pointless lies about my childhood. I told him how Dad and I used to make model boats together and then sail them on the Serpentine in Hyde Park. I told him that we went to Midnight Mass every Christmas even though we weren't religious at all, and that I was once grounded for winning a game of Scrabble using the word "clitoris". I lied about how Dad threw me a surprise twenty-first-birthday party in our local pub. I don't know where these stories came from, but they made him laugh. He suggested books for me to read, too, and I started to make my way through his library.

The residents of David's block were mainly Mexican or Armenian, but there was the odd student and actress living there too. Armenian teenagers sat on a tattered wall outside David's apartment in the afternoon, lifting their hooded eyes to scrutinize the passers-by, like ogres at a concrete drawbridge. They spoke in hybrid Armenian-American, but their language was really a series of glances, frowns and lugubrious adolescent shrugs. They knew that Belle, a fat Texan woman with a sausage dog, was in love with Yuri, the building's Armenian manager. They listened to Yuri as he played the viola for two hours every evening, the strangled sounds of his imagination spreading musical nostalgia over Los Angeles streets. The boys knew that Belle sat at her window every night wearing a baseball T-shirt and filled Sudoku puzzle books while listening to the aching viola from the floor below. The boys knew that sometimes Belle cried, and that a bald Spanish hipster was a secret smoker, hovering like a hooker on the corner of the street and then stuffing his face from a tin of Altoid mints so his all-organic actress wife wouldn't find out. The Armenian boys would watch and comment with their eyes on the amalgamation of the skinny models with fake breasts, the male actors who wore different fedora hats every day, the retired Armenians, the Thai cooks wearing white overalls, the film students wearing tortoise-shell Ray-Bans.

Like the area he lived in, David wasn't easy to understand. He cleaned the glass top of his coffee table with Ajax at least twice a day, yet if there were no cigarettes in the flat he'd rummage through last night's ashtray, digging through the dislocated smiles and frowns, looking for something to smoke. If you walked out of his tidy and minimalist living room, there was a balcony packed with broken air-conditioning units, rags, a rusted mini-barbeque, a fan and a gaudy plastic Christmas tree with a white plastic angel. The floor of his balcony was thick with a weird white dust, and the one time I ever went out on it I left footprints in his own personal beach. The balcony detritus was left there by the previous occupant of his flat, and he hadn't got round to moving it yet, six years after moving in.

I told David that I was looking for a job as a waitress or in the tourist industry. But most of the time I wandered around the streets in the heat, among the Armenian grandfathers playing checkers on the pavement and grandmothers in brightly coloured deckchairs wearing ill-advised swimsuits, flicking through soporific magazines like the ones that David did most of his work for. It was as if the social layers of the adults in Little Armenia were parallel universes. The Armenian grandmothers didn't glance up to see the jogging porn stars, who didn't seem to register the quiet Thai couples squatting outside the nail parlours. The Armenian pseudo-gangsters who sold little bags of marijuana outside Starbucks in the nearest strip mall only noticed Armenian women. I could have walked by in a miniskirt and no bra, and they would see me but they wouldn't react, because I didn't walk through the same dimensions as they did. The pseudo-gangsters listened to their own music on earphones and wore white trainers, which they used to try and trip up pretty Armenian girls wearing tight jeans. Nearer to the doors of Starbucks there would be chess games spread on tables and furrowed fingers twitching over black or white wooden pieces. It smelt like coffee and stale sweat out there, but I enjoyed watching those earnest games. I'd feel content, less aggressive than usual, like I was watching through a crack in the door. It was only the younger generations, the newcomers, who saw the layers.

David had no idea he even lived in Little Armenia, which was really a pocket of Los Feliz and melted confusingly with the slightly more visible, beauty-parlour-and-take-out-famous Thai Town. "I live in Los Feliz," David said, bored, glancing out the window and seeing a platinum-blonde yummy mummy with a three-hundred-dollar stroller walking past a hissing traffic jam of smoking SUVs. He didn't see the watchful Armenian adolescents sitting on the wall. He was aware that we lived near Thai Town, but only because of the speed with which greasy chilli-and-coconut polystyrene would arrive at his front door. He only saw the layer of his surroundings that affected him.

After two weeks, the middle-aged Armenian women who lived in David's building seemed to see me, too, and they became my friends. I needed friends, because otherwise I found myself sitting at David's window watching for Richard or the thuggish man with the schoolboy haircut and the nose stud. The friendly Armenian women were the mothers of the adolescent voyeurs who saw everything and the pseudo-gangsters who saw nothing, although I could never work out who belonged to whom. Perhaps they were also the daughters of the deckchair grandmothers, but that was too complicated.

"I was born in a village at the base of Mount Ararat, that very same mount, child, where Noah came to moor his boat after the Great Flood," one of them told me while we smoked next to the fetid courtyard swimming pool that nobody ever dared jump into. "I lost a father, a cousin and a brother to finding Noah's mythical shipwreck, which was meant to be just there where we lived. Why they need to find it, huh? That's what I always said, but they kept climbing and climbing for the damn thing, so there was never any peace. My sister married an ugly man from the Bible Archaeology Search and Exploration Institute when she was eighteen. He left her pregnant with a boy that she named Noah, just like the other twenty-five Noahs at the local school." I smiled at the woman, who dabbled her dirty feet in the water. Little ribbons of tattered dust lifted up from between her toes and dissipated in the water.

"Oh what a hoo-ha, child, when some local troublemakers claimed they'd found the ark years ago, found it and walked it and played it since childhood. What a hoo-ha, child, really, about a few bits of old wood they'd pulled off a barn and buried in the snow for a few weeks. They claimed to play tag in the sacred bowels of God's vessel, which my father and brother died searching for." I offered the lady a cigarette, and she took short, sharp puffs, like she thought it was going to be taken away in a moment. Her knees were worn ragged like leather pouches full of different-shaped stones. Mine were white with jigsaw pieces of white scar tissue from football and fights.

"How did you come to America?" I asked her politely.

"My twin sister and I, we weren't interested in marrying men named Noah, you know?" she said, a slight American twang entering her speech as another woman from David's building leant over the motel-like balconies that framed the courtyard. This woman was smaller and slightly balding, which accentuated her already high forehead.

"Dalita telling you 'bout Noah?" said the balding woman from above.

"Nah," said Dalita.

"Dalita was crazy 'bout Noah, would have followed him to the bottom of the ocean any day."

"Would not," said Dalita, looking at her knees. These women never asked about what I was doing in Los Angeles, but they liked to tell me things about myself.

"You're anaemic, child," said one of them, looking at the bruises on my body.

"That boy you live with has done some wrong things," said another.

"Haven't we all," said another.

"You must not be scared," said one.

"You mustn't be angry," another said to me.

"Your soul is lonely," another said.

"Things are going to fall apart," said another.

22

Three weeks after Lily's wake I did a handstand for David, showing him how straight I could get my back and how I could walk on my hands across his living room. I was wearing jeans and a T-shirt, my bare toes stretching up against gravity and the tendons in my feet arching forwards. An hour later we were fucking, but I don't remember it clearly. I remember the childishness of doing the handstands in front of him – how the blood rushed to my head and my spine tingled as it stretched upwards. I remember that it was evening, and that he said I should have been a gymnast. I said gym class was for pansies, it was all about football, but then there's a big blank space, an explosion of noise and eradicated synapses in which we must have kissed and touched properly for the first time.

The absence of any lasting recollection of these moments makes me think of my mind as a city, and that first evening with him as one of those bulldozed Los Angeles buildings. There is the outline of a memory in the rubble, but it's sunken and tumbled. Amongst the burnt-out foliage and gang graffiti of it I have no idea how we got to the point of me itching black cotton knickers off my ankles, like a cricket playing music, and realizing with horror that I was still wearing blue cotton socks. There is no lasting memory of how we got from the over-lit living room to the darkened bedroom. I couldn't tell you what he looked like naked that night, or what I felt like naked in front of him. I couldn't tell you who did what to whom or the patterns of our bodies on the bedsheets. I couldn't tell you if it was scary kissing someone whose body was so oddly large compared to mine. I couldn't tell you how that worked, logistically. I couldn't tell you what I was thinking about, what it smelt like, or what noises happened to be going on in his building at the time. I couldn't tell you if we were silent or loud.

The next thing I remember was sitting on the edge of his bed and knowing, without looking, that he was watching me while I put Lily's tan-coloured lace bra back on and tugged a white T-shirt over my head. I sucked my tummy in slightly because he was watching, and when I lifted up my arms to pull the T-shirt on, I smelt him on my skin. Together, we had an entirely different smell than apart. It was deodorant and wet flesh, dampness and unwashed sheets, dried saliva and jogging in the dark. I smiled happily to myself at the thought of the last hour, knowing David was watching me smile.

23

Daphne was always telling me "not to be so angry". Daphne moved in with Dad when I was eleven. For some reason she thought I was going to be something she could play with, but I wouldn't be a doll or a daughter or even a friend to her. A few months after she moved in, I was already ignoring her existence, and she was already talking about me in the third person. "Why does she have to dress like that?" Daphne would say, with me standing right there in front of her. "Why doesn't she help more at the café? Why can't she smile sometimes, huh? Why is she always so bloody angry?"

The only thing that Daphne and I had in common after she moved in was an addiction to sleep that I copied off her. She had always been a compulsive sleeper, I think, but for me the dependency only came the year after Grandma and Grandpa died. Daphne moved into our flat the same week Grandma moved to the hospice. For those few months while Grandma was still alive, two important people in my life were desperate to be unconscious. Grandma would talk at great length in her nonsense-poetry language about how she couldn't understand her surroundings any more. She wanted desperately to die, squirming darkly to herself in a hospice room that smelt of damp flesh and antiseptic soap. She wanted to be "out there". She wanted to be "no". She wanted to be "dust" and to be "gone now please". Meanwhile there was Daphne, who would come upstairs after her waitressing shifts, pop a Valium or two and not wake up until twenty minutes before her next shift.

Daphne and Dad's bedroom developed a thick, acidic smell. At breakfast time most mornings before I fell in love with sleep, I'd stand at their bedroom door and inhale the edges of that tangible sleep bubble. Every step into that scented blister sent adrenalin into my brain: I was scared that at any moment she might wake up. She'd be all tangled with limbs akimbo and cocooned in limp sheets, a look of concentration on her face as if she was counting out change in the café. Without even touching her, she'd radiate this thick heat that made me feel pleasantly claustrophobic. There was one time when I wanted to ask her something, but couldn't bring myself to wake her up. It was around 5 p.m. and she was napping, an activity that ate up most of the afternoon. Her waitressing shifts at the café seemed to diminish rather than increase after she started sleeping in Dad's bed every night. I snuck bravely through the creaky door, which used to be Grandma and Grandpa's creaky door, then tiptoed through the bubble-of-sleep smell and extended my fingers over her body. Where should I touch her? My fingers hovered, doubtful, towards her pale shoulder, when suddenly she flinched and grabbed my wrist. She held it tight, without seeming to recognize or even see me. She looked me in the eye as if I was an unpleasant creature from her unconscious, and I froze, appalled. The moment hung there in the air for enough time for me to notice some mascara residue lodged in the crow's feet around her eyes, then her painted fingers peeled away from my skin and she started to snore again, while I backed out of the room into the corridor.

Oddly enough David did nearly the same thing to me once. David mostly had insomnia, but when he did sleep he fell into a coma-like trance and was nearly impossible to wake up. No amount of music or coffee-making or telephones ringing worked. There was one time when his mobile phone kept ringing and he wasn't waking up, so I stepped hesitantly into his bedroom and stretched out my hand to shake him. He looked sweet, asleep. Then suddenly his big hands grabbed and held my wrist hard enough to leave a clumsy bracelet of heart-shaped bruises that he claimed he didn't remember creating. He looked me bang in the eye, and then let go of my hand. I'd been leaning away from him, scared, so when he let go of me I stumbled backwards onto his carpet. He nonchalantly turned away from me and started to snore.

"She's copying you!" I remember Dad shouting at Daphne six months after I started my obsessive sleeping, when he finally realized that I'd been missing school several times a week and not seeing my friends. "You're a role model now, babe, you can't just be a lazy slag."

"I'm not a slag," said Daphne, missing the point. She wasn't very bright.

"The doctor says she's not got mono and she's not got narcolepsy. She's not addicted to sleepers, either," said Dad pointedly to Daphne. "All I can think is she's copying you."

"I'm not her mother. I never signed on to be a fucking mother."

"I'm not asking you to be a mother! I'm asking you to be conscious. Occasionally."

After Dad started to take an interest in my sleeping, it became even more obsessive. If he made me go to school, I would fall asleep at my desk or in the playground. Teachers would find me asleep in the stationery cupboard, sweating like I was having a seizure. I'd fall asleep behind the games shed, or in the cafeteria, or curled up in the girls' locker rooms. My favourite feeling was the sinking sensation between being awake and asleep, when I could only half-control my thoughts and they half-controlled me. Eventually Dad took me to a big white hospital in the suburbs, where I tried to tell a moustached Asian doctor about my interest in half-thoughts. I tried to explain to him that colours were stronger in my unconscious. The doctor made notes while I told him that within twenty minutes of closing my eyes each evening after school, deities would fall in love with me over candle-lit seances in the jungle. On other nights I invented perfect languages, full of perfect onomatopoeic words, which united continents of warring tribes in a mythical version of Africa. I explained how I often murdered evangelical dictators and escaped capture by climbing into train carriages full of corpses, or became the zookeeper at a miniature zoo full of calf-high giraffes and ankle-high gazelles in my dreams.

"Do you ever think about falling asleep for ever?" asked the doctor. The doctor's office was full of mahogany furniture and waxy pot plants that made sinister shadows on the walls. There were bookshelves in all the corners and books on shelves above the desk – *John Locke and the Paradox of Forgetting, Freud's Unconscious*, that sort of stuff.

"Like, dying?" I said, looking at a poster of a sleeping baby behind the doctor's head. Half the baby's head was open to reveal his brain, and there were anatomical descriptions of each sleep-related section of the brain.

"Do you think that death is like being asleep for a long time?" he said.

"No," I said, narrowing my eyes, "I don't think about dying very much."

"Do you miss your Grandma and Grandpa?" he said.

"Yes," I said. "But I don't believe in Heaven."

"So where are your Grandma and Grandpa now?" he said.

"They're in a box under Dad's bed," I said, "cos they were cremated."

"Do you miss your mother?"

"No," I said.

"You never wish you had a mother?"

"No," I said crossing my arms.

"Does it make you feel bad that she left you?"

I shrugged, nonplussed.

"Does it make you feel unlovable?"

"What?" I said. "What do you mean?"

"Does it scare you when people leave?"

"What's that got to do with liking to sleep?" I said, and promptly lost interest in the whole conversation. He was a weedy man with thick glasses. I imagined the doctor as a child while he tried to tell me that it's important to keep a hold on reality, however banal it seems.

"Reality is very important," he said. I imagined the doctor being bullied at school, being put into rubbish bins and spat on. He told me that I was obviously very creative and that I had a high IQ, but mustn't let myself slip away from the tangible world and the people around me. I imagined the doctor falling asleep in bed with his boyfriend or wife, snoring just slightly.

The doctor made me stay overnight in that hospital, with electrodes attached to my wrists. The hospital room was the colour of pale eggshells, and there was a white porcelain lamp with a pink floral shade next to the bed along with a plastic mug of water and a box of tissues. There was a window that looked out onto another part of the hospital. I could see a middle-aged man asleep in bed and a nurse tucking the covers in around him. In another window there was a nurses' station with a skinny lady filing her nails while watching a tiny television. In my bedroom there was a video recorder attached to the ceiling, which could see every bit of the room apart from a little triangle of space directly behind it.

Dad was livid with me when the doctor told him that I hadn't slept for a minute all night. I'd spent the entire evening drawing pictures of dolphins on the wall behind the camera, out of view, or making rude faces at the camera.

"Do you know how much that night cost me?" Dad shouted at me when we got on the train the next morning. I shook my head. "Now they want you to come in for weekly therapy sessions. They think you're crazy, but I won't have it. We'd all like to spend our lives falling asleep and swimming with dolphins, but we have to work. You're just an attention-seeking little girl who doesn't know how to behave. That's all. Do you know that? You only think about yourself. You're just like your fucking mother," he said. "And you're going to snap the fuck out of it," he said as the train moved off.

I didn't say anything in retaliation, and I stared out of the window at suburban rooftops, torn in places by crumbling walls and graffiti – "bite", "slum", "ideal", said the walls in kaleidoscopic bubble-writing. The sky slipped by above the chimneys and our train fed itself into the city. "Abluvion", I thought, imagining Grandpa's dictionary again. As the train slipped underground I begrudgingly decided to stop sleeping all the time, mostly because going to see the boring doctor once a week was a grim prospect. Although legitimately tired, I stayed awake through the entire train journey and watched a B-horror flick called *Curse of the Puppet Master* with Dad until midnight that evening, long after Daphne had popped Valiums and passed out on Dad's lap. For the next few years I sometimes woke up in places other than where I fell asleep, or dreamt things that I thought were true when they weren't, but I never spoke about these sleep demons to him again.

24

On the whole I slept unexpectedly deeply in David's bed, falling
into a well of nervous unconsciousness while he was sleeping
next to me, but also while he padded around the flat reading
magazines and fixing his cameras. He told me that I whimpered
in my sleep, which embarrassed me, but I wouldn't tell him
about the dreams of fainting and falling, or of the bleeding
sunsets and the mouthful of goo being disgorged from the lips
of a newborn baby. I also wouldn't tell him about a new recurring dream, a horrible Enkidu-Gilgamesh-and-Lily-inspired
nightmare that started in the idyllic few weeks after David
and I started sharing the same bed. The dreamscape was a
desert village of concrete houses with barren cactus gardens.
I'd be playing with the desert geckos and chameleons a little
way from the town, letting their little webbed toes crawl all
over my body and face while I lie on the floor. Then with a
rush and an intake of breath, a sudden panic comes over me
as I remembered: we are meant to be moving house that day!
I immediately start to run towards my house, bare feet panting over hot sand and brambles, geckos tumbling backwards
off my skin, but when I get to our kitchen it's empty. I run
out front just in time to catch sight of David and Lily driving
away in David's new black SUV. Sometimes they kiss before
driving away, but they never look back. The worst part of the
dream was how as time passed and nobody came back for me,
my flesh began to crawl with metallic-coloured scales. They

came painfully out of my skin like teeth from raw gums. My spine grew lengthways, and I screamed when it broke out of my lower back, becoming a tail. My tongue grew while my legs shrunk, and when a new family came to live in the desert bungalow, nobody took any notice of the gecko in the garden.

I'd wake with a sudden gulp of air, pleased to see David. Sometimes he'd stroke my hair and I'd pull away from him, not wanting to be patronized. Sometimes we'd make love after my nightmares, and I'd feel even more like a strange animal. Occasionally he even held me in place on the bed or the floor. If he held me too tightly I'd buck against him, my hips squirming on impulse and the palms of my hands pressing neatly into the groves of his shoulders. He'd pin me down hard, like we were fighting or play-wrestling. I'd push him away when he came close, and he'd drag me back in, then he'd push away and I'd pull in, yet we hardly moved at all. I loved him. My skin would itch for him to hurt me, but I didn't ask him to. I knew I was with him, kissing him, touching him, but sometimes I wanted more proof of our connection and my physical existence. I was more existent when he touched me. I wanted pain, though. I wanted the proof, the pain, the sure rush of being connected to another human being. All I could do was buck under him and fight, though, and could never quite articulate my interest in feeling pain.

The closest I ever got, somewhat comically, was once asking him:

"Have you ever killed a chicken?"

I wasn't bringing up the subject of pain, only I'd seen a documentary about the sex lives of animals. When a female otter is in heat, for example, the male glides towards her under the stream water, and they copulate while swimming slowly forwards together in the river.

"Can't say I have," said David, lighting a cigarette and lounging. He tipped ash into a silver tray.

"You press their backs so they think they're going to have sex," I said, "and then you snap their necks."

"I'd never hurt you," he said.

I laughed at his earnestness, and kissed his shoulder.

25

Two of Lily's ex-patients lived in a rundown Spanish villa in Laurel Canyon. The address was on the "contact sheet" that I'd found in the plastic zipped compartment of the red suitcase. Even from the road you could see paint peeling from the chalky stucco in the midday sun. It was cool up in the mountains, though, different from the polluted heat of Thai Town and Little Armenia. Gobs of sunlight ran around on the road as trees shivered above me. There was a massive Toyota people carrier in the driveway, and the sound of a dog yapping behind a garden door that seemed to be the only entrance to the house. It had been over two weeks since my rucksack got stolen, and I was beginning to stop looking over my shoulder for Richard or his friend. That morning I'd telephoned all of the people on Lily's list of work contacts. Only one of the contacts from this list had offered any useful information about Lily. The first number I called was a wrong number: either it had been typed wrong or it was no longer in service. The second number took me through to a young-sounding Canadian man whose grandmother, one of Lily's patients, was at a hospice now. The Canadian didn't remember much about Lily, and seemed eager to get off the phone, back to whatever daytime television show was booming in the background of our conversation.

"She was only here a couple of weeks," the Canadian man had said. "Don't think it worked out or something, but I can't remember."

The second-to-last phone number belonged to Teddy Fink, presumably the same Teddy from the photo of him and Lily outside the place labelled "Malibu Mansions" in biro on the back, and from the greetings cards Lily had saved.

"I'm afraid Mr Fink died four years ago, and I have nothing to say about Mrs Harris," said the woman who picked up the phone. "I'd rather you didn't call here again, thank you." And the woman put down the phone, so that wasn't very successful at all. She sounded irritated and busy. Then the last number on the list was answered by Ms Bianca Forbes, who was immediately excited to hear that my mother was her former nurse and that I was looking for information about her.

"Oh! Well she came over every afternoon for years and years and years, we knew her well," said the chirpy voice. "Of course we remember. I was so sorry to hear that she died. Poor thing. Why don't you come up for iced tea this afternoon and we can tell you all about her? It'll be fun." So that's how I ended up standing outside the garden door in Laurel Canyon with no one answering the door. I definitely had the address right, because I'd taken a taxi for the first time since being in Los Angeles. Lucy and Bianca Forbes lived right at the top of a road called Eden Drive, off Wonderland Avenue, which isn't the sort of address you forget.

I knocked on the door one more time and then rang a doorbell that didn't make any sound. The dog started to bark louder, though, and eventually I heard footsteps traipsing towards the door.

"Hello?" said a woman's voice through the door. She opened it an inch, stretching two door chains like saliva on an oversized mouth. The woman I saw through the crack was small and wide-eyed and middle-aged with peaked eyebrows and black hair. A poodle yapped at her feet. "Miss Lily's daughter, right? They mentioned, yes," the woman said in halting English, and unlocked the door. She grabbed the poodle aggressively by its collar and dragged him off away from my ankles. The woman was wearing a black T-shirt and black leggings, with her hair tied neatly up in a shiny jet-black bob around her head, looking almost identical to the poodle. "They're on the porch," she said, and walked the dog away. Down some stone steps was a sloping walled garden that smelt of foliage and chlorine. At the lower end was the swimming pool, and at the top was a large Spanish-style porch with two identical old women sitting on colourful wooden chairs. They both waved at me, and I walked up towards them, trying not to trip over bits of crazy paving and tree roots.

"Hello, hello!" one of the women. "You made it!"

"Let's have a look at you, then!" said the other. They were clearly twins. Perhaps one of them was a little more hunched in her chair and the other a little more wrinkled at the neck, but essentially they'd aged at the same rate. They were pixie-like, both wearing oriental pointed slippers and cotton dresses with matching gold earrings hanging heavily off their ears. "Eldritch," I thought, which means "unearthly and weird", but the word always makes me think of elderly elves wearing lots of golden jewellery. The house seemed massive behind them. There were four white pillars holding up a second-floor balcony, which had elaborate wrought-iron railings that wound in the shape of flowers. Then the third floor was topped off by a sloping tiled roof the colour of rust that matched the colour of their slippers.

"You don't look a thing like her, do you?" said one of the women, peering at me over a pair of tinted spectacles.

"Yes she does," said the other woman. "Now, turn to the left a bit," she demanded of me. "Now isn't that Lily's pout, just there, that curl at her lips?" And both women fell silent, studying my profile, the angles of my lips.

"We had no *idea* she had a daughter," said one of them.

"I don't think many people did," I replied.

"Now why is that then?" said one of the twins.

"She was only fourteen when she had me," I said.

"That's terrible," said one of the twins.

"It's all right," I said.

"Well my name's Bianca," said the hunched twin, "and this is Laurie Lee." They both grinned at me. I noticed that the poodle-faced woman hadn't gone far. She was sitting on a deckchair looking our way. "And Lily came to work for us years ago, when she was just starting as a nurse. We recommended her to all our friends," Bianca continued.

"Thanks for seeing me," I said. "It means a lot."

"It's no problem at all; we were so upset to hear that Lily died. We read it in the papers."

"Laurie Lee always reads the death notices. It makes her feel like she's achieved something with her day," said Bianca with a wink.

"Not dying is an achievement at this stage," said Laurie Lee.

"Who would have thought we'd outlive one of our nurses?"

"Did you go to the funeral or the wake?" I asked.

"Oh no," said Laurie Lee, "Bianca has such a trouble breathing nowadays, and I have this damned arthritis. We saw the death notice, that's how we found out. We sent flowers. Brightly coloured flowers."

"How long did she work here?" I asked, looking around at the muddled opulence of the place. The poodle woman was definitely watching us, and the poodle dog was chasing bits of blossom as they fell and floated on the still air from the trees above.

"Maybe three years?" Bianca said. "Although she worked for others as well as us of course. She was great fun. She was, what? Laurie Lee? What was she?"

"Vivacious," answered Laurie Lee.

"She had a marvellous sense of the absurd," said Bianca. "That's one thing. For example, when we were a bit more mobile we used to go on a lot of church tours, you know, stained-glass windows and altarpieces and stuff. One time Lily came along on a particularly boring tour, and there was this sign – what did it say?"

"It said – 'For the Sick and Tired of the Episcopal Church'," said Laurie Lee. "It was for some free health-care assessment. But Lily was bored, so she stole the sign and we all got helpless giggles in the car back home, because she was the one 'Sick and Tired of the Episcopal Church'!"

I smiled politely, and the twins grinned with nostalgia.

"She was fun," said Bianca. "That's the thing."

"How come she left?" I said.

"Well, it was a bit awful, in the end," said Bianca. "Oly down there, the one who let you in, she's our housekeeper. Been with us for years. She was always saying Lily stole things – objects and cash and what not, but we figured Oly was just jealous."

"Turned out Lily really was stealing, though," said Bianca. "Not a lot, mind you, so don't worry, and we didn't really mind. We have enough money, God knows, we didn't even notice that she pinched some now and then, but I suppose it was the principle, and we had to let her go."

"It shouldn't have been such a big deal, but we'd written letters of recommendation, and it was a little embarrassing when those people realized things were going missing."

"I phoned some other people she worked for earlier today," I said. "They wouldn't talk to me."

"Who'd you call?"

"A couple of people. One was Teddy Fink?" I said. "But he's dead. I spoke to a woman who sounded really irritated that I'd called."

"Daughter, maybe," said Bianca. "Lily worked for Mr Fink while she was working for us. Did Tuesdays and Fridays with him, the rest with us even after she got married. We'd hear stories about him, that Mr Fink. He liked her a lot."

"He adored her… the daughter *didn't*." Laurie Lee giggled.

"A lot of the people she nursed loved Lily, just as much as we did, but obviously you can't keep help if they're dishonest. You just can't," said Bianca, turning her palms outwards.

"Do you think she wants to know this about her mother?" said Laurie Lee to Bianca, then turned back to me. "I mean we still cared about her in a funny sort of way, we really did. Even after we found out. You know? We were heartbroken to see her go, and she still came around for lunch every so often. She was troubled, that's all."

"Do you remember when she set the Christmas pudding on fire and her hair got caught in the blaze?" said Laurie Lee to her sister.

"Whoosh! Up it went," said Bianca with a smile.

"She bought five different-coloured wigs from a dress-up shop. One day she'd have a neon-blue bob—"

"The next day she was a blonde bombshell."

"And we missed her when she was gone."

"It wasn't the same after."

I think the twins continued to reminisce, but I lost track of the conversation. My mind went to Richard, and to thievery, and then to David's part in all this.

26

I shared a sundae with David a few nights later. It was raining, like the night I met August properly, but the rain seemed
hotter this time, and more dramatic. Los Angeles isn't built
for the rain, and everyone panics. The air gets saturated
with ambulance sirens as oil rises up through the suddenly
soaked tarmac highways, causing crashes. There was a flat-
screen television in the corner of the diner where David and
I sat, which broadcast the news. A smiley blonde presenter
explained about blocked traffic and fatalities. A car fell off
the edge of a road towards Malibu, killing a socialite on her
way back from a charity gala. In Englewood earlier in the
evening, a bus full of children had crashed on the way back
from a field trip to the science museum. One died, twenty-
two others were injured. There'd also been a gang bust-up
outside a club that night, killing five gang members and two
innocent bystanders.

David and I were both thoughtful that night. I played around
with a computer game on his mobile phone. It looked new,
and all the contacts on his phone were celebrity hairdressers
and department stores and stuff, not people.

"I threw out my old phone when I gave up drinking," he
said. "A month and a bit ago. It's easier without my old friends
leading me astray." I looked up from the game and straight
at him – with this revelation about giving up alcohol, things
started to make sense. It was six weeks since Lily's wake. It

was four weeks since David's birthday dinner at the Thai restaurant. It had been an intense month that felt like longer, and I'm not sure I'd ever known someone so intimately as I thought I knew him then. Still, certain puzzle pieces didn't quite connect. He seemed awkward and adolescent sometimes, but I guess that was because he was used to being drunk. He didn't have many friends, but I guess that was because they were drinking friends. Even his scars, his weight loss, his sadness.

"You quit drinking when Lily died?" I said.

He paused.

"Yup," he said.

"Because Lily died?" I said.

He paused again, and massaged his big shoulders slightly. He looked much better than he did when we had our first lunch in the car outside the Platinum Club. The bags under his eyes were thinning, and he didn't look so gaunt. He swallowed a mouthful of ice cream and chocolate sauce.

"I sound like a Hallmark card," he grinned, but it was a fake grin that immediately collapsed back into a frown again. He didn't know where to look as he spoke to me. "I've done a ton of shit that I regret, that's all. I've messed up. And I don't want to regret anything else. I don't want my life to be… *regrettable*." He looked away, over at the television. "You've made a difference, is what I'm saying." He stumbled, not looking at me. "You've helped," he mumbled, and stared over at the TV.

I raised my eyebrows, and stuttered: "And Lily?"

"What about her?" he said, looking confused. I knew he wanted me to say something about what he just revealed, either the alcoholism or my impact on his sobriety. It was like a mental tick, though, and I asked:

"Was Lily an alcoholic? Is that why she died? Was she addicted to drugs or alcohol or something?"

David's big green eyes rested steadily on me. He looked oddly beautiful, his shoulders hunched in front of the dripping window and his mouth curled into his trademark lopsided frown. I remembered the sight of him sitting on Lily's bed at the top of the Pink Hotel during the wake, sucking his thumb after he cut it trying to get Lily's photograph out of the frame.

"I don't know," he said. David glanced at his hands, then out of the window. Then he looked back at me. "I wish I hadn't said anything."

"Why?" I said.

"Does everything have to revert back to some party you happened to wander into?" he said. "I understand why she stays on my mind, but why do you bring her up? She has nothing to do with you."

"Cos she has something to do with you," I lied guiltily. "I don't know. Because she meant something to you, because I wear her clothes – a million reasons."

"What do you mean you wear her clothes?"

"I realize you were drunk when we met, but I stole her clothes – remember? You called me a grave-robber."

"Of course I remember that. But at the café you said you sold them. You turned up at my door with a plastic bag."

"A plastic bag full of her clothes, some of them," I said. "The ones I didn't sell."

"You said you sold her clothes. I assumed they were new clothes. The plastic bag was from that clothes shop above the supermarket. I thought they were new clothes. You sold her clothes."

"I said I sold some of her clothes."

"Fuck."

"What's the big deal? I thought you knew."

"What are you wearing now?"

"Hers," I said, and we both looked down at my white cotton dress with the black buttons up the front, the same white dress I'd been wearing when I came to his house. "Her shoes. Her bra. Her knickers."

He went pale, white as Lily's dress. And I felt sick too, because I was deep in now.

"You're insane. That's disgusting," he said.

"Don't say that."

"You're actually fucking insane."

"Don't say that. You just admitted to not remembering half your life. Don't call me insane."

"You said you sold them."

"You're like a scratched record. *Some – of – them*. I sold some of them, David, and kept some of them. They're just clothes," I said. "What's the problem?"

"The problem is they belong to a dead woman."

"You wouldn't be here with me if I was still wearing polyester sports clothes and a dirty baseball cap!"

"That's the most ridiculous thing I've ever heard," David said, and pretended to smile. Again, the smile collapsed.

"I know you wouldn't, though," I snapped at him, "cos you walked away from me that morning."

"I didn't want to vomit on you! It wasn't your fucking clothes. You really think I'm that shallow?"

"I think you like Lily's taste. She had style. I don't."

"But I don't give a fuck about Lily's style. I give a fuck about you. Maybe it wasn't instantaneous at the beach, but I was about twelve days gone at the dreg ends of a bender. If I'd been sober I would have fallen for you then. The clothes didn't matter."

"You don't think they matter," I said. "But they do."

"Those clothes belong to a dead person."

"I'm not arguing with that," I said. "I know they do."

"I'm trying to do something really difficult. The last thing I need is a tourist in stolen clothes sleeping in my apartment," he said.

"You invited me," I said. "The hostel was just fine."

"Whatever," he said.

"I'll leave in the morning," I said.

We drove to his place in silence, my bottom sticking to the wet leather seats of his SUV. I thought about him saying he would have fallen for me at the beach, if he hadn't been so legless.

"Did you ever write her love letters?" I asked David in the car.

"No," he said grumpily. I didn't know if I believed him or not. Everything felt static as I undressed later in the living room, listening to him tug damp clothes off his body in the bedroom. We waltzed around each other. I turned on the bath water. He turned on the TV. He boiled the kettle on the stove. I got into the bath. Then ten minutes later he came into the bathroom and brushed his teeth while I was floating in the rising heat and heavy steam. I closed the sticky plastic shower curtain abruptly with my toes. I have long toes. They're sort of funny. My second toe reaches out further than my big toe. Dad has the same thing.

"David?" I said.

He grunted and spat toothpaste out into the sink.

"I thought you knew," I said, "I thought it didn't bother you or, maybe, you were OK with it."

"Why would I be OK with it?"

"You said I looked better the second time you saw me. Less feral." The water looked bright green around me. "I'm sorry," I said.

He paused for a while. He put his toothbrush back on the sink and took a sip of water from the tap.

"You stumbled in on all this," he said eventually. "It's not your fault. And I'd rather have you in weird clothes than not have met you at all." I sunk my head quickly under water and emerged again. "Which I guess is the toss up," he said, "since we wouldn't have met if you weren't a thief."

"Or if you weren't a mean alcoholic," I said.

I could see his shadow through the shower curtain, leaning on the sink. We were silent again.

"You know, I'm ten years older than you," he said after this moment of quiet. "That's no good thing." I wondered if this was time to reveal that I was five years younger than I claimed, but of course decided it wasn't.

"Close your eyes, I want to get out of the bath," I said instead.

"I've already seen you naked, little thief," he said.

"You've never seen me naked when you're angry with me. It's a completely different thing. Go away or I'll dissolve."

"Dissolve into what?"

"Into the dirty bathwater," I said.

"I don't want you sliding down my plughole with the troll people and the iguanas. You might clog the pipes," he said.

"Charming."

"My eyes are closed," he lied. I peeked my head around the curtain, where he was clearly staring at my hunched silhouette beyond the frosted-plastic curtain. He smiled and picked up a towel from the rack, holding it out in front of him like a football banner.

"Have you turned into a mermaid?" he said.

"You wish," I smiled, getting up. "As it happens I'm half human, half dove," I rose from the water, stepping into the waiting towel.

"That sounds like something that ought to be explored," he said, wrapping the towel around me.

27

A week later I found piles of carefully chosen women's clothes arranged on David's bed. Laid out like shadows were a pair of sturdy jeans, five high-necked cotton T-shirts, black and white cotton knickers, a brown jumper made out of some synthetic woollen material, a knee-length chiffon skirt, some tights and slip-on shoes with little heels. There was even a pair of faux-pearl earrings. Everything was from an outlet mall in Fresno, and each piece had something wrong with it – you could see a squelch of glue where the faux pearls had been sunk into their platinum shell, and the jumper had a hole in the sleeve.

"I'm sorry it's nothing extravagant," David said as he came in the room, making me jump. I touched the sweetly chosen clothes. He must have looked absurd in the dress shop, his big Gilgamesh hands picking up little shiny kitten heels and tiny white cotton knickers. Warmth came into me with the most phenomenal surge. I imagined him looking lost among the aisles of silk and zips and buttons, getting everything completely wrong. Is this the girl he wanted? Pearls and knee-length skirts? Or was this what he thought I wanted? The sensation that filled me up at that moment felt like hunger, or desperation. In retrospect, it was love, but at the time it was a sudden, overwhelming nausea. I couldn't even look at him.

"You don't like them," he said. "I'm sorry."

"I do, I like them," I said.

"They're not you," David said.

"They are," I said. "They could be."

The day before he bought me the new clothes David had got me a day job working as a script supervisor for a man named Sam, who had the face of a prematurely balding child. He was tubby, with kind eyes, and he wore oversized T-shirts emblazoned with creatures from *Star Wars* or *Buffy the Vampire Slayer*. David said Sam came from a wealthy family, and his uncle had put up some of the money for his latest films. Although I didn't have any experience on movie sets, Sam took David's word for it that I was observant and could do the job. I was to be paid cash.

"Close your eyes," said David to me only a few moments after we met Sam in a Silver Lake bar with big chunks of plywood nailed to the floor. "What colour are Sam's shoes and is he wearing a belt?" David asked me.

"He's wearing white Nikes," I smiled. "The left lace is trailing on the floor. He's not wearing a belt, but he should be, cos I can see the top of his boxers."

"What colour are his boxers?" David laughed.

"Blue." I smiled, the knuckle of David's right hands resting on my nose.

"Awesome," laughed Sam. "That's pretty awesome."

"She's oddly observant," said David. "It'll be perfect."

"How'd you two meet?" said Sam.

"At Venice Beach," said David.

"Guess that's why we haven't seen you for weeks," he said. "We going to party tonight?"

"I've got to work," said David.

"Where you been the last two months, though, dude? We haven't seen you."

"Cleaning up my act a bit," David said.

"Well come to Vegas with us next weekend and we'll get you good and dirty again."

"I'm in AA," said David. I looked at David. He hadn't told me that he went to AA meetings.

"I'm hoping you're talking about American Airlines or the Car Insurance, dude," said Sam.

"No more booze," said David.

"No more weekends?" said Sam, taking off his hat for a moment and rubbing his balding head. "Ever?"

"Not if the weekends include getting wasted and waking up in gutters. I want to remember the second half of my life. Thought it might be a nice change."

"You're not even staying for one drink tonight? To toast your girlfriend's new job?"

David tilted his head to the side, indicating "no".

"There was this one time," grinned Sam. He looked at David, then cheekily at me: "Right? We're on a bender in San José. We haven't slept for twenty-four hours but we're on fire. Like, blazing. Then we realize, where's David? We're like, dude, he was here a minute ago. Then my cellphone rings and it's David telling me he's woken up in, like, some chick's bedroom in Mexico." David smiled somewhat nostalgically at the memory, then looked nervously at me as if I might be retrospectively jealous or angry. "This man," continued Sam, nodding at David and ignoring the awkwardness, "is downright the best dude to have at a party. The best."

"I don't really want to know," I said blankly.

"Oh, feisty," said Sam, looking at me and then glancing over at David. "So has she tamed you, then? You whipped now?"

"Give it a rest man, can she have a job?"

"Course. Anything for a buddy," said Sam.

It turned out that I was a very good script supervisor. I notice the details. Being a script supervisor made me think of the comment about solar eclipses being "coincidences of geometry", which Lily's anonymous lover talked about in one of his letters. This is what the day-to-day construction of movies seemed to be about. In order to make it appear that people were having a natural conversation on screen, the geometry had to be perfect. It was a mess of angles, of eye lines that needed to "match up" and coverage that needed to slot together. Everyone on set was always talking about the "180-degree rule", where two people in conversation should have the same left/right relationship to each other at all times. If the heroine is on the left and the hero on the right, then she should be facing right at all times and he needs to face left. Jumping to the other side of the characters on a cut would be disorientating. A script supervisor is someone who details the geometry of continuity. I'd note down whether the actor exited stage right or left, whether his shirt was tucked or not, whether he was wearing a watch or whether his cuffs were buttoned up.

Sam hardly ever looked directly at anyone, let alone noticed anything that went on around him. Los Angeles is a city of sideways glances – over shoulders, through car windows – and Sam epitomized it. He had an anxious sideways glance for when he wanted to escape a conversation, an upwards tilt when he was lying, a burrowing stare when he was embarrassed or anxious, and a sharply flung sideways look when he was trying to be flirtatious. Mostly Sam and I talked while he was driving me back from set, both staring straight ahead at the battalion of armoured worker ants zooming down the freeways. It was in cars that he told me his secrets, hardly noticing that I never said a word. He told me about the hundreds of women he'd slept with in San Francisco before he moved to Los Angeles and lost all his hair, and about how his ex-wife cheated on him during their annual Christmas party.

"Actually during the party?" I asked.

"In our bed," he said. "But a couple of months before that I did a chick in the kitchen while my wife was listening to Tracy Chapman in the bathtub."

"Huh," I said as we merged into the freeway.

"You're such a good listener," he said earnestly.

"Did you know Lily?" I asked Sam, once.

"Lily who?" he said.

"Harris. She and David were friends."

"David's not particularly charitable with information about his private life. Guess you've found that out," Sam laughed. "I chalk it up to him not remembering most of his private life! Drunk fuck. Was she a girlfriend?"

"Think so," I said.

"Are you checking up on him?" he said.

"Just curious."

"Curiosity killed the cat," said Sam.

As Sam started to like me more and more, he stopped asking anything about me. I listened to him endlessly constructing his identity, telling me what he was and what he wasn't. His mother had an all-consuming obsession with true-crime novels, so she saw everything as a potential crime, which made Sam a very jumpy child. Sam hated: pushing past people in movie theatres, crumbs, seeing people eating, any sort of white sauce, seafood, conversations about cheese and missing the first or last second of a movie. He literally had to sit in his seat until the credits were over and the screen went silent. Every evening after work and after long, monologizing drives across glittering Los Angeles, Sam would drop me off at David's place. I never told David about Sam's confessed fetish for wearing designer women's underwear, or how Sam no longer had sex with his girlfriend because she had a mole on her lower stomach that made him feel physically sick. The mole was mountainous and had two hairs, Sam said, like television antennae. It was difficult to have sex without touching it, so he didn't have sex any more. I didn't even tell David when Sam parked the car outside the Starbucks on North Vermont and Franklin one morning and told me that he loved me. Nobody had ever, in my life, directed the words "I love you" at me, and the first person who did say it was someone I'd only met a few weeks before and I didn't care about in the least. I would have liked to ask him what colour my eyes were, or where in London I was from. Why didn't I live in England any more? What did I want from life? How old was I? Instead I smiled stiffly and told him that I didn't feel the same way as he did.

"You're living with David," Sam said.

I nodded.

"You're a brave girl," Sam said.

"He doesn't drink any more, he's different," I said.

"I understand," he said, not looking at me. We both stared forwards at a row of cars, a burrito stand and the back entrance to a large, flat-roofed, beige Starbucks. Both Sam's window and mine were rolled down in his little car, and we were smoking anxiously out of them, our elbows dipping from the car, both of us sipping iced black coffee that felt amazing in the heat. The air was heavy and the car smelt horrible because we'd started using a Coca Cola can to throw our cigarettes into since yet another forest fire was raging through the hills above us.

Every time we blinked that strange summer, fires hit the headlines. More often than not the dry air was thick with soot. The heatwave had finally ignited, and LA had a halo of fire over it. One of the fires even came close to consuming the zoo, and they had to relocate all the animals before the fog and soot in the city turned into the smell of an exotic barbeque. One of the fires started when I was watching television at Sam's house. His living room looked out on a layer of rooftops, and then out towards Griffith Park Observatory. Sam's flat was a bric-a-brac of collectable figurines trapped in packaging. Each little Vampire Slayer, Darth Vader, Spider-Man and Princess Leia was poised in earnest combat with the stale air still in its box, its panic-stricken painted eyes threatening mutiny. Apparently the toys were worth a fortune, though. He once told me that he had a comic-book collection worth more than his penthouse. When the fire started I was playing with the wax from some rose-scented candles. Sam was working in the other room. With red eyes and slow reactions, I dripped the wax onto my knee and made a dotted line up the inside of my thigh. Each blob of pale wax burnt my shaved thighs and left continent-shaped raw skin as I peeled off the wax puddles. Wax doesn't turn me on. I like that immediate surface-level sting of it, but mostly it makes me feel nostalgic for crayons. In autumn I used to spend hours tracing around leaves from London trees, copying their veins like a cartographer. But hot wax did have a certain appeal, in relation to pain. Unlike cutting, wax burns didn't leave a scar or any telltale droplets of blood in between the bathroom tiles. Wax was a clean, frivolous pain. While I dripped wax on my thighs I noticed the grazes on my knees had healed. I wondered where Richard was now, and if he'd forgotten about looking for me and looking for the suitcase. Vanessa said nobody had come to the Serena since the day the man stole my bag, so perhaps Richard had forgotten about me.

I can't remember what was on television at Sam's place the night the crazy fire started, but the programme was interrupted to show footage of Griffith Park starting to burn. Then I looked up through the big window behind the television and saw the actual fire spitting up in the middle distance.

28

"The sky is blood-red outside my window tonight, and I'm thinking of you," I read, closing my eyes to feel the sun on my body while imagining the anonymous author of the letters. I'd read the letters so many times, now, that the words were becoming familiar.

"The first time we met you were holding a small red umbrella," the man wrote. "Remember? And now the colour red makes me think of you." I tried to concentrate on the words. "Later, I came to know your little red dresses," the letter continued, "and the army of incendiary lipsticks on your dresser. That first sight of you made me think, immediately, of red-light districts, of the bullfighter's tempting rag, of revving engines, of battle decks stained red from the start, so that the sight of blood would cause no alarm. These images flashed in front of me as you turned and smiled at me. Right now the sky outside my window is the colour of that nail polish you have called 'The Battle of Magenta'. It's making me think of you, but also somehow, of childhood.

"I made paint once when I was boy,' the typed words continued. "Carmine is a particularly deep red colour, different from Magenta, produced by boiling dried insects in water, then treating the resultant acid with alum, cream of tartar, stannous chloride or potassium hydrogen oxalate. Sometimes egg white, fish glue or gelatin were added, but since I had no fish glue or gelatin, I stole eggs from the fridge. What fascinated me most, apart from a natural boyish interest in boiling bugs, was that the quality of the carmine was affected by the temperature and the degree of illumination present during its preparation, sunlight being essential for a perfect hue. The colour red, then, in my eyes, was made from dead insects and sunlight. Perhaps I would have forgotten about sunshine and dead insects, if it wasn't for that moment outside the café when I saw you, beautiful, swinging your red umbrella. And perhaps if I'd been unlucky enough never to have known that carmine was made from death and sunshine, I never would have fallen in love with you. With love, for ever, for always."

29

The next day David was out, while Sam and I weren't filming, so I sat around the swimming pool with the Armenian women again. They all wore faded swimming costumes, great big sunglasses, and sat with their feet in the chlorinated water until lunchtime most days, shelling peas or peeling potatoes into metal mixing bowls. I was wearing a navy-blue bikini that the Armenian ladies leant me, with a white T-shirt on top. Over the last weeks I'd started to sit with the Armenian women nearly every day, either reading Lily's notes or one of David's books.

"I've lost my tea strainer," one of the Armenian women yelped from inside a first-floor flat at the corner of the swimming-pool courtyard. "Has anyone seen it?"

"Look under the bed, that's what my mother always used to say. According to my mother, everything that got lost could always be found under the bed," said another woman. "If I lost my religious faith or my virginity, it probably would have been under the bed with the TV remote and my father's dentures, as far as she was concerned."

"It's a tea strainer, why would it be under the bed?" said the first woman, humourless.

"Ah, you were lucky," said Dalita to the woman whose religious faith was under the bed. "Just one thing to remember! My mother, yes? She had a continual monologue, a waterfall, yes? Of advice. Whatever we were doing, she had advice." Dalita put on a high-pitched know-it-all voice that was meant to be a parody of her mother: "See that flower, yes? That's an Aratararicum. Lovely flowers. If you ever keep them indoors, remember not to over-water them. They're delicate, yes? They're delicate and they need a lot of sunlight." Dalita continued, getting into the role and making her friends laugh. "Talking of which, aren't you hot in that T-shirt, little one? Take it off or you'll get heatstroke. If you ever do get heatstroke, put ice cubes under your tongue and on your wrists. Don't believe anyone who tells you to take a cold bath, you'll catch your death, yes? Talking of which, never bite ice cubes, you'll break your teeth. It's important to look after your teeth if you want a good husband…" Dalita took a breath. "She could go on for ever, a regular panic of strange advice."

"High heels ruin the shape of your feet," remembered another woman. "Which is gobbledygook. I wore heels all my life just to spite her, and my feet are just fine."

"People don't get what they deserve," said another, "they have to fight for it."

"Do everything once," said another woman, "was advice written by a dead man."

"Be careful what you wish for, it might come true," said another of the women.

"What about your mother?" said Dalita to me.

"She told me never to start smoking," I lied, somewhat randomly, lighting up a cigarette and offering them to Dalita. Dalita cackled, and took a cigarette from me.

When I went upstairs, David was already back. He was in a playful mood. He had his camera out, and the minute I walked through the door, all sweaty from sitting by the pool, smelling of chlorine and sunlight, he snapped a photo of me. He smiled. It reminded me of the morning after Lily's wake, when he wouldn't stop taking photos in the dusty early light. I wondered if it reminded him of that too.

"Don't," I said to him.

"Smile, beautiful," he said.

"No," I said, and turned around so my back was to him. We were both quiet and still for a moment, neither moving. I loved him. God, I did. Nothing mattered, not even Lily. Not Richard, not the Pink Hotel. Nothing. I knew the glass eye of his camera was on my back. I felt like a deer caught in range. My spine tingled underneath the sweaty T-shirt. My toes wriggled. Then I broke, and peeked over my shoulder at him. He immediately took a photo. Flash. I was dead.

"Whatever happened to the photos from the beach?" I said after I turned away from him again and stood with my back to him, silhouetted by the window.

"What photos?"

"After the wake," I said.

He shrugged.

"Probably at the office," he said. His expression clouded for a second, then brightened again. "I'll have a look. Take off your T-shirt, lovely thief girl."

"No," I laughed. "Hey, David, why don't you have any personal photos around the flat? Like the photo in your sock drawer of you and your friends in that car?"

"Have you been snooping?" he smiled.

"What happened to all those people? Like Sam and stuff? How come you don't want to see them at all any more?"

"I don't remember those moments except from the photos. I don't much remember the people, they didn't mean anything. I dumped that ugly car. It reminded me of being drunk."

"And you dumped the friends, too?"

David was silent for a moment.

"If you take off your T-shirt then I'll put photos of you all over my walls," he said eventually. "To make up for my lack of personal history."

"Please don't," I laughed.

"Come on," he goaded. "Please get naked."

"No," I laughed. "You take off *your* top."

So, of course, he took off his top without a moment of hesitation. He took off his T-shirt and then his trousers and then his boxers, until he was standing there starkers in the living room, just wearing mismatching socks. I laughed and glanced out of the window, because the living room looked out on the corridor. Anyone could have walked past and seen his tan line, his hairy legs. He had amazing calves: big, hairy, sinewy.

"Now your turn," he said. His gaze relaxed and unnerved me at the same time. His eyes were always mischievous, like he was thinking of a joke and I was the punchline.

"Not going to happen," I said, shaking my head. He took a step towards me and I took a step towards the door.

"Please?" he said. "How about just one flip-flop?"

So we laughed and he took some photos – of me laughing, of my head lost inside my T-shirt, of me taking off one flip-flop, then the other, and soon I was only wearing bikini bottoms, laughing for David in the living room. He kissed a freckle on my shoulder, and kissed my spine.

30

Sometimes I'd go to Julie's Place when David was out. It was like I was tempting fate now that Richard hadn't bothered with me for a while. I'd go back to the hostel and dress up in Lily's clothes first – the fuchsia sundress and teardrop earrings, or the tight black dress and the red stilettos – then I'd change back into David's dresses and wipe off Lily's lipstick before I went home. Vanessa and Tony thought it was hysterical. They smiled when I went into the back room dressed in jeans and came out in high heels and dresses. I don't know what they thought I was doing, but they didn't seem to mind.

I was fascinated by the way Julie was beginning to look at me. It was so different from her derisive shrugs the first time I came to the bar. Now she looked at me in this strange, searching way, like a fleeting version of the way that David looked at me. She looked at me like she could see me, while before she'd looked at me like she was waiting for me not to be there. Now she would cock her head to the side and smile knowingly at me like she was my best friend. And she didn't tell me I was too young to drink. Perhaps it was because I wore Lily's clothes with more confidence. At Julie's Place I found myself asking people questions all the time. How long would you wait in a restaurant for a date? Have you ever been arrested? Would you rather have a bath or a shower? What superhero would you be? If you had to lose one of your senses, what would it be? If you had to lose a limb which would it be? Do you have any piercings? There are mountains of people in my memory of those semi-drunken evenings, plus an insatiable desire to know what made each one of them happy or sad. The bravado of those conversations scared me, though, because no one told the truth. I don't think it was their fault, though. I think the truth is actually very difficult to know about. It's as hard to tell the truth as it is to see it in other people. These people presented bite-sized chunks of their identity, and wittily irritating one-liners that meant nothing to anyone.

"Piercings? You can look for them later…"

"I'll be Batman if you're Cat Woman…"

"I'd wait for ever for you, baby…"

It felt like I'd spent each evening trying desperately to conjure cardboard cutouts into 3D form.

Julie either spoke slowly, like a mouth on the moon, or a mile a minute, without punctuation, as if I were a tape recorder coming to the end of my capacity. Mostly she filled me up with a tizzy of words. "You know when I knew I was a heroin addict?" she said to me one evening, her jagged elbows on the bar and her wrists gesticulating wildly. "Cos, believe me, at first it was recreational. But then it was New Year's Eve and I was wearing a red Yves Saint Laurent dress on the F train into Manhattan, and there was a hobo next to me who'd just had a hit – but he's nodding in and out, do you know what nodding is? He was happy. He was blitzed. And I knew I had to get help, because I wanted to be him. I didn't want to wear silk blend and go look at paintings in an Upper East Side apartment, I wanted nobody to watch me shoot up in a corner some place, I could pass out easy enough when I wanted…"

"Did you lend Richard and Lily money particularly to buy drugs for the parties?" I interrupted. "Were they drug dealers or something? Maybe that's why he just, you know, disappeared?"

"Richard?" she said. "Richard?"

"Lily's husband," I reminded.

"I know who Richard is!" she said. She was high as a kite that night. The pupils of her eyes were dilated, bursting, and she was pouring vodka down her throat at an alarming speed. "They had amazing parties," she said. "I hope he's OK."

"Has anyone heard from him?"

"Nobody's heard from him since the wake."

"Did a guy called David Reed ever come to the bar? Maybe he met Lily here sometimes?" I asked.

"I never forget a name," she paused, then continued: "But there were lots of guys. Richard knew that. She was beautiful."

"Affairs?"

"Sure. Of course. My God."

"With who?"

"She and I weren't tight like that, not after she divorced that pretty boy and started to understand the world. She followed me around like a dog when she first started working here, thought I was awesome, but she learnt fast. Anyway she wouldn't have told me about her indiscretions, didn't tell me about the men she fucked, cos Richard was my friend more than she was."

"Are you sure she had affairs?"

Julie nodded and made herself another drink.

"She modelled, right? Did she date her photographers?" I asked, smiling at Julie.

"Richard didn't like her modelling. He liked her being a nurse, you know? Fair enough. Her ego didn't need fanning.

And she had a good time as a nurse, it worked out well for them. God, Richard loved her."

"Lots of people seemed to," I said.

"And then they got the hotel, so she stopped nursing too," Julie said. "I think then they were happy for a while."

"When did they buy the hotel, exactly?"

"Oh," she said and, just then, her elbow slipped off the bar. She nearly hit her chin on the metallic surface before righting herself with a giggle. The upward tilt of her thin lips didn't suit her: it sort of stretched her face in all the wrong places. She was so thin, like a wig on a clothes pin. I never knew quite what was true in Julie's ramblings. Sometimes she drank Coca Cola at the bar and looked haughtily at the youngsters around her drinking harder things and coming out of the bathroom with glittery smiles. Occasionally she'd get roaring drunk or high and whisper at me with pale lips that chewed the air and spat it out as mangled words. She'd talk of the buttercups in her garden at home, the time she wiped her arse with poison oak during a camping trip and nearly died, her compulsive fear of cockroaches, which reminded her of her father. One night Julie got paralytic, and I ended up taking her home in a taxi while one of the blue-eyed barmen locked up. Julie lived close to the bar, in the smoggy hills above Griffith Park. Her place looked small on the outside, with paint peeling off the stucco and big clumsy umbrellas of trees lolloping across the windows. We finally found her keys from the tissue-laden depths of her snakeskin purse and stumbled into the hallway. The ground floor was the top floor, with a worn red carpet and a framed promotional poster of *The Nutcracker* at the New York State Theatre twenty years ago. Then there was a narrow staircase that opened out onto a living room with hard-wood floors and yellow lace curtains covering a breathtaking view of winking late-night Los Angeles. It smelt like soup, just like Julie did, and there was no living-room furniture apart from a grey Pilates exercise ball, a blue foam mat and a black-leather bench press. There was drug paraphernalia – a syringe, a lighter – on the marble kitchen counter, next to some carrot sticks. There were lots of framed photographs all over the walls, of Julie at different stages of her life. There was Julie grinning behind the bar, Julie on a rowing boat with a man, Julie blowing out birthday candles at a small kitchen table. One picture caught my attention, of Julie and Richard and a bunch of people I didn't recognize all posing outside Julie's bar with their motorcycles. Richard's motorcycle was slim and elegant, with a visible engine and leather seats just like the one in Lily's photo. The other bikes were bigger, like most of the bikes in the mechanics shops I'd trawled through a while back.

"So Richard was really into bikes, then?" I asked Julie.

"I'm sorry to cause trouble," slurred Julie.

"Don't worry," I said. "Do you and Richard still ride?"

"I sold my bike years ago," she said. "I never rode it any more, wasn't worth the hassle."

"Does Richard still ride, then?"

"Sure, Lily, sure. You know he wouldn't give that up."

"I'm not Lily," I said. I was wearing the tight black dress and her red stilettos, which were uncomfortable and made me stand very straight.

She was silent. With her tiny body resting against my shoulder, I went in search of her bedroom. Two doors escaped off the living room. One contained a futon, a collection of shoes – over a hundred pairs – and a small collection of children's books: Lewis Carroll, *The Famous Five*, *Eloise of the Plaza Hotel*. The other bedroom had a quaint four-poster bed covered with colourful scarves. There were ballerina shoes hung on the wall and ballerina memorabilia placed neatly, on lace doilies, over every surface. There was a teddy bear bleeding stuffing from his ear on her bedside table, next to a copy of Aesop's *Fables*, a cut-glass tumbler of water and a thermometer. I carefully flopped Julie down amongst the throw pillows and pink silk blankets on the bed, wondering if she'd always been that thin. She was beautiful, though, like an ageing doll.

"Who are you?" Julie said. She stared at me and frowned.

"I'm not Lily," I said. The arches of my feet ached in Lily's stilettos.

"No," she said. "No I guess you're not," she said. Julie's bloodshot eyes fluttered closed.

"Did you have an affair with Richard?" I said.

"No," said Julie. "He loved Lily. It's such a pity they broke up, they made a great team."

"What do you mean, broke up?" I said.

"Oh, you know. They got a divorce not long before she died. A month or two, maybe. Not too many people know that I guess. He told me though. He was my friend."

"How come they broke up?" I said.

"Her affairs, his depression. Money trouble, too, I think. You're so lovely, though," Julie purred. "You're divine. You two should make another go of it; see if you can make it work. He loves you so much."

"I'm not Lily," I said again.

"I know you're not, I know you're not," she slurred.

I stepped out from the acidic smell of vodka sweat and restless sleep that was creeping up in Julie's bedroom with every breath she exhaled. I wondered if what she'd said was true, or just the drugs messing with her head. I looked at the photo of Julie and Richard with their motorcycles, both looking young. I padded over to Julie's living-room window and leant my hot forehead against the cold glass, then opened the window and breathed the smell of pine needles and night air.

The radio earlier had said that it topped a hundred in the valley that afternoon, but the evening was cool and still with a perfectly black sky shot over by a firefly orgy of street and billboard lights. If it was true they were divorced, I wondered if she'd left Richard for David, and I wondered what I felt about that. Who wrote the letters about umbrellas and love? Did Richard hurt Lily because of her affairs, or perhaps because of their money trouble? I felt very small and perturbed, and for a moment got my mind off Lily by letting myself think about the café. It would be 11 a.m. there, and Dad would be in a cloud of heat as chip-fat bubbles burst on the meniscus of grease and strips of potato browned in front of him, or he'd be getting bread out for sandwiches. He'd have hired some kid to take my weekend shifts. If it was a boy, it'll take him a few weeks to notice that his acne is getting significantly worse and his skin reeks of bacon grease. Dad and the boy probably wouldn't talk except to grunt over balancing the register at seven every evening, but Dad would give the boy more than his fair share of the tip jar. I tried to stop thinking, but my mind kept going – café, Daphne's fingernails, Grandma's swollen ankles, Lily's love letters, Julie's toes, then I thought of the little girl falling through the air and smashing on the floor. I opened my eyes with a jolt and tried to blink all my thoughts away, but couldn't clear my head.

31

One night David and I compared scars, and continued the conversation we'd started in the car outside the Platinum Club a month and a bit ago. First I kissed the scar that split his right eyebrow and one on his cheek under his eye. They were just little indentations; slightly more textured than his skin, but not ice-coloured like my scars.

"Where's this one from?" I asked, touching his cheek with the tip of my finger, my other hand resting across his torso.

"Bar fight," he said, turning his head slightly to kiss the scar under my chin near my ear, which was shaped like Italy. "This one?" he asked, touching it.

"A savage game of Red Rover when I was ten," I smiled.

"This one?" he said, and pointed to a curved Cheshire-cat-smile shape on my shoulder.

"I smashed a window by mistake once," I said.

"Jesus," he laughed.

"Yeah," I blushed and kissed the soft space on David's hand, between forefinger and thumb. He kissed the raised white globe under my right lip, where I bite down when I'm nervous. I showed him the scar on my bottom from when I was thrown in a skip and metal cut through my jeans, and the slice on my wrist from when I fell on a shard of metal during a scuffle at the football field. I even showed him the four-inch blue knife line inside my thigh, and he kissed it. Then I kissed the snake-shaped scar on his lower back, from falling off a balcony when he was wasted with Sam one night. One or two scars, like one on the side of his forehead, and one on his neck, looked fresher than the others. They'd healed, but they had that shiny, slightly raised look of freshly formed scars.

"What about your limp?" I said.

"The scars seem strange now," he said to answer, touching his ankle, where there was a scar on his Achilles heel.

"Why?"

"I guess cos for the first time in my life I'm not drunk," he said. "That's why everything is so… empty, in my apartment. I got rid of everything that reminded me of alcohol. The scars remind me of alcohol. I think the ankle's from… walking into a window, something dumb."

"Do you miss her?" I asked.

"Who?" he said.

"Lily."

He turned to look at me, but didn't get angry. We were silent for a while. He touched his forehead.

"I think about her more than I'd like to," he said. "But I wish I didn't. I don't want to have to think about her."

"You must have loved her a lot," I said.

"I said I don't want to have to think about her," he snapped, sitting up in bed and facing me. "I wish you wouldn't bring her up. It's so nice here with you. Then you have to mention some other woman."

"Did she used to come with you on your drunken weekends, ever, outside LA?" I said to him.

"I'm not talking about this," he said, and I thought for a moment that he was even going to hit me. My skin lifted, tingling, bracing itself, eager, but he deflated. His fist fell back onto the pillow, and he sunk back into the bed sheets.

"Sorry," I said, and looked away from his sunken body. We were silent for a while, then he put his hand on mine. From his bed we could see a panorama of rooftops, washing lines and palm trees.

"Tell me a story," David said.

"What sort?"

"Any. A story. Whatever you want. Tell me how you turned into a half-human, half-dove hybrid? Since you're no mermaid."

"My mother took off her dove costume and did it with my father at the back of a theatre," I said. Then I thought for a moment. "No," I said. "It happened when I was kidnapped by bandits."

"Bandits?" he smiled.

"Bandits."

"How were you kidnapped?" he asked.

"From a bar in the little village we're travelling through with… It's stupidly hot and we've been arguing all day…"

"You and I?"

"No. Not you and I. Just a boy," I said.

"What are you and this boy arguing about?"

"Mostly about how he left the top off the toothpaste and now all our clothes smell minty."

David smiled.

"One cut can unravel a jumper," he said.

"We're drinking Coca Cola in a local bar, which is empty apart from a crouching old man, a barman with skin like dehydrated beef, and a tiny television set showing Olympic reruns of 100-metre sprinters. All the doors and windows are open, but the air is heavy and giving me a headache. All the humidity from months of travelling has finally soaked through my skull. My brain is damp laundry, mildewed wood, or week-old bikini bottoms found screwed up in some forgotten crevice of a suitcase. I excuse myself, the boyfriend has one eye on the sports channel anyway…"

"Bastard," David added.

"And I step outside onto a little dirt courtyard behind the bar."

"What country are you in?" David said.

I shrug.

"It's a country in my imagination."

"OK."

"Anyway, outside the bar there's a man smoking a cigarette. He glares at me and I look away, over at the tips of the trees reaching out into the jungle. The man offers me a cigarette, and I hesitate, but he seems nonchalant and I'd like to inhale something, so I take it. He lights it for me, and as I kiss the filter to my mouth there's a look in his eye, an unpleasant look. It's a split second, but I know from the look in his eyes that everything in my life is about to change. The smoke rolls down my throat, and it suddenly feels like I've swallowed a bag of marbles and can't breathe. I turn away from him."

"A poison cigarette?" he said, raising his eyebrows.

"Shhh," I replied. "The next thing I know, I'm vomiting on myself and trying to stand up while three men help me out from the boot of an oversized car."

"You've jumped in time."

"I passed out. I don't know where I am and I pass out again. When I wake up for the second time I'm on a small white bed in a small white room with no windows."

"Who is the boyfriend?" David asked.

"What do you mean?" I said.

"If it's not me, who is it?"

"He's no one. He has blue eyes and a slightly frizzy, dusty brown ponytail. Even when we're sitting in the bar, he's already disappearing in my mind. I mean, I'm already forgetting who he is before we've even broken up, and he's in my imagination. Do you know what I mean?"

"Your imagination is very detailed."

"Are you jealous of a fictional character I just made up?"

"Perhaps you'll meet him for 'real' one day, Mr Pony Tail. He sounds like an idiot, but perhaps one day you'll meet him in a bar, or Whole Foods or something, and recognize him, recognize him as a future memory. Or he'll recognize you."

"Shall we kill him off right now? Just to make sure he doesn't turn up in the vegetable section of Whole Foods and want to take my digits."

"Sure."

"Fine," I smiled. "After I smoke the drugged cigarette and am folded into the boot of the car, a crazed jungle pirate with solid gold teeth robs the bar and guns down everyone inside it. It's a completely unrelated and very unfortunate incident. The pirate kills the crouched old man, the barman and my fictional boyfriend, all for a small television and the equivalent of twelve dollars and fifty cents cash."

"They assume you met the same fate, so nobody looks for you."

"Nobody would look for me anyway."

"Of course they would," David said. "I would."

"As an odd point of interest," I replied, ignoring him, "although slightly off the subject, the pirate slept with his wife that night and they conceived a kid, who twenty years from now will end up winning a bronze Olympic medal in the 100 metres."

"Huh. But back to the bandits."

"I wake up in a dirty bed that smells a little bit like piss and mildew. My body is dirtier than it was when I passed out. There are ecosystems of jungle dirt in the frills of my belly button, and dried sweat clinging to the creases of skin at my armpits. My short blond hair is a helmet of grease and dirt, at the same time greasy and brittle to the touch. My skin is a shade darker than it was when I passed out."

"You're turning me on," David said.

"The words 'greasy and brittle' turn you on?"

"No," he laughed.

"Dirty?"

"Yes."

"You're a cliché," I said.

"All men are clichés," he said, and kissed me.

32

David and I walked back from one of his favoured 24-hour Thai restaurants. It was around midnight, and the air was still, smelling like pollution and burning. On a balcony somewhere above our heads there was a baby screaming, and in the distance a car engine revved. There was some music from a nearby door, and cars going by on the main road. "Euphonious," I thought to myself. We turned onto David's block, and immediately saw a skinny coyote outside the gate, its body half-flooded by a street lamp and half in darkness. The coyote was in the middle of an almighty yawn when he saw us. He froze in mid-movement with his strong back arched, one knobbly grey paw stretched out in front of its body. He held himself still for a minute, his whiskers quivering in the lamplight and his ears pricked back. His tail was chopped off halfway, so it was more like a stump, but that was the only clumsy thing about the creature. After a drawn-out moment he drew his chest upwards with an inaudible sigh and stepped backwards out of the lamplight. I thought of a ballet dancer stepping out of the spotlight, or a reluctantly retreating thief in a pantomime.

"We interrupted his yawning," said David quietly, neither of us moving a muscle, and we heard bushes rustle as the coyote disappeared back into the undergrowth. The coyotes had been smoked out of the hills by the fires, and were stalking rubbish bins like common foxes.

"In order of preference," said David, "orgasms, ice cream or yawns? What do you think?"

"It's an impossible question," I smiled at him, but then at that same moment I felt like someone was watching me. I turned away from David's smile and, sure enough, at the end of the road I saw the thug-faced man with the gold nose stud and schoolboy haircut. I stepped forwards, and he was gone before I even blinked.

"Hey!" I shouted after the man. "Hey!"

"What's wrong?" said David, shocked by the sudden outburst and looking around the empty streets. "Shh…"

"Did you see that Mexican guy?"

"Who?" he said, following my finger pointing towards the end of the road.

"That guy who just turned the corner? It was the guy who stole my rucksack."

"Really?" David said, not believing me.

"Yes," I said. We both hurried to the end of the road, in the direction I thought he'd gone. Of course, we couldn't see the man anywhere. We could see the United Methodist Church on the corner, which looked like a factory building. We could see smoke from fires in the hills and a bunch of men at the bus stop, but not the one who stole my rucksack. There were people I might have mistaken for him, but I didn't say that to David. I bit my lip.

"Maybe I imagined it," I said, looking around.

"Maybe it's just that you're a horrible racist and all people with different skin colours look identical to you?" he smiled.

"I'm not a racist," I said. "I saw him."

"Racist," David nodded, kidding. We stared around us, and then suddenly David became serious. He glanced sideways at me, and I turned towards him. "Sometimes I think you don't always tell me the truth," he said. "You can be very secretive."

"I'm not secretive," I said, and when he faced me I put my arms up over his shoulders. I had to stand on tiptoe to inhale him, along with the smell of sap in the trees and late-night air.

"I was driving around the other day and I saw you go into that hostel you stayed at for a while. Why'd you still go there?"

"I have mates there," I said, without skipping a beat. "I made friends with the manager while I was staying there. Her name's Vanessa. Were you spying on me?"

"You're not keeping her clothes there?" he said. "The suitcase?"

"I said I got rid of them, didn't I?" my heart sped up.

"Yeah," he said, and I bounced up to kiss him on the corner of his mouth. He bent down to kiss me properly.

Later that night, when neither of us could sleep, David said: "You never told me the rest of your story, after you woke up covered in dirt."

It was the hottest night of the year, and the fires were spreading, causing the air to taste thick and feel close. We'd kicked off the sheets, and both our skins were sticky inside all the sludgy air. We had two fans going, clacking away in the silence. I thought for a moment, turning stories over in my head.

"So I'm covered in dirt," I said, "and groggy from the drugs they gave me in the cigarette. I can smell something funny in the air, like blood and mud."

"Ominous."

"And I can hear clucking."

"Clucking?" he laughed.

"Clucking and mooing and naaing, all around me."

"A farm," he said.

"Will you let me tell the story?" I said, elbowing him, bad tempered and anxious in the heat.

"Why are you on a farm?" David asked me.

"It's more like a meat factory," I replied. "A massive meat factory owned by a great Fat Rich Man with lots of rings on his fingers. He's a vegetarian himself, and has taste in art and literature. He owns several Monets, a Van Gogh and a library of classic novels."

"Who runs the farm?"

"Farmhands. Native of the unnamed jungle in the unnamed tropical country. He treats the natives well and considers himself not only a very just employer, but also a civilizing influence. He lends out books. He pays fairly. Before he started his empire of meat, there weren't enough jobs. Now there are jobs for anyone willing to work. Even the animals live well in his empire, fattened with the best food, allowed to run around in what he considers a 'free-range' environment. He only has one problem."

"What's that?"

"He has a secret."

"What's his secret?"

"I can't tell you. It's a secret."

"I don't like secrets," he said, and looked at me.

"All right then," I said. "When the Rich Man first started out in the meat business, he persuaded his childhood sweetheart to marry him and move out to the farm. Unfortunately she wasn't used to the heat or the germs, and she died within a year. The Fat Rich Man was distraught, and although the meat business was thriving, nothing made him happy. The Fat Rich Man started to drink, and one night he was so lonely, so dizzy from the heat and the stench of blood, that he went down to the farm in the middle of the night, and guess what he did?"

"He fucked a pig."

"A horse, actually, but good guess."

"I'm a sick fuck."

"This was a sick fuck," I said.

"Very funny," he said.

"Anyway, the horse became pregnant and bore the Rich Man a son, who grew up into the secret apple – and secret guilt – of the Rich Man's eye. The Rich Man named his boy Enkidu, after the legend of Gilgamesh, and Enkidu grew up to be a brave, strong boy, who looked almost human if it wasn't for how the boy walked around on all fours and refused to eat anything except milk and hay."

"You really have the strangest imagination," said David, stroking my hair.

"Now I'm self-conscious," I said. My mind went blank. "You'll never know how the Rich Man planned to civilize his son and drag him from the animal kingdom."

"I'm sorry, go on."

"No," said.

"Don't be bad-tempered. It's the heat making you angry?"

"I'm not angry," I said.

"What happened to Enkidu?"

"I'm not telling you," I said. "Why did you follow me today, when you saw me at the youth hostel?"

"I wasn't following you. I just happened to pass on my way to taking a photo of Mary Fodder coming out of the gym."

"What did you do after you saw me?"

"I got the photograph of Mary Fodder. Then I drove around. Please tell me about Enkidu," he said.

"No," I said, and turned my back to him.

I couldn't fall asleep though, and we both tossed and turned in bed for another hour before starting to talk again. When David tried to touch me, I batted his hand away. Another hour or so passed.

"When you masturbate," David asked eventually, still stifled by the ridiculous closeness of the air and the rhythmic pulsing of the fans, "do you think about me?"

I looked at him. David was staring at the ceiling, where the fan was catching nuggets of light from the rising sun outside the window and throwing them against the wall.

"Of course," I lied, thinking of the indistinct strangers who populate my dreams. It has always upset me to see men in pornography. They look so painfully ridiculous, with their muddy shadows of prominent muscles that shout out like a biology diagram – Thorax! Abdomen! Gluteus Maximus! And those eager faces looking so pleased with themselves, nodding up there on top of clenched shoulders like one of those dogs on car dashboards. The men in my dreams and nightmares are so much less distinct: they are almost without edges, more like distant memories than anyone David could be jealous of. It's strange that I'll happily watch pornography involving women, and that in my dreams I am distinct down to the position of my legs and the taste in my mouth, but I will not watch men in pornography, and the men in my fantasies are ideas, not people.

"Really?" asked David, pleased. "What do we do?"

"It's not like that," I laughed, blushing in the dark. "I don't know. Yesterday, when I was in the bath, we did it on a washing machine."

"There's a washing machine in your head? How domestic. Did you come?" He smiled. I loved his smile.

"Of course," I said, and didn't mention that in my fantasy I was left naked on the washing machine for a full cycle, my hands tied behind my back. It wasn't domestic, or even funny. The backdrop of the washing-machine fantasy was actually a Laundromat near David's office, where I washed lots of Lily's clothes while I was looking for him. Another problem with my fantasies, which I didn't tell David about, was that they often ran away from me and didn't result in my touching myself at all. They also often involved me being left alone and scared. Like my dream of the beach where I wash goo out of the baby's mouth while someone drowns on the horizon, I'll begin somewhere perfectly reasonable and end up all alone, in tears, not turned on at all any more, but horrified at my own mind. In reality I won't be crying, because I haven't cried in years, but in my imagination I'll be watching my fantasy self in floods of unattractive tears, tied to a damn washing machine. I often think that if I could make my mind do what I wanted it to do, if the girl in my dreams sat up straighter and smiled more and did what I told her to do, my life would be easier.

"What sort of washing machine?" asked David playfully, turning his head to me.

"I don't know," I said.

"Fast or slow cycle?"

"Fast."

"Colours or whites?"

"Whites, for sure. Higher heat," I said.

"Would your clothes be in the machine?" he asked.

"Of course."

We paused, sleepy as the sun was rising outside the window.

"What happened to Enkidu, then? I won't be able to sleep until I know."

"I was brought into the farm in order to drag him into the human world."

"To make a man of him, like in Gilgamesh," said David.

"Exactly," I yawned. "But I'm too sleepy to make a man out of anyone tonight."

"You live in a state of perpetual unreality," he said.

"Says the alcoholic," I replied.

"Harsh," he said.

"Pots and kettles," I kissed him.

"Let's run away somewhere," he said.

"Sure," I smiled.

"Let's run away somewhere tomorrow," he said.

"Where?" I said.

"Rio, Mexico, the moon?" he said. "I really don't care. I just want to get out of here. That woman from downstairs keeps telling me that things are going to fall apart."

"She tells me that too," I smiled.

"Are you as good at lying as you are at story-telling?"

"What do you mean?" I said, confused by the sudden change in tone and subject.

"Are you a good liar?" he said.

"My Dad could always tell when I was lying, cos my left eye twitched," I lied to David with a small smile. He held his thumb under my eye.

"Do you love me?" he asked.

"I really do," I said. "I love you."

"I love you, too," he said, watching my eye for a twitch.

33

We didn't go away the next day, of course, although I wish
we had. Instead we woke up in the heat and had a few hours
together before Sam picked me up for work. David and I
walked up to Griffith Park Observatory. The city and the
Santa Monica Mountains stretched out glinting below us
like a saucepan of water that was just about to boil. When
we got to the top, through all that thick dry heat we could see
the bald patches of burnt earth where the fires had been put
out only a few days ago. Smoke was still rising, not even very
far away, shattering the blue sky into grey and shifty pieces.
I watched a dehydrated fly swim in delirious circles and then
land on a metal railing, which must have been insanely hot,
because the fly fell dead to the floor a few seconds later. David
wore a pale-blue T-shirt, slightly torn, and got a triangle of
sweat on his back as we climbed. I could smell him. He told
me about how one day when he was twenty-five he woke up
outside the observatory at nine in the morning with no idea
how he got there, surrounded by Dutch tourists who were
poking him with their guidebooks. I laughed, although it was
a pathetic image.

"You ever woken up in weird places?" he asked me.

"I don't think so," I shrugged, "I don't like getting drunk
much." David laughed. "But I did have a brief love affair with
drowsy berry-flavoured cough syrup – but that's about it." I
smiled.

We were silent for a bit, walking around the circles of the building. David said he was going to spend his afternoon out on some photographic mission or other, stealing private moments from famous people. He said he might develop the photos he'd taken of me a few weeks ago, the ones of me posing in my bikini around his living room.

"Ah, no, don't," I cringed. "Please don't."

"Why not?"

"They'll be silly," I shivered.

"They'll be lovely, I promise," he said, smiling, and held my hand as we made our descent back down the hill. I wondered what he saw when he looked at me, and contemplated how much dishonesty there was in perception, anyway. He might not know my real age, but he still saw me. He might know things about Lily that I didn't, but I still loved him. He turned to me and said: "I might try to find the roll of film from ages ago, the photos I took when we first met, when you were a thief asleep on the beach," he said.

"That's not fair," I said. "I might look ugly."

"You never look ugly," he said.

"Liar," I said.

34

The first set I worked on with Sam had been on a fake suburban street, and the second was a Korea Town pet shop. There was a front area full of spider-webbed plastic castles, fake seaweed and rancid dog chews, then two long corridors – one lined with fish and the other with yelping dogs who looked like they were about to drop dead, their little paws scratching at their glass walls. Every night the owners and their two teenage sons would climb up a wooden ladder to a small attic above the shop. They slept up there on four tidy futons while we filmed. In the morning, when the light was just beginning to ruin the continuity of Sam's shots, the family came yawning down the wooden ladder in matching blue cotton pyjamas to make tea in the kitchen, where they also cleaned out the daily mulch of a hundred animal cages. The family seemed entirely at ease with the camera crew. We learnt later that they'd had other film crews in over the years. Only in Los Angeles is every mom-and-pop shop also regularly a film set.

There seemed to be a lot of crazy people in that part of town, their presence amplified by our shooting through the night. The shop was opposite a Kentucky Fried Chicken branch, one built in the shape of a giant, dirty, concrete KFC bucket on North Western Avenue. When the crew arrived in the evening, religious zealots would be preaching of martyrdom out in the strip-mall parking lots, while Korean men skulked in and out of a 24-hour convenience store. The convenience store smelt of aerosol cans, and the shopkeeper sat behind a safety cage. Next to the store was a tanning salon with a blown-out neon sign outside, which I can't imagine attracted many customers, and above it was a window display full of dusty wedding gowns and taffeta prom dresses the colour of dried phlegm.

"Maybe there's a meth lab in the tanning salon, and they deal from the shop," suggested Sam on the first night of shooting when I mentioned that the tanning salon and the dress shop couldn't possibly make any money. "That would make sense."

"What about the dress shop?" I asked.

"That's where they live," he said, "with wedding dresses for duvets and veils for pillows." I smiled at him. A year or two later, after all of this was over, I stopped by at the strip mall and peeked in at the dress shop. There was a sign on the window that said "appointment only", and through the dusty glass I could see a woman changing her baby's nappy on the counter. I could have sworn they were even the same dresses in the display, so perhaps Sam was right.

We worked till 7 a.m. that summer morning. Sam gave me a ride home, and it was around eight when I let myself into David's flat. The first thing I noticed was a wooden chair missing from around the kitchen table and dents in the kitchen walls, where a confetti of paint was drizzling off. It was quite a small mark in the wall, but I couldn't help noticing that the laminate kitchen floor was dented now too. David got out of the shower just as I walked in, and he smelt clean like a baby or a shampooed dog. I walked through the slightly askew living room and into the bedroom. I kissed him on the cheek, but he turned away from me and started to dry himself with his back to the bedroom door. Perhaps there was a faint hint of alcohol in the air, but mostly all I could smell was shampoo.

"How was your night?" I said. My voice sounded relatively calm considering the adrenalin suddenly in my brain. I hadn't been to the Serena for over a week, not since we saw the coyote and David accused me of keeping secrets.

"All right," David said as he dropped his towel and started to get dressed. He seemed to be moving slowly, in a slightly odd way: swampy and thick. The atmosphere was very different from our talks about going on holiday to the moon.

"Want me to make you breakfast?" I asked him.

I didn't mention the little cuts on his knuckles, or the fact that several plates were missing from the kitchen cupboards. He was looking at me strangely while I made scrambled eggs in his little pink-tiled kitchen. There was a gap between us that I couldn't put my finger on. He was definitely drunk, or he had been. Maybe he'd just fallen off the wagon and it was nothing to do with me, I thought hopefully, but something was certainly wrong, and I could feel his angry thoughts while I whisked up the eggs in a ribbed-glass cup and added milk. The eggs lolloped around in the glass, and I broke the yolks against the sides with my fork, merging them like bleeding sea creatures into the thick surrounding water. I concentrated on feeding crumbs of salt into the mixture and turning olive oil to fume in the saucepan before I poured the mixture in and watched it sizzle.

I pretended not to feel this horrible itch on my skin where he was looking. I turned and smiled fakely at him across the kitchen table. I'd been wearing one of his T-shirts all night on Sam's set, from some death-metal band I'd never heard of, and the jeans he bought me rather than Lily's stonewash skinny pair. My hair was long enough to be up in a ponytail now, although there was only a tuft of blond hair caught up in the rubber band. He had got dressed in his normal ridiculous fashion – tracksuit bottoms with holes in them and visible elastic at the waistband, a nice pressed shirt with blue stripes, a pair of purple plastic sunglasses on his shorn head. His hair was still damp, and his camera lay dormant on the table next to his hand.

"You want cheese in your scrambled egg?" I said to him.

"Is that an English thing?" he replied gruffly, and I turned to look in the fridge, just so that I could use the door to shield myself from his look. He'd been irritated with me before, for moments, but never for long, and it never felt as heavy as this. We didn't have any cheese, and when I turned back to the eggs they were already setting in the saucepan. I gave them a quick stir, scraping the yolk from the sides, and put toast in the toaster. If I'd known this moment was so important, I would have done something interesting with the eggs.

Perhaps I did know what was happening, although not how or why. Perhaps I was stretching out the time before I had to make contact with the problem, or perhaps I was waiting for him to speak first. While scrambling eggs in David's little kitchen, the trouble seemed to be contained beyond a glass wall. I felt groggy and feline, like someone had weighted down my ankles with sandbags, but I didn't feel like it was the end of the world. All I wanted to do was curl up and be unconscious, preferably near him. Instead I buttered his toast in the kitchen. The smell of coffee filled the kitchen from the gurgling machine.

"How's Sam's set?" David finally said to me as I tumbled the scrambled eggs onto his toast and turned to put the plate in front of him. Then I swung my back to him again and busied myself arranging the remains on the eggs onto another piece of toast for me.

"Yeah, fine," I said. "Bit crazy."

"It's in a pet shop, isn't it?" he asked.

"Yeah," I said, picking at my food. "What you been up to?" I wasn't hungry. Neither was he, it seemed, because he didn't even pick up his knife and fork.

"Just developing photos at the office," David said.

"Anything good?" I said nervously.

We paused. David looked at me, then shrugged and glanced back at his hands. I felt all brittle and jumpy. Film sets often ran on a prescription drug called Adderall, which I'd never taken until Sam gave it to me. Nobody takes it in London, or at least I'd never heard of it, but Los Angeles seemed to use it like morning coffee. It's meant to be for people who find it difficult to concentrate. It makes you speedy and focused, but after a while it makes you hollow and sleepless. Everyone took it on Sam's set.

David didn't touch my scrambled eggs. He looked like he was hardly awake at all, and his body reminded me of a tethered bull or a tranquillized horse. His tanned shoulders were hunched forwards slightly over the table, and his heavy eyes followed me languidly as I moved around the kitchen.

"What's wrong, David?" I said finally. "What was wrong with the photographs? You're scaring me."

"When are you going in to work today?" he replied, pale, formulating his words with care.

"Sam's picking me up at three," I said. "We could say fuck it. Go to Mexico today. Can we go away to Mexico today? Or the moon, or Rio, or wherever? Sam can find another script supervisor, it doesn't matter at all. What's wrong?"

David looked like he was holding his breath or biting his tongue.

"I don't want to talk to you now," he said. "I need to go out, clear my head. OK?"

I felt like we were in one of Sam's movies, only the eye lines didn't match up. Or like I was trapped in a game of charades and we hadn't read any of the same books or watched any of the same movies.

"What's happened? How did it happen?" I said.

"When will you be home?" he said, not answering.

"The film wraps this time tomorrow. I don't have to go, though."

"Let's talk tomorrow then."

"Are we actually arranging a date to argue? Let's just do it now," I said.

He was standing up, within touching distance of me.

"No," he said.

"Why not now?" My voice was getting high-pitched.

"Cos neither of us have slept, and the sight of you is making me feel sick," he said, and lifted his hand in a way that made me flinch, although it turned out he was merely reaching for his bag on the hook behind my head. "Plus I have a hangover," he said. My skin lifted where I thought it was going to be hit, blood rushing to the surface and making me flush.

"I'm sorry," I said.

"You're a liar," he said.

"I should have told you," I said.

"I've really fucked up," said David.

I wasn't really sure what was going on. If I could do it again, I'd make him hit me. It would have been nice to add David's anger to the physical map on my body. Through all our bedtime wrestling matches he never left a scar, and I badly wished that he had.

"I'm not going to hit you," he said, measured.

"Why aren't you shouting at me," I said.

"Valium," he said, and there was almost the trace of a smile on his lips. He'd got drunk and lost his temper earlier, and now he was sedated.

"I'm so sorry," I said again. It was all I could think of to say. It sounded lame and beside the point. I wished I'd been there when he smashed the chair to pieces and smashed plates on the floor. Some physical pain would have been better than the absence he left me with instead.

"Just get some sleep," he said. He hesitated at the door before he left, a funny look in his lopsided green eyes.

35

I went to the pet shop as planned that afternoon, believing David would be home when I got back and we could somehow talk everything through. Even though I was about to spend the night on a sweaty film set, I wore David's favourite navy-blue dress, black kitten heels and the little pearl earrings he bought me. In our breaks during shooting, Sam and the crew huddled in the strip-mall car park clutching cups of coffee and taking pills from the cinematographer, whose girlfriend was a narcoleptic set dresser. We'd just shot a scene where the main actor was trying to choose from a tower of translucent plastic jars, each containing a nearly identical blue tropical fish with a chiffon-like tail. They put blue dye in each jar of water, so it looked like a parody of water.

I told Sam that David was angry with me, but Sam didn't say much. Sam just gave me a hug and wink, and told me that his bed was always open for me. I was standing with Sam in the car park when everything suddenly started to melt in front of my eyes. I'd been exhausted and tired and tearful all night, of course, but by 5 a.m. I was feeling sick. Some others – a gaffer and an extra – had gone home with food poisoning earlier in the night. It's amazing how your life can hinge on one moment of awful timing, like bad film-set pizza toppings. I tried to keep my surroundings steady, as if I was holding up a falling bookshelf. The flat sky, the concrete buildings, the cars winking by the pet shop – everything began to lose its definition, and suddenly I desperately wanted to be horizontal, with my hot cheek resting on the cool early-morning tarmac. All my dreams of fainting that summer didn't prepare me for that feeling of wanting to pass out.

"What's wrong?" said Sam, taking coffee from my hand. I felt nauseous, but I could have remained standing, I thought, if it wasn't that I wanted so badly to fall.

Before I passed out, I didn't think about David or Lily or the fainting game, but about fish. There was a time, when I was little, when Dad said he was going to the fish shop. I knew that Grandma and Grandpa's café downstairs had fish on the menu, but somehow I'd missed a link between the things that swam around in the nursery-school aquarium and the white flesh caked in batter that we sometimes sold drenched in vinegar and riding on a bed of yellow chips on the café menu downstairs. In retrospect we were probably at the fish market so that Dad could speak with a supplier, but of course I thought we were going to get a pet fish. I imagined my own private underworld of plastic treasure chests and seaweed arches like the bowl we had at school. I was very quiet and good all the way to the market, where we walked through corridors of fruits and vegetables – plums and apples and baskets of fresh strawberries. Then we turned a corner into a funny smell. Suddenly I saw a mausoleum. Hundreds and hundreds of heavy eyes stared. There were tiny little ones overflowing their boxes, big silver monsters with damp pink flesh hanging from sliced open stomachs, ignominiously open-mouthed, salivating ice and blood. Each one was staring at me accusingly. I lost Dad like I often did in crowds because he walked so fast, but he looked behind in time for me to run forwards and grab his hand.

"Bad fish," I said to Dad after some mental gymnastics, deciding they must be bad, because they had been killed. Good fish couldn't possible end up like that. What I remember most is a bit of a fish's face that I picked up from my father's feet as he talked to one of the vendors. It was half a head, the eyeball very much intact, with a visible spinal column coming out of the neck for a few centimetres before snapping. The flesh that was still clinging to the spine felt sopping wet, the texture of conditioner-soaked hair in the plughole after bath time. Then the scales were drier and firmer than expected, as was the eyeball itself, which I touched with appalled glee.

36

After fainting I woke up abruptly and found myself at the Kaiser Hospital in Los Feliz. Out of the seven of us who got sick that night on set only I was still in the hospital four days later. David wasn't in the hospital with me, and when I asked where he was, the nurse said she wasn't aware that anyone called David had come in to see me. The other people from the set who got food poisoning from the same pizza toppings had been discharged two days earlier. There had been "complications" in my situation. The nurse explained that she was afraid I'd "lost the foetus" – for some reason I just laughed. The air smelt of disinfectant. Then with baffled pride I nodded solemnly and frowned, pretending to her that "the" foetus was an entity I was even vaguely familiar with. It was only a few weeks old, so nothing really, but nausea overwhelmed me again. The nurse also told me that my friend Sam was coming to visit me later that afternoon, and that he'd been very worried. They assumed Sam was the dad of this empty space in my tummy.

It didn't matter at all. I didn't think about what might have happened or could have happened or what I would have done if it weren't for the Adderall and the food poisoning. "The" foetus only existed for the fraction of a second after she told me it was dead, since only then did I acknowledge that at one point it had been alive. There was a sweet old woman in the hospital room with me who'd just had a stroke. She kept sticking out her tongue at me and telling me the beginning of a joke about how many Jewish grandmothers it took to screw in a light bulb, but she couldn't remember the punchline. She looked terribly confused, and I wanted to telephone Dad, but didn't know what I'd say to him. I think I would have liked to tell him that it was suddenly apparent to me that he'd done his best and failed. That I should have tried harder to stay out of trouble at school and that I wouldn't be going back.

I picked up Lily's suede shoulder bag and left the hospital early that morning without waiting to see Sam. I took the bus back to David's. It was just getting light when my clumsy fingers shoved the key hurriedly into David's gate and swung it open. I walked upstairs. "Broken bird," David had said once while he kissed my shoulder blades, which stuck out just like broken wings from the bones of my back. I was most fond of David in the morning, when he was grumpy and clumsy. I liked his moments of brokenness, too, just as he liked mine. I loved him when he burnt his fingers, spilt coffee on the business section of the *New York Times*, bumped his head, forgot to close the fridge. It was in these living moments that I saw an amalgamation of his past and his present, momentary visions of what he might have been like as a child or during gawky adolescence. I loved David most during the moments I pretended not to notice, when he dropped cereal on the floor or when he lost his car keys and had to hunt through the wash basket for yesterday's pair of trousers. Perhaps this is how love works – in flashes of banality that become brilliant because of love. One night, when we lay bedraggled in bed, he read the beginning of *Paradise Lost* to me with a sonorous and theatrical voice. There's a bit when Satan has just fallen from heaven into hell

227

and is described as having "baleful eyes", with which he glances around the sordid place he's fallen into. I thought that "baleful" meant woebegone, because that's how the word sounds. To me it suggested that the fallen angel had melancholy but purposeful eyes. For a while after he read me that, I thought that David cast "baleful eyes", just like Satan's, especially in the morning, when he had to confront a broken light bulb or a burnt piece of toast. I checked in a dictionary, though, and the word actually means "hostile" and "menacing".

I got to the top of the stairs and noticed that the window of his flat, which looks into the balconied corridor, seemed different. Before I opened the door, I saw through the window that the flat was empty. The sofa, the glass-topped coffee table that he cleaned so lovingly twice a day, the flat-screen TV, the saucepan I'd cooked him scrambled eggs with, it was all gone. There were shadows of his possessions, like indentations in the carpet where his furniture used to lie, but this only intensified the absence. There were rectangles of bright paint where his pictures had hung, surrounded by faded white. The flat looked much bigger without anything in it, and the fitted carpet looked uglier. There were balls of red fluff from his carpet, paper clips, kirby grips and stray rubber bands in dusty corners. The bedroom was empty too, as was the bathroom. He was gone. He had evaporated.

I went and stood where the kitchen table had been, and bent down to touch the dents in the laminate flooring and the skid marks on the walls from where he must have attacked the chair a week earlier, when really he ought to have been attacking me. The dents in the floor looked like dimples, the marks on the walls looked like scars on very pale skin. I walked to the kitchen and took a sip of water from the familiar tap. I drank from my hands, because there weren't any cups. I didn't wait for the water to cool down, and glugged it lukewarm from my skin, which still tasted slightly acidic, like illness and hospitals. I don't actually remember falling asleep, lying on the pressed bit of carpet where the sofa bed used to be. I didn't dream of anything. Not animals or dust or sunsets.

"Excuse me," said a voice. I opened my eyes. It was Yuri, the Armenian building manager, standing at the door with his arms crossed over his belly and his earphones half attached to his ears, as always. It was funny that he always stood as far away from other people as he could. It meant I had a very clear sense of his shape – the too-short T-shirt over his belly, his out-turned legs and slumped shoulders. I rubbed my eyes and sat up, still lying where the sofa ought to have been.

"What happened?" I said groggily.

"What, um, do you mean?"

"Where is he?" I clarified, as I stumbled to my feet in front of Yuri. Perhaps I looked a little feral, because Yuri frowned and took a step back as I took a step forwards. He looked like one of the scared younger boys who used to watch us play football at the Swiss Cottage football pitch, too nervous to join in.

"Where did he go?" I asked.

"I think," Yuri said, "he moved out."

"Clearly," I said, frowning. "When did he go? Where?"

Yuri shrugged, helplessly. "I don't know," he said. "He didn't give forwarding address. I don't know."

"He can't have just... gone," I said. "When?"

"Three days," said Yuri.

"Three days," I repeated. Something awful must have happened. If he'd known I was in hospital, however angry he was, he wouldn't have left. I know that. My voice remained steady, but Yuri looked like he was watching a necklace break at his feet, bits falling everywhere. Yuri was looking directly at his trainers, not at me.

"He left your clothes, though," Yuri said, pointing to a couple of supermarket bags in the corner. I hate it when the voice inside your head is different from the image you're presenting. I believed myself to be standing in the empty flat looking a little impish, a little crumpled as I noticed David's shopping bag of clothes. I believed myself to look righteous and perhaps just adequately pitiful, but in fact I probably looked more like one of those alley cats that skulk around dustbins at night with their fur fraying. My skin and hair were dull, my body was anxiously thin, my lips chapped, and I was holding onto the wall as if I was about to collapse at the knees and cease to exist.

I almost laughed at myself as I stared at the neatly folded clothes in the bags at the corner of the room, but the fizz of false amusement got stuck in my throat and turned into a shiver as I glanced at the clothes he'd bought for me at the outlet mall. I walked over to the corner and bent down. There was my pink toothbrush, some lipstick, some "volumizing shampoo", my hairbrush, my little pearl earrings. Lily's white dress with the black buttons, Lily's jeans and T-shirts and scuffed grey ballet pumps. My baseball cap. My Adidas jumper. Lily's teardrop earrings and lipstick and sunglasses. From one of the bags I unearthed a bunch of photographs that I'd never seen before – the ones he'd mentioned that he was going to develop when we were walking up to the Observatory. Some of the pictures were of me in my red baseball cap and sports clothes from that first day when I arrived in Los Angeles, and some from when

David took playful photographs of me laughing that day when he'd persuaded me to take off my clothes in the living room.

"Fuck," I said, and felt a little dizzy. My eyes stung as if tears were brimming there. "Fuck, fuck, fuck, fuck."

"Are you all right?" Yuri asked.

"Fuck," I said, and Yuri quietly left the room.

I flicked through the photographs. There were dozens of them, at least thirty. Most of them are like the rest of the photos around David's flat: weird, anonymous, disembodied. One was of the skin on my hand clutching a cigarette, and an ugly hangnail; another was the shadow of my baseball cap obliterating my eyes, my back to the camera. In the third photograph I was asleep on the bench with my hat slightly askew and my cheek pressed onto Lily's Play-Doh-red suitcase. It was before I woke up that first morning after the wake, ten weeks ago, when I was dreaming about drowning. One of my tracksuit legs was rolled up, and you could see the scabs on my pale knees. Then there was a close-up of my face, which looked like a baby's face. It's funny to imagine how tough I thought I was, because in the photo I looked exhausted and innocent.

The next three photographs were from only a week or so ago, of me in various stages of undress. They made me cringe. There was a photo of just my belly button, a photo of my nipple, a photo of my smile. There was a photo of me with my back to the camera turning around to smile at David, but the one he meant me to look at – the one that changed everything – was a photograph of me wearing a white T-shirt over a bikini and laughing at the camera. After that laughing photograph, the next photograph in the pile was one of Lily. It was the photograph David stole from the Pink Hotel on the night of the wake. In the stolen photograph Lily had her legs crossed under a tree, wearing a white T-shirt over a bikini and laughing, her pale eyebrows crouched playfully over dark eyes. She was a bit older than me in the stolen photograph, with much longer and darker hair. She was sitting under a tree, and I was standing inside a shadowy apartment, but comparing the two photos Lily and I looked eerily similar. The colour and shape of our eyes were the same as we laughed, and our mouths were folded into the same shape. It was also something about the gesture, both our hands hovering up near our mouths slightly like we were embarrassed to be laughing so hard. I imagined David watching as the photo of me developed in the darkroom he used at work. I wondered how long it took for him to realize how much I resembled Lily. I felt sick again, and dropped the photographs onto the carpet.

37

Yuri let me sleep on the floor of the empty apartment until the afternoon, when the Armenian mothers came to hover around me in the empty flat. They brought a smell of chlorine and slow-roasted garlic with them into the sticky air. Dalita was in her faded tropical bikini with a T-shirt from some pizza restaurant, plastic bangles jumping on her brown wrists as she consoled me with a cup of home-made nettle tea. The first sip was bitter and boiling. It burnt my tongue, and the shock made me blink.

"You're too good for that son of a bitch," said Dalita, looking solemnly around while my tongue blistered.

"He was too old for you," said another, leaning her bony shoulders on the door frame and artfully flicking cigarette ash back onto the corridor floor.

"He was packed full of darkness," said another of the women, with her bottom perched on David's windowsill.

"In the name of Bartholomew I swear, that man, he wasn't any good at all," another chimed in. Nobody had anything constructive to add about David's disappearance, except for admitting that they'd been pleased with the domestic booty he quietly passed onto them.

"We thought it was you who told him to give us the stuff, though," said Dalita carefully, shrugging her freckled shoulders. "We thought you were getting married or something, yes, and moving some place nicer than here. We were expecting you to come and say goodbye."

Dalita apparently received a slightly dilapidated microwave, a wooden salad bowl with matching spoons, and even the IKEA sofa bed that I slept on for the first week in David's flat. Another mother got David's television, another his crockery and cups, but no one got an explanation about where he was going.

"Dalita didn't like the man a bit, of course," one of the Armenian housewives said, "but she'll take his sofa bed."

"It's IKEA!" said Dalita in protestation. "You can't leave psychic traces on IKEA furniture. Not possible."

"Is that a fact?" Dalita's friend giggled.

"He looked drunk, though," said another of the women to me knowingly. Then the woman glanced quickly away.

"Oh," I said, pained.

Even the voyeuristic contingent of teenagers on the wall outside the building didn't have anything much to add about David's abrupt disappearance.

"He scrammed on Monday, dawg, when you were at work. Just with a bag, though. Didn't think much of it. He came back, again, what, two days later?"

"He asked if we'd seen you. We said you must have run away or sommit, cause you hadn't been back."

"He came back for me?" My blood thinned and everything lifted. I noticed that one of the boys was wearing a shirt of David's, an orange one with a silky black collar. Another was wearing a pair of David's massive brightly coloured trainers.

"He came back for his stuff, dawg," said one of the boys. "Guess he thought you'd left him."

"Packed all his shit and handed it around the building," said another boy. "Loaded the rest of his stuff in his car. He gave us a whole bunch of his shirts. He had rad clothes, man, rad."

After that I called David's mobile from the strip-mall pay-phone. I called three times, but it was disconnected, just like Richard's phone. There was a dial tone, like the phone was off or out of range. I put it down and dialled Sam's number instead.

"Where the fuck are you?" Sam snapped. "I just went to the hospital. They said you checked yourself out."

"I don't like hospitals."

"Nobody likes hospitals."

"The woman in the bed next to me was crazy."

"*You're* crazy."

"I'm fine," I said. "I feel better. Thank you."

We paused.

"I managed to smuggle you under the company emergency insurance," he said. "Lucky girl."

"I can pay you back," I said.

"It's covered now, don't worry," he said. "No harm done."

"Do you know where David is?" I said. "He's not at home."

"I couldn't get hold of him," said Sam. "His phone's off."

"Did you call?" I said.

"Course," he said.

"The first night?" I said.

"I didn't think of it the first night, to be honest," Sam said. "It was hectic."

"When did you?" I asked.

"The third night, but his phone was off," Sam said quietly. I was silent on my end of the phone and could hear my heart beat. Sam started to talk quite fast: "I felt bad about not calling earlier, so went around to his place and stuff, but he wasn't there. I even called his work a couple of times. They haven't heard from him either. I thought it would be fine. I looked after you, right?"

"You called his work?" I said.

"I tried to find him," he said. "I really tried hard."

My hands shook as I lit a cigarette.

"We had an argument the night before," I said to Sam. "I told you he was angry with me. Why didn't you call the first night?"

"I'm sorry," Sam said.

"He wouldn't have left if he'd known I was ill," I said.

"I know," said Sam.

I put the phone receiver away from my mouth for a moment. It smelt sort of like oily fish, or maybe that was a smell from one of the take-out restaurants around me.

"Let me come see you," he said. "Where are you?"

"I can't, Sam, I don't want to."

"Please," he said.

I was too tired to argue about it, so ten minutes later Sam met me at the Starbucks on the corner of North Vermont and Franklin, but I didn't get in the car with him. He parked and looked up at me from the driver's seat.

"Let's go get something to eat," Sam said.

"Thanks for looking after me, but I just want to be on my own right now," I said without getting in the car. "I'm sorry, I'm a mess. I need to think."

"Get in the car and talk to me," said Sam, but when I didn't move he climbed out of the driver's seat into the sunshine. He leant his elbows on the top of the car and didn't come any closer. "We'll think together."

"I can't, Sam, I have to go now. I don't want to get in the car with you."

"David didn't even look for you," Sam said. "Have you thought of that? If you didn't come home to me one night, I would have looked for you."

"He was angry with me that first night," I said. "He found something out about me. He must have thought I'd left him."

"What did he find out?"

"It doesn't matter, Sam. I'm sorry to have caused you so much trouble."

I didn't walk away, because I knew Sam would just follow me. I didn't want to give him an excuse to make a scene or to touch me. My skin felt raw, and the sun wasn't helping. I shouldn't have arranged to meet Sam at all, but everything just felt strange. I didn't have the energy to fight or even be angry, although if he crossed over to my side of the car I thought I might actually just run. Instead I stood there in the heat for a while and felt drained. Neither of us moved.

"Go away, Sam. Please, I just want to be on my own," I'd say every so often in variation.

"Please get in the car," he'd say.

I promised to call Sam the next day, and he eventually conceded to drive away. As he rounded the corner, a bus pulled up to the stop just outside Starbucks. I ran to follow two schoolgirls through the sliding doors and climbed on after them.

38

Pregnancy was an alien idea, like some tribal fable about how tortoise shells came to be cracked or a creation myth about primordial soup and golden eggs. There was no possible way I could have made a creature inside my stomach. On the bus I got a window seat and tried to remember creation myths I'd learnt about at school. The concrete LA streets slid by under the window, and I dredged up memories from a school project about weird "beings" that created themselves out of nothing. They were sleeping entities, nothings, who broke out of their own subconscious to roam the desert as kangaroos or emus or lizards or whatever it was they imagined themselves to be. These dream beings were not only shape-shifters of the mind, but sculptors who set about cutting man and woman from rock that they imagined into existence. The imagination creatures slithered and sliced and licked humanity into existence.

The other story I remembered was about an Aztec goddess who was impregnated by a knife and gave birth to a daughter who became the sun and a litter of boys who became the stars. The sun and the stars all walked with their mother on earth until the mother goddess found a ball of hummingbird feathers that took her fancy. They were so pretty that she put them against her breast, and suddenly found herself pregnant again. Presumably the sun and the stars thought that she was pregnant by the actual hummingbird, because the kids weren't best pleased about the idea of their new bestial and birdish stepbrother. My school-project memory is that Mother Nature gave birth to the God of War, which doesn't quite make sense. A hummingbird fathered the God of War, while a knife fathered the universe? Anyhow, the God of War set the sun and the stars ablaze before banishing them to the other side of the universe, where they burn today. I know that she got pregnant with a knife at some point, because I remember getting in trouble for illustrating that particular moment of the story rather than, say, the hummingbird feathers or the night sky.

At the front of the LA public bus was a pregnant middle-aged woman with rugged cheeks wearing a shiny top with a sequin-coloured halter neck, the kind of thing a teenager might think she looked precocious in. She was all dressed up. The fashion for leggings instead of tights left a swollen flash of pink skin between her lower calf and the straps of her heeled sandals. She wore glittery lipstick, and must have been in her early forties. I had a vivid, vile split-second visual image of her lying open wide on a mattress, in a tastelessly furnished suburban apartment, being impregnated by the long vibrating beak of a monstrous mythological hummingbird. I blinked the image away.

I hadn't been to the Serena for over two weeks. It smelt of mouldy laundry and ham sandwiches as I stepped up into the lobby. There was a girl with blond cornrows drinking a can of beer at the top of the steps, and a skinny man with a Jesus beard playing solitaire on the coffee table in the communal TV area. Vanessa and Tony were both behind the desk, and they looked up at me sharply as I came in. Vanessa was wearing her trademark black dress and had backwards halos of sweat under her arms. Her hair was up in a shiny ponytail that didn't do her any favours and looked almost like a helmet sitting on top of her head. Tony meanwhile was wearing a tight T-shirt, flashing the tattoos on his massive arms. He'd grown a little goatee since the last time I saw him.

"Where've you been?" Vanessa said to me.

"I've been ill," I said.

"She looks like shit," Tony said to Vanessa.

"Are you all right?" said Vanessa, cocking her head to the side. "What's wrong with you?"

"Food poisoning," I said.

"Bad luck," said Vanessa, then there was an awkward pause, broken only by a bunch of European travellers watching American football in the lounge. I got the sense that something was wrong, just from the hesitancy of Vanessa's smile.

"Someone already settled up for you," said Vanessa, grimacing a little and cocking her head to the side in an expression of apology. "Did you know that?"

I didn't reply. I thought about the chalky letters and all the photographs, the unreasonably heeled shoes and the dresses that smelt of flowers.

"He came for the suitcase again?" I said.

"It was Miranda on shift, not us," said Tony in response to my blank expression.

"It wasn't the same guy as last time, though," said Vanessa. "Miranda said this was a nice guy. *Charming*, is what she said. He was picking up the suitcase cos you didn't drive or something?"

"What about the locker key?" I said. "He didn't have that."

"He told Miranda you were going to drop it around when you came to say goodbye to us. Obviously, when you didn't come…" Vanessa trailed off, and frowned. "I guess Miranda fucked up."

"I wouldn't have sent someone to get the suitcase without me," I said. "Not after all that shit a month ago."

"Miranda's not the sharpest knife in the drawer," said Tony.

"When did the guy come for it?" I asked. David must have come to the hostel to check if I'd been lying to him about keeping the suitcase, and of course discovered that I was. I wondered if this was before or after he'd got the photos of me developed and recognized the similarities between Lily and me.

"Ten days ago," said Vanessa.

"Are you sure?" I said, and Vanessa nodded.

Ten days ago I was walking up to Griffith Park Observatory with him. He hadn't got the photos developed yet, and he hadn't seemed angry with me. But perhaps even then he knew I was lying about the suitcase, he just didn't know why.

"What did the guy look like?" I asked.

"She just said he was charming," Vanessa shrugged.

"Charming," I repeated.

"That's all she said," Vanessa shrugged. "I'm sorry."

That night, back in Little Armenia, I dreamt about the desert. Dalita had put the sofa bed back in David's flat while I was out, along with other comforts like towels and sheets and toilet paper, so that I could sleep there and think for a little while. The manager pretended not to notice. Other than the bits from the Armenian ladies, there was nothing in the room except the plastic bags David had left for me. Of course, it took me for ever to sink under into sleep. I lay there on the lumpy IKEA sofa bed feeling absent. And when I did sink beyond the grey area of half-sleep, the sleep that came was in ragged fits and starts.

I kept waking up breathless. I tried to vomit in David's toilet once or twice, my fingers wrapped around the porcelain bowl. I banged my knees on the tiles and on the edges of the toilet. There was nothing much inside me except cigarette smoke and nettle tea anyway, so I couldn't throw up. The dream was about Laguna Highway. In my dream the sky was flashing by my face as if the air was solid like I was pushing through translucent layers of jelly and falling forwards into a landscape that could have been a tunnel, but really must have been a desert road. I couldn't stop falling, but I couldn't wake up either.

39

"I'm going to come home now," I said blankly to Dad over the phone the following afternoon.

"Great news," said Dad. There seemed to be music on in the background of our flat. Every so often something crashed in the kitchen, and there was laughter coming from the living room. "Someone keeps calling for you," he said.

"Can you just tell him you haven't got a clue where I am?" I said. "None of it matters any more."

"It's not that Richard guy calling. He only called once. This other guy keeps calling. Aaron Sotto or Spoto or something. Wait a second, I have the number."

"I don't know who that is," I said. There was the sound of crashing and shuffling as Dad looked for where he might have written down the telephone number.

"I can't find it," he said.

"It doesn't matter," I said.

"Why don't you get the fuck home and you can talk to these people yourself. I'm not your fucking secretary," he said, and there was a loud crash in the background, then the sound of people laughing again nearby. "I don't know what I did with the number," he mumbled, and I didn't press him for it. I wondered if Aaron was the guy with the nose stud.

"What are you *doing*, Dad?" I said, because I could hardly hear him for the music and the noise.

"Making… fuck," something crashed in the kitchen again.

"Ouch. I'm making margaritas. Your stepmother went and invited people round, didn't she? But I'm the one who's slaving away with the fucking drinks."

"You're making *what*?"

"You know, those ice-cocktail things? I didn't know what they were either. It's ice and tequila and whatnot. Daphne dragged me to a dancing class a while back, believe it or not. Now she's bloody invited them over, so I have to work out how to make these damn drinks she wants."

"Huh," I said. He turned a blender on in the background and suddenly I couldn't hear what he was saying. I think he was grumbling about the people who were coming over, but I couldn't hear a word. That must have been a new appliance. It was hard enough finding a mug with a handle in our kitchen at home, let alone a blender. "And then Tom fell over his own shoelaces and landed in the famous punchbowl!" Dad said, finishing the story I hadn't heard.

"That's great, Dad," I said. "Cool."

"So we'll be seeing you soon. Your bedroom's a bit of a mess. Daphne's been spring-cleaning, organizing shit. Plus that old fridge from the shop, you know? It stopped working a while back, but we have to pay to get rid of those things, you know? Haven't got round to it."

"That thing's huge," I said.

"Yeah, yeah, you can sleep with a fucking fridge in your room for a week or two if we say so, amount of fucking trouble you've put us through."

"I don't have any money left, Dad."

"Oh?" he said, and sounded almost happy. "When you know what flight you want, then let me know and I'll book it for you, but you're going to pay me back every penny with interest, and then some. Got that?"

"Great," I said sarcastically, then stopped myself. "Thanks, Dad. I'll call you tomorrow," I said. I was wearing David's blue dress and kitten-heel shoes again. The little faux pearls in my ears were rubbing against the phone receiver and irritating me.

"See you soon," I said to him.

That night Julie gave me a pill of something – ecstasy, I guess – and I danced all night with this low thump in my abdomen and a peculiarly brittle sensation of happiness. It was wordless, like my panics, but it wasn't full of terror. The music fed through me, and I danced for hours wearing David's prim little navy dress and kitten heels. Perhaps I took more than one of Julie's pills. I certainly drank, too. I found my brain working in strange, pleasant, unintelligent ways. There was this one time when I ate hash brownies at a friend's house after school and noticed that my thoughts became very pictorial and literal. Someone was watching *Easy Rider*, and Peter Fonda wants to give some girls a ride on their bike. Dennis Hopper says, "We're not no travelling bureau," which made everyone laugh. I laughed too, but only because I imagined these two men dragging a mahogany bureau down the open roads, spilling knickers and bras in their wake. The commonest metaphors became a phantasmagoric horror movie – she caught his eye, he wore his heart on his sleeve, the earth stopped – everything had literal and unpleasantly physical dimensions. It made me wonder how different people formed their thoughts, whether they could feel themselves thinking, or whether thinking just occurred fluidly to most people. Did other people have uncontrollable actors in their conscious imagination, like peripheral shadows speaking unexpected and unscripted lines? Did other people have distinct architectural spaces in their brain? My sexual fantasies often occurred in a minimalist white house, built with as many windows as a conservatory might have. There's a kitchen made of black-marble counters with a matching black-marble table in the middle, and all the floors are made of pale, varnished wood. In reality, this house belonged to a wealthy school friend who I knew when I was eight. She lived in Primrose Hill, fairly near me, but much posher, and I used to sleep over there sometimes. In reality, my friend's mother would make bread on the marble counter in the middle of the kitchen, the white flour making patterns on the black marble. In unreality I have made love on this counter in many unreasonable, embarrassing and gymnastic positions. Behind the kitchen was a breakfast nook surrounded by windows looking out on a patchwork London garden of rosemary and lavender. I never enjoyed the reality of my body before David, but I did enjoy my imagined body. Sometimes my dreams bled out into this garden, into the herbs and the thorns and the mud, but mostly they revolved around the trendy, nearly empty living room where my school friend and I used to put on theatrical events based on *Alice in Wonderland* or Suzanne Vega songs. Who knows why this is the stage set of my mental gymnastics. Nothing sexual ever happened in that house. I don't remember the girl's father ever being around, nor do I remember any older brother. I remember that it was always too hot, because they had the heating on full pelt, and the mother made us drink tall glasses of cold milk so we'd grow tall.

The pills made me very aware of how my brain worked, especially as I found myself in a rooftop beer garden downtown, lying flat out on the grass with the same superb thump of emptiness in my stomach. There were other people around, people I'd met while dancing, and we were all drinking beer in a sort of circle. Around me were knobbly grey trees the same colour as the winking chrome-and-glass building behind. There was a small guy called Justin with a big nose and chipmunk cheeks. He looked mean and confused and very high. Another boy was tall and had this vast, bobbing Adam's apple. Everyone in the group was talking intently about "vanishing points", the space where perspective lines converge, and everyone was tracing the vanishing points around themselves – where paths disappeared beyond foliage, where walls ended and sky began. They were all student film-makers. I thought to myself: this is a vanishing point, this moment in time, but I didn't say anything. My mouth wouldn't have worked anyway. The boy with chipmunk cheeks asked me how I felt, and I had difficulty verbalizing the sensation of emptiness in my gut. More than that, it actually took me a moment to physically feel my body, at which point I worked down from my head to my toes without speaking. My jaw was uncomfortably tight, but the beer went down pleasantly, softening my tongue and the rigid muscles. My shoulders were solid and locked, my stomach was empty, my womb was empty, my legs ached. The boy with the chipmunk cheeks put his hand on mine and I took it away as if stung.

"Hey, hey, chill," he said.

"Sorry," I said, and the morning yawned forwards. Everyone around me seemed strangely elegant for this time in the morning and this state of ecstasy and alcohol. At least it seemed that way. People smiled slowly, discussing the nuances of the morning's light as it knotted against the reflective windows of the building opposite, or dissipated from a shiny metal Buddha in the corner of the garden. They must have all been camera guys, because all they talked about was different kinds of luminosity.

40

Later that day I took a Greyhound bus out to the desert, to near Laguna Highway. I wanted to see where Lily died. In the phosphorescent East Los Angeles terminal there were army boys with buzz cuts and high foreheads, an old man with a white beard and a sullen, tidy girl staring over from a computer game she was playing in the cafeteria. Behind me, an obese Japanese woman in a velour tracksuit was talking to an elderly Southern lady. The Japanese lady's name was Saigo, which she told her friend meant "end" in Japanese. She explained that she got her name because she was the last of twelve children, after which the woman's mother moved into the guest bedroom and refused to get undressed in front of her husband ever again.

"Now boarding for Indian Wells, Bermuda Dunes, Palm Desert, Rancho Mirage and Cathedral City and Indio," the automated voice said. I climbed on behind the group of army boys. They sat in front of me and played a card game called Go Fish while talking about their kids. They'd all been to Iraq, and just got back on leave. One of the youngest soldiers, with a high forehead and stocky shoulders, had a daughter living in Fresno. A boy with acne had a pregnant girlfriend living in Van Nuys, and another had a four-year-old son with a woman who was now married to another man. As we fled through the desert, I imagined that the bus was driving across David's sun-tanned skin. There was a broken pane of glass winking on the sand, smashed into twenty or so slices of reflected sunshine.

It reminded me of the scars on David's shoulder. I tried to remember the other scars, the one across his hand that he said was from a bar fight, the one on his lower back from falling off a wall. "Matrix," I thought, imagining the mass of fine-grained strings of skin that made up a scar. The word came from the Latin for "womb", which seemed fitting: an environment in which something develops, a mould in which something is cast or shaped, an organizational structure.

I touched my tummy and looked out of the window. Laguna Highway was near Palm Springs, a few hours out of Los Angeles. The Greyhound bus eventually stopped bang in the middle of nowhere, where khaki desert crevices met a single hot-tarmac road, and the driver told me that this was where I wanted to change buses. There was a forest of windmills against the craggy mountains. The bus stop was powdery pink concrete with a goods train passing behind it in a parade of graffiti-caked wrought-iron freights in faded red, blue and green. Someone had tagged the word "ECHO" onto several of the crates, and the repetition had a calming effect as every third or so façade "echoed" and kicked up dust with the methodical clack – clack – clack of metal on hot metal. A young man with dusty ankles and chapped lips was asleep in the shade of concrete, surrounded by a fortress he'd built from army-regulation camouflage bags. There was also a man riding a children's bicycle, his big body unstable as he stumbled into view over the horizon. Everything was a little wobbly. On the other side of the pink concrete structure appeared a uniformed man. He stubbed out a hand-rolled cigarette as he shielded his bloodshot eyes from the sun to glance up at me and grin broadly.

"Where you going to?" he said. I guess maybe he was stoned.

"Laguna Highway," I said.

"Don't know it," he replied, and turned abruptly away from me to pick up a sci-fi magazine.

"It's the road that runs through Laguna Town, north of here. Can I look at a bus schedule or something?" I asked. He stared at me as if I was insane. Behind me the man on the bicycle had stopped, and his face was exactly the same colour as the sand, like a beach sculpture. He was panting from the ride, and his breath smelt vaguely of salt, too, probably the remnants of a tequila shot or salt-rimmed margarita on the rocks. I thought about the smell of alcohol on David's skin the other day.

"When's the next bus east?" the sand man asked the uniformed man.

"Should be here in an hour," he said.

"Mother-fucker," said the sand man, and kicked the kerb with broken trainers.

I had to stay the night in Palm Springs, which is the nearest town to the little pink bus stop, and also the nearest town to the mysterious Laguna Highway. The town was full of elderly people with sun-scorched skin. I found an information booth with an elderly woman inside, wearing big sunglasses I could see my reflection in.

"What you looking for, love?" she said.

"I want a bus that goes down Laguna Highway?"

She ran through the schedule. There were funny little water-spritzer machines attached to the roofs of most buildings in Palm Springs, which sprinkled onto your skin and occasionally left little watermarks on people's sunglasses. The air smelt of fried meat from a burger restaurant nearby. The information lady eventually decided that there was a bus that went up and down Laguna Highway from a town called Burrow, not far from Palm Springs, towards a town called La Toro.

"Where you wanna get to, then?" the woman said.

"I don't really want to stop anywhere," I said, and the woman frowned, losing interest in me.

The La Toro bus didn't leave till 2 p.m. the next day, from a different stop than the pink one near the train tracks.

The inside of the bus smelt of burnt plastic, and there was no one on it except for a bedraggled woman wearing a headscarf, clutching bags of shopping and staring straight ahead of her. I'd bought a sunflower from a flower shop in Palm Springs, and it sat limply in my lap. After ten minutes, the bus turned from the small road out of Palm Springs straight onto a big highway marked with a sign saying "Five miles to Laguna", so I guessed this was Laguna Highway. I held my breath, expecting to feel something at the sight of the road Lily died on. It was just tarmac and sand, though, and it looked nothing like my nightmare or my imagination. There would be no way to know exactly where the accident happened, of course, so I'd just have to get off at some point. The road disappeared occasionally around craggy corners, jumping out of sight. There were squat little shrubs poking out of scorched and bearded rocks.

I wouldn't have known we were entering the town except for a lopsided sign that said "Welcome to Laguna Town", and a minute or so later we came to a huge plastic Mexican cowboy, taller than the bus, only the cowboy didn't have a head on his shoulders. He wore an off-white shirt with denim pockets and a denim collar, but his head lay in the muddy sand next to his boots and had flies buzzing around it. Then the bus trundled past a solitary grocery store offering 99-cent tacos: outside there was a crowd of men drinking coffee from blue plastic camping mugs. All of their heads turned to watch the bus pass the shop, and nobody smiled.

I looked straight ahead, and decided not to get out of the bus just yet. At worst I'd take the bus all the way to the end of the road and then come straight back. Each flattened shop or bungalow was miles from the last, and there was some sort of factory in the distance, kicking up curls of grey smoke into the perpetually corrugated white sky. Some of the buildings had little wire fences around them, and bony dogs yelped at the bus from their cages. We passed a burnt-out caravan on the right-hand side of the road, and I was so focused on this strange skeleton of black metal that I almost didn't see a dusty blue warehouse-type building with a sign saying "Eagle Motorcycles" lying on the floor in the sand. The windows of the building were boarded and bedraggled, but I immediately recognized the shop sign from the picture in Lily's suitcase, although in the picture the sign had been elevated above the door and the paint hadn't been peeling. I got up off my seat and took a step towards the front of the bus.

"Could you stop?" I said, and stumbled to the front of the bus, where the driver glanced at me in the wing mirror. His eyeballs were off-white, the colour of a fried egg. He looked around at me.

"Here?" he said, not stopping.

"Yeah, sorry, I want to go to that Eagle Motorcycle place we just passed," I mumbled, staring back at him in the grubby mirror. As the driver begrudgingly put his foot on the break and curled to the side of the road, I scanned the surrounding area for David's SUV. "Do you know if anyone lives there?" I said. The bus shuddered to a stop.

"Don't know. Think it's been closed for years. You getting out or not?" he replied gruffly, opening the folding bus door. For a town with such a pretty name the air there smelt like singed skin, sand and petrol.

"When do you come back?" I said to the driver.

"Not till this time tomorrow," he said. I hesitated on the steps of the bus, Lily's suede shoulder bag on my arm. We were two hundred metres away from the shop.

"Really? Someone said you came back this way today. At the information booth they said this was your route."

"The *information booth* was wrong," he said laconically. "I don't have all day," he said.

I glanced out into the desert and hesitated. Then I swallowed and figured – fuck it, there's not much to lose really – so I stepped off the bus, but I was scared as the doors closed behind me, and all I had was a suede shoulder bag and a sweating sunflower that had lost half its petals in the vicious desert heat. Almost before my shoes hit the tarmac the bus started up again in a beige bubble of sand.

There was nothing around for miles except smoke trawling up from cumbersome horizon-level buildings. I didn't feel sad or moved or curious or lonely. Nothing came into my mind, so I turned away from the road that she died on and walked the two hundred metres or so up to the closed doors of the Eagle Motorcycle building. I stood exactly where she'd stood in the photo. The sign was at my feet, while it had been over Lily's head, and there was empty space to my left where her motorcycle had been. The air was so hot it was difficult to swallow, even though day was turning into afternoon as I stood up on tiptoe to look through the windows of the building.

"Hello?" I said. There was something lodged on the inside of the front doors, a bit of metal that may have fallen down from the roof or wall and made it impossible to open.

"Hello?" I said, louder. "Is anyone there?"

It didn't look like there was anyone in there, and I felt nervous about how on earth I'd get back to Los Angeles. Perhaps I could walk to the 99-cent-taco place and call a cab. Eventually the door of the Eagle Motorcycle shop squeaked open a bit and I could slide through. Something clattered outside the mechanics shop, and I jumped. A ragged little kitten chased a Coca Cola can over the stubble. The kitten followed the can out of sight again, and I held my breath.

The front door had been held shut by a fallen bit of machinery – a ramp. There was half a motorcycle suspended from the ceiling, and another motorcycle was gutted in the corner. The bikes looked similar to the one in Lily's photograph, but both of these bikes were covered in dust and rust like they hadn't been touched in a long time. They were nothing like the muscular pieces of metal that I saw at the mechanics shops. These ones had smooth lines and simple shapes. The back wheels were smaller than the front wheels, so the bikes looked like yawning animals, both arching their backs. I thought of the coyote David and I watched outside his flat. "In order of preference, orgasm, ice cream or yawns? What do you think?" he'd asked me, and I never answered.

Around the bikes there was a mortuary of parts. There were thick black tyres, handlebars, sprockets, greasy chains and wing mirrors all glinting as the sun struggled through dusty windows.

The seats and mudguards looked like they were made of onyx. I jumped at the sight of an eagle on a bookshelf, but it was stuffed. It was a taxidermy eagle, like the taxidermy cat above the door of August's bar. The bird's spine was arched just like the bikes. His head was high, beak polished to a knife point. There were bottles with viscous and chemical-sounding names like Autoglym and Mamatec. I wondered who invented those names, some aspiring poet stuck in the branding of cleaning chemicals? Two massive industrial fans sat in two corners of the room. A pile of dust covered each blade. Across one cork-lined wall hung a few wrenches, pliers and screwdrivers. Along another wall were planks of wood, untidily littered with a few dusty books. They weren't all vertical like the little army of alphabetical books in David's flat, but spewed out in horizontal and diagonal piles, front covers akimbo, wrinkled pages folded out all over the place and interjected occasionally by the odd ornament – a metal lion head, a small wooden totem pole, a souvenir Venus de Milo. I noticed that some of the books had front covers like the Enkidu novel I'd taken from next to Lily's bed at the wake and lost when my bag was stolen. There was a whole bunch of these books, and I fingered their dry pages: one was called *Prometheus Bound*, with a drawing of a naked man in handcuffs; another was called *Leda*, with a picture of a half-man, half-swan creature. I flicked through books on astronomy and books on art history. Stuff had fallen off the shelves to the floor. There was a complimentary mug from a gas station broken on the floor, and a pink conch shell. I touched the smooth seat of one of the bikes. Maybe one of these bikes was the one she died on.

"Excuse me, is anyone there?" I said to the nothing, and wondered where and if I'd sleep that night. I would stay in the workshop I suppose, but I'd be cold. I looked around for blankets, and saw some plastic sheeting with frayed edges. I shivered and fondled a chunk of smooth, half-welded metal from one of the work desks. There were streaks of colour in it, and it was a perfect weight.

Apart from the two windows at the front of the workshop, there was one little window at the opposite end. Through it I was surprised to see a bungalow tucked right behind the work-shop, out of sight from the road. There was garden furniture outside it, including a rusty barbecue and some discarded barbecue utensils. Behind the barbecue there was something that looked like a dry pond, except it was made out of a plastic rowboat, sunken into the sand. Colour was just beginning to drain from the desert as midday turned to late afternoon. The massive expanse of sand around the building did look a bit like a lagoon, and the boat could have been a ship in low tide. There were no vehicles around, so I guessed it would be as empty as the workshop.

I walked up to a wire-mesh gate that framed a garden of cactus plants and shrubs around the bungalow, a bit like the garden in my gecko dream. Inside the wire mesh, the bungalow windows were dark, and I knocked hesitantly before trying the door handle. "Anomaly," I thought. "Mendicant, gran-diloquence," and raised myself onto tiptoe to stare through a broken window, which was open a crack. I couldn't see anything through the glass, because it was darker in there than it was outside, and the sunlight made rainbows on the surface. What is glass made of? Is it just sand? It was only a small window, about the size of an A3 piece of paper, reflecting light particles back into my face.

"Hello?" I said, mostly to myself. Then, as my eyes became accustomed to the darkness, I saw that there was the silhouetted outline of a man on the other side of the window, apparently staring straight back at me.

41

I thought for a second that the man in the window might be David, and I stepped backwards, nearly losing my footing on a rock behind me. Then, as my pupils dilated, I realized that it was the man with the schoolboy haircut who stole my bag. He smiled at me from behind the glass, and instead of running I glanced absently around at smoke rising from the chimneys of far-away bungalows.

"Hola," the man said through the glass. "How'd you get here?"

He disappeared from the window. I considered walking away, perhaps to the 99-cent-taco place, or another bungalow, but I stayed put.

"Guess who's at the door!" the thief shouted back into the darkened bungalow. There was a pause as doors opened and things shuffled inside, then the front door unbolted and opened a crack. I stood three metres from the door with my kitten heels embedded in sand. The person who opened the door had holes in his grey sports socks, and tattered linen trousers that dragged slightly in the dust. They were too big for him, and his white vest was yellow at the neckline. His gold chain was matted in his chest hair. A little smile appeared and then disappeared at the corner of his chapped lips, and he put small-framed sunglasses down over his green eyes. His red hair was longer than it had been at the wake, and he had a beard now. He took his time looking me up and down, with interest, and then he smiled at me.

"Well then, hi at last," he mumbled. I blinked. He stared at me through his sunglasses for another second, and then turned abruptly inside the bungalow and left the door open for me to follow him. "You better come in then, it's a million degrees out there," he said in his nasal New York accent while he walked away across the room, sticking his chest out and clenching his fist like he'd done at the wake.

I wavered on the doorstep for a moment, but saw through the door that Lily's red suitcase was lying open in the middle of the living-room floor. The "charming" man must have been Richard after all, not David. Lily's dresses, boots, Christmas cards, letters and all the rest were lying there on a dirty white shag carpet in front of a fireplace. From the doorway the bungalow smelt slightly of paint, a bit like how Laurence's fingers used to smell after he'd been out tagging London with spray paint. The front door led into a tiny kitchenette, but you could see over the counter into a messy living room. There was a taxidermy crow on the mantelpiece, and a taxidermy eagle on the coffee table. The crow's beak was tilted upwards in a haughty smile, and a string of rosary or carnival beads glinted around its neck. There were beer bottles, some with candles shoved down their necks, some broken and used as ashtrays. A huge road map hung on one wall, just like the various doodled-on road maps in Lily's suitcase of memories.

It was the road map rather than the suitcase that made me follow Richard into the bungalow in the end. The map on the bungalow wall was of California, and as I got closer to it I saw that the coastline formed the basis of a naked woman's spine, and her knees were crouched up near the border to Nevada, at Death Valley National Park. One of her nipples seemed to be made out of Lake Tahoe. The woman's head was drawn up near Oregon at a place called Eureka, which was sort of funny. Jazz played quietly from some old speakers in the corner of the room, and the man with the pierced nose seemed to have disappeared into one of the doors off the living room. Along with the bits and pieces I recognized from the suitcase, there were other girlish things around the bungalow that suggested a woman's presence, or the remnants of a woman's presence – a bracelet on the counter, some moisturizer cream and a lipstick on the floor next to the sofa. On the coffee table, amongst Lily's photos, was the one of Lily standing with her bike under the sign saying Eagle Motorcycles. You couldn't see much except for powder-blue walls, a door and the dusty-looking sign, but of course I now realized that she was standing against a backdrop of desert. Her face looked sultry, but sort of eager, like she was impatient to go for a ride. Also open on the coffee table were the bunch of maps with their labyrinthine erotic doodles, the Christmas cards from Teddy, the legal documents and the love letters.

All of the lights were off inside the bungalow, but one of the walls had a sliding door, which was open and led onto a patio made of packed sand and half-moon car tyres. There were two metal chairs on either side of a table made out of a worm-scarred wooden door, which was covered in engine parts like springs and cogs and different-sized screws. A big metal awning threw shade over the patio. Richard was already sitting in one of the chairs, and he didn't turn around or tell me to have a seat.

"I'm not going to hurt you," Richard said, not looking at me. "Nor is Jorge. I wanted Lily's stuff back, that's all. It's not so unreasonable," he said.

"You got your friend to *mug* me," I pointed out.

"Don't be so melodramatic," said Richard. "I would never have anyone hurt Lily's daughter," he said. "He just went to retrieve my property."

"Why did you wait so long before you tried again, once you knew where the suitcase was?"

"Jorge clearly wasn't very efficient. I had some shit to sort out, but when I went to the hostel all I had to do was ask and the nice lady gave the suitcase over. Easy."

"I tried to give the suitcase back, you know," I said lamely, staring at the back of his head and then around the dusty landscape.

"You didn't try hard enough," he said.

Richard rolled a little metal screw around between his thumb and forefinger, then picked up a tiny nail file. He held the nail file to the end of the screw and stared at it as if about to start filing it down, but didn't do anything. In profile he looked both rough and effeminate, like some sort of violent and graceful desert creature. At the wake he'd reminded me of a snake, but his face looked less vicious and startling now. In front of the bungalow were miles of desert and the occasional burnt-out or abandoned building, their scorched wooden beams raised in surrender. One was a house with a sloping roof and a rusted RV outside it, another was just a skeleton of a building rotting in the sunlight.

"Were you reading Lily's Enkidu book?" Richard said.

"I didn't get to finish it," I said.

"Nor did she," he said. "Why are you here? I didn't think I was actually going to get the pleasure of meeting you."

"I came to see where she died," I said. Richard unclenched his freckled hands and moved his body around slightly to face me.

"My name's Richard Harris," he said, but I didn't take his freckled hand, or sit down in the chair next to his. However well spoken and "charming" he seemed now, when I looked at him I couldn't shake the image of him lying unconscious on Lily's unmade bed with cocaine in his nostril hairs and drool around his mouth.

"Is there some way to get away from here apart from the bus?" I asked Richard.

"You won't shake my hand?" he said.

I didn't move or touch him. Touching Richard, even his hand, seemed repulsive. I missed David.

"Will a cab come out here?" I asked.

"Doubt it. Jorge can give you a lift somewhere, though. He lives near here and has a car."

"A green Volvo," I said. "I know."

"Dirty thing," said Richard. I didn't say anything.

"Jorge is a great friend," Richard continued. "He's a good guy. He makes the taxidermy birds." I lit a cigarette. "He wasn't going to hurt you. He just wanted to find out where the suitcase was and bring it back to me."

"Did you know she had a kid?" I said.

"Yeah," he said.

"She talked about me?"

"She asked your dad if she could have you come to LA once, you know," said Richard. "She wanted to take you to Universal Studios or something ridiculous. I listened to the conversation they had. Your Dad said that if Lily came to London she was welcome to take you to the cinema and pick you up from school and see how it went, but there was no way he'd let Lily hurt you again. So it was a no for Universal Studios."

"Fair enough," I said.

"Indeed. I agreed, to be honest. He told Lily he felt sorry for her cos she was missing you growing up, and one week in Los Angeles wouldn't solve that."

"Sounds like Dad," I frowned, and Richard looked at me. I remembered how August had glanced furtively at me in his flat that first night, like he couldn't place me and didn't know whether to be familiar or distant with me. Richard was doing the same thing, stealing sideways looks and pretending not to.

"Is that the only time she tried to contact me?" I asked.

"She wouldn't have been a good mother," he said.

"She wasn't a good mother," I said.

We sat in silence for a couple of minutes. I put down the sunflower I'd bought to put on the road. It had lost a lot of petals, and the ones that were left seemed to be turning brown at the edges already.

"Is that for her?" he said.

I nodded, but my nod turned into a shrug. I thought about poor Dad, not knowing what to do with me all those years, and I looked around at the landscape of sandy hills and burnt buildings beyond Richard's little bungalow.

"What is this place?" I said.

"A little business venture that fell through a few years back," he said with a shrug, letting his eyes meet mine and stay there for a beat. "We were meant to sell it, but for one reason or another it became our secret little holiday home."

"Someone told me the two of you divorced?" I said.

"Did Julie tell you that? You've certainly done the rounds, haven't you? Yes, Lily and I were divorced when she died. In fact, that's one of the reasons we were out here the weekend she died," he said. "Sorting our shit out."

"Did you have an argument that night?" I said carefully. "I mean, why was she driving so fast, late at night?"

"Oh, she always drove fast," he said. "She went out to clear her head." He paused, thinking about it. "Can I give you some advice?"

"I guess."

"It's a bit sentimental, this advice. I've been getting quite sentimental in my old age, or since she died. Since she died I feel like I've aged."

"OK." I shrugged.

"There are a finite number of people who will ever *see* you," he said carefully. "Really *see* you. Lot of people loved your mother over the years, which you've probably worked out from your little paper-trail treasure hunt. But I *saw* her. We had a lot of the same flaws, which made it hard sometimes. Eventually we were making each other insane, but I'll always love her." He paused, like he was a little embarrassed by his lyricism. I couldn't decide if it sounded phoney.

"Stay for a drink?" Richard said after a while. "I only have whiskey."

"Whiskey then, OK," I said. "Thanks."

He slid back through the doors into the bungalow. I turned my chair around to face inside the bungalow and watched him make the drinks. There was a photograph on the kitchen wall that I hadn't noticed before, of a miraculous red sunset that looked like grenadine spreading through a glass of lemonade. Richard broke ice out of ice trays from the freezer, smashing solid water on the granite countertop. One of the ice cubes spun onto the floor and almost immediately began to melt there. I remembered the anonymous letter writer's typed words. "I feel sometimes as if I'm fictionalizing you, as if you're a figment of my imagination," he'd written to Lily.

"Did you write those love letters about red sunsets and umbrellas?" I said as Richard walked back to the patio with two glasses of whiskey on ice.

"Sure," he said. "I didn't know she'd kept them. They're quite embarrassing," he said.

"I liked them," I said. The whiskey tasted strong and cold on my tongue, so I took two gulps in a row, trying not to wince as it burnt my throat. The coldness contrasted the desert heat and made my teeth ache slightly. I thought to myself: "Carmine is a particularly deep red colour, different from magenta, produced by boiling dried insects in water. The colour red is made from dead insects and sunlight." I lit another cigarette, and the whiskey calmed me down a bit. I thought of the word "entanglement" and how the letters described that Lily liked words. Richard had tangled lines on his face, around his eyes and downward-sloping mouth. His irises looked heavy like nuggets of metal. I wondered whether he was planning on going back to the hotel after he'd sorted his life out, and whether he regretted being the one who truly "saw" my mother.

"I like your maps, too," I said to Richard.

"Thanks," he said. "They were Lily's idea. We used to take road trips occasionally, on the bikes – we'd decide where the elbow of California was, for example, and go there. Or the eyebrows of Nevada. We wanted to have a picnic on the nose of every big city in the world." He smiled.

"What body part is this bungalow?" I said, looking over through the sliding doors to the map on his wall.

"Dunno," he said. "The toes?"

"What about the Pink Hotel?"

"Los Angeles is sort of the belly button of California, don't you think?"

"Guess so." I smiled slightly.

We paused, and he looked solidly at me for a moment.

"It was days before I remembered someone had walked off with Lily's suitcase," Richard said. "I was looking for all this missing paperwork and suddenly – bang – I remembered some ghostly kid in our bedroom with a suitcase in her hand. The deeds to the Pink Hotel were in the suitcase, you know? It made my life a nightmare. It took me a month to come get the suitcase myself, because I declared bankruptcy and everything was a bit fraught. Turns out I owed too many people money, so even if I had inherited the hotel I would have had to sell it."

"You didn't inherit it?" I queried.

"You didn't look at the deeds?" he said.

"I saw some legal stuff, but I didn't understand it."

"Lily inherited the hotel from a guy she nursed, called Teddy Fink. Did you get that far?"

"No. I didn't read them. I read the Christmas cards and saw the photo of Teddy Fink, and I know he died, but I didn't know he left her anything when he died."

"It was always in her name. And because we were divorced when she died, the hotel doesn't come to me. It comes to her next of kin. So that's you."

He raised his eyebrows at my completely blank expression. The words hung around in the air for a while, and I fumbled to open a new cigarette packet from out of Lily's suede bag. I put one in my mouth.

"I thought you knew," he said.

"Wouldn't someone have tried to contact me?" I said.

"I think the lawyer left messages with your father," Richard replied. "But as I discovered, you're not an easy person to track down."

"Aaron Soto?" I said.

"That's it," said Richard.

"Are you angry?" I said to Richard as this information slowly sunk in.

"There's nothing I can do, I would have contested it maybe, if I'd had the fucking deeds when I needed them," he shrugged. "But then it was too late, I had to declare bankruptcy, and after that it didn't really matter. I only went back to get the suitcase for sentimental reasons. Anyway, I've started from scratch before. It's probably better this way." He paused, and turned to face me in a way that made his eyes look almost kind. "In the end I came for the suitcase because I wanted my memories back," he said.

I remembered Julie saying that Richard used to sell old cars, and it struck me that he seemed exactly like a used-car salesman. He was charming, like Miranda said, but furtive. He didn't seem as scary as people kept saying he was, but I could see how he might turn. I wished David were there: he'd know exactly what to say. A gecko crawled near my feet, its skin glinting. It was so very gecko-like and so perfect. It made me think of one of my favourite words, from when Grandpa was still alive. Grandpa taught me the word "quiddity", which is like "essence", only better. It's a word that describes exactly what is so compelling about good words. A good word captures the quiddity of its meaning, the drippiness of dripping and the phosphorescence of a phosphorescent light. The geckoness of being a gecko. The trouble is, in the day-to-day reality of life, things are so much more complex. It's hard to pinpoint the quiddity of people or relationships or conversations, because as soon as you do, it will shift slightly, and the quiddity will be different.

"She wasn't happy the night she died. We were sorting out our things, separating, not really talking much. Maybe it would have been better if we'd argued. She could have let out steam," he shrugged.

"What happened, exactly?" I said.

"She drove off too fast, turned a corner and knocked into some drunk in a big car who happened to be out there that night. And that was that. It's usually so empty around here. It wasn't directly my fault, but maybe I should have known she'd drive recklessly if I let her go out. Maybe I did know she would." He lit a cigarette. "The drunk phoned an ambulance for her, then drove off. They couldn't trace the number. Big old American car drove right past the bungalow even, not that I knew what had happened until the ambulance turned up."

"What make of car?"

"Buick, I think," he said. "A big gold Buick."

I stopped smoking my cigarette and then forced myself to breathe quietly. It was really quite dark now out on Richard's patio, and the embers lit up our faces. You couldn't see into the distance any more. There were stars, but I've never had any interest in stars: I don't care that they're pieces of the future or the past or whatever, I don't care that they're dying. They're just pinpricks that make patterns if you stare for long enough. "They remind me of school outings to the observatory," I'd said

269

to David once when he tried to mumble something romantic about the sky, and he'd fallen about laughing on the floor. "City slicker," he'd laughed at me.

Richard and I sat up nearly all night in the end, chain-smoking awkwardly and drinking his whiskey. I looked through Lily's suitcase, but it didn't seem magic any more. I thumbed the comforting silk of the fuchsia dress, but it didn't feel as addictive as it had done on Venice Beach after the wake. Instead it felt sort of thin and dry, like my skin used to feel if David kept the air-conditioning whirring all night. I missed him. Nothing smelt of Lily any more. Her perfume, whatever it was, had worn off the clothes. I looked at the greeting cards signed "Teddy" and the photograph of Lily wearing pink scrubs standing next to the debonair old man. I looked at the legal documents, too, and Richard explained what they meant, but I had no way of knowing that Lily's name on the deeds meant I would inherit the hotel. Jorge came out and sat with us for a bit, but he went to bed early. He said his car was parked a while up the road, and he'd drive me home the next morning if I wanted, but I glared at him and said I'd get the bus.

There were half-eaten sandwiches on the coffee table, burnt saucepans in the sink, beer bottles full of stale dregs and floating cigarette butts all over the tables. Richard and I sat on opposite ends of the living room and made awkward conversation about Lily. We both drank too much.

"Is that the typewriter you wrote the letters on?" I said, pointing to an ancient machine in the corner.

"Sure," he said.

I have no idea if somewhere in the baffled heat of my belea-guered brain that night I was thinking about David's big gold car from the photographs in his underwear drawer. Certainly it turns out that memories aren't racked up like souvenirs on a mantelpiece or words on a page. I know that I did a handstand for David the first night we made love, and I felt utterly happy. Yet it's hard to remember how we argued in the rain and kissed to make up when I got out of the bath, bubbles on my nose, or how I felt when we saw a coyote yawning under a street lamp. Those memories were corrupted by the details of Lily's crash. You'd think the past would be stable, even if the future and the present were unpredictable. You'd think there would always be that wonderful hour when we ate Oreos in his car. But there are so many factors: the smell of new leather, the scars on his body.

That night, drinking whiskey after whiskey with Richard long after the ice ran out and the liquid was warm on my tongue, nothing was clear. Thoughts were trying to work their way up into my consciousness, and I didn't want them there. I sunk them in alcohol, and by the time I fell asleep on Richard's manky sofa I was too drunk to dream.

Many things scare me: sirens, silence, insomnia, sleep. Memory never scared me until the next morning, when Richard gave me the number for Aaron Soto, Lily's lawyer who'd been calling Dad, and we called from the bungalow telephone. It was a very bright morning, and my head throbbed from the night before. Jorge was frying bacon in the dirty kitchen, where the tap was dripping onto a pile of greasy plates. The light from the windows was hurting my eyes, and I was biting one of my ragged fingernails as I dialled the lawyer's number. I tore a hangnail off and couldn't breathe for a second when he said the drink-driver had handed himself into the police a few days previously, and that his name was David Reed.

42

I peeked through into a crazy-paving courtyard full of palm trees and children's toys. It was a concrete-coloured condominium on Long Beach, ten minutes from Long Beach Airport and an hour or so out of Los Angeles. Every few minutes the clear sky hummed with aeroplanes taking off or landing, and I swear the air smelt a bit like diesel. It was a wide suburban street like you see in American movies, but the fences were made of chrome rather than painted wood, and all the gardens were dead from that summer's heatwave. There was a lot of background noise – cars and aeroplanes and children – but it all seemed a million miles away as I sat on the corner of the wide road with Lily's Enkidu book in my lap, leant to me by Richard so at least I could finish it, and my eyes flicking from the page to the condominium gate every two seconds. People came out. There was a mother wearing fluffy slippers and pushing a pram, then a construction worker carrying a thermos in his hard hat. I read the same sentence from Lily's novel a hundred times, something about Gilgamesh building a wall to protect his people, but couldn't concentrate on the words.

"Get bananas too, for Lucy's tea, all right?" someone shouted from a balcony window inside the gates, and I looked up to see David stepping out of the gates wearing grey tracksuit bottoms and a creased green T-shirt. He was two hundred metres away and blended into the variations of grey and green lining the street, but even from far away I could see that his socks didn't match. There was a flash of purple under the elastic of one of his trouser legs, and a flash of white under the other. It was amazing how his clothes never fitted him. Perhaps it was because his proportions were so vast, but he was always a little bit more than averagely crumpled. He glanced up to the balcony.

"Sure," David said back to the woman. His voice sounded hoarse and distracted. "You want me to get you some cigarettes?"

"Got a pack this morning," said the woman's voice. "No worries."

I followed David at a distance as the wide suburban road turned into a busier street, flanked with shops and palm trees. David limped in his big scuffed trainers, his head down. The police had given me the address of David's cousin in Long Beach, and told me he was on bail. It was only ten days since I'd seen him, but it seemed longer. Jorge gave me a lift back from Laguna Town to Los Angeles a few days before, and since then I'd felt angry with David in a way I've never been with anyone before or since. It was partly sadness, but the feeling made my stomach ache and my skin sting.

From the way David was walking I wondered if he was drunk, but even when sober David walked with that lazy gangster lollop. I wondered if the limp was from the crash. He limped his way past a schoolboy holding a rat-terrier dog, and a bag lady pushing a shopping trolley full of her possessions. There were DIY shops, coffee franchises and crappy-looking teeny-bopper clothes stores on either side of this main road, none of which David looked up at. Without glancing from the pavement, he eventually turned into a convenience store on the next corner.

It was one of those flat-roofed buildings with stretched-out windows and big doors like yawning plastic mouths.

I peeked through the window and saw David holding a list in one hand and a shopping basket clumsily in the other. The phosphorescent lighting accentuated the tiredness of his eyes. He was picking up things like canned soup and dried pasta from the shelves, putting them hesitantly in his basket. I'd never seen David buy anything that needed cooking. He ate Oreos and buttered ham sandwiches with the crusts cut off, or Thai takeaway, so he must have been doing the shopping for his cousin. I watched him take a while choosing from different sorts of pasta sauce, then moving onto mincemeat and eggs, but he forgot the bananas.

When he came out of the store I was standing by the window to the right of the door, ready for him to see me immediately as he stepped out. I couldn't help it. I wasn't sure what I was going to say to him, or how I felt, but my skin tingled with wanting him to look at me. But instead of seeing me outside the convenience store, David turned in the opposite direction from where he'd just come and walked with his head down into a public garden a few yards down.

The sign outside said it was a garden, but really it looked more like a square of dried grass between two buildings. There was a bench and a broken swing set covered in seagull or pigeon droppings. Graffiti plastered the crumbling brick walls, and rubbish was heaped in the corners like maybe it was used for teenagers to hang out in at night rather than for children to play in.

David put the shopping bags down in the shade under a tree and sat on the bench for a moment, leaning his elbows on his knees and his head in his big hands. I just stood there at the mouth of the garden, watching him. People walked past the gates, but nobody walked inside. I had my school rucksack over my shoulder and was wearing the jeans David bought me, with a black T-shirt and the little pearls with glue visible in the fitting. He only looked up from his stupor when the sound of an aeroplane throbbed in the air. He glanced absently into the sky, frowning, then noticed a shadow standing at the garden gate and turned to me.

My heart pounded when he looked at me. Perhaps love is stupid, more than it is blind. The feeling certainly remained vivid despite everything that had happened. I waved hesitantly from the gateway, and he didn't move, just stared at me.

"You forgot the bananas," I said after a long silence. It wasn't what I meant, obviously, but it would do. He smiled very slightly at me, and didn't say anything for a long moment.

"Shit, yeah," he mumbled eventually. "Guess I did."

I took a step forwards, into the little garden.

"That your cousin?" I said. "At the balcony."

"Yeah," he said. "She's OK."

"Are you OK?" I said.

"Yeah. You?"

"OK," I said. Another plane flew over our heads and made a throbbing sound. The noise got caught between the buildings, tunnelled between the garden walls, and I used the moment to sit down on the bench next to him. He straightened his back, and I wondered if his skin bristled like mine did. I had images of his skin sweating into mine while we lay on his bed, his hands on my wrist and my hips bucking against his body in the darkness. I didn't tell him about the hospital or the Laguna Highway.

"When's your court date?" I said.

"Two weeks," he said, and blinked.

"She was upset. She was driving too fast," I said, but the words felt irrelevant. "She wasn't wearing a helmet." He didn't reply, and we sat in silence for a few minutes, an inch or so apart from each other on the bench.

"I'm so sorry," he said. "I can't even..." he trailed off.

"Don't," I said.

I offered him a cigarette. We each lit our own and stared at the wall in front of us for what seemed like ages. I tried to think of something to say, anything.

"I used to love planes when I was a kid," he said eventually. "Did I ever tell you that?"

"No," I said, turning to him.

"I used to beg people to take me to the airports on Saturdays."

"Geek," I said.

"Yeah," he said. We fell quiet again. His big hands were resting on his knees, and the fingers of my right hand, the one closest to him, stung with the proximity.

"Your socks don't match," I said to him.

"You got your rucksack back?" he said, nodding at the doodled-on school bag at my feet. I shrugged, lifting my hand from the bench for a second, but not putting it back down on his hand like I wanted to.

"I didn't have the courage to hand myself in," he said. My hand snuck a little closer to David, still resting on the bench. The tips of my fingers touched his trouser leg. I could feel his heat through the material, and he glanced down at my hand resting there.

"Why is your phone off?" I said.

"No reception," he said.

"Liar," I said.

"Let's not talk about liars," he said.

"No," I said.

"When I took Lily's photograph, years and years ago, we hardly exchanged a word. I never would have thought of her again if it wasn't for what happened on the highway. She and I were never involved, you know that?"

"Let's not talk about it now," I said.

"You shouldn't have come," he said, but he let my hand rise up and rest very lightly on top of his hand, between his fingers. My fingers looked pale, and his looked dark. His hand twitched as our skin touched, but he didn't move away. It felt like sipping water when you're thirsty, or a first cigarette of the day.

43

The windows were all boarded up, and the blonde concierge girl was long gone from the crepuscular lobby of the Pink Hotel. I breathed in a lungful of dust and flicked a light switch, which popped quickly and remained dark. In the communal area to the left of the lobby an anxious bee was jumping against gaps in the taped-up window panes, chasing little nuggets of California sunlight that were subsumed into the darkness almost as soon as they touched it. The beat-up-looking sofas were still there in the corner of the large room, but the vending machines and television were gone. The floorboards were covered in cigarette butts and broken glass, which crackled against the bottom of my trainers when I walked over them.

In the corner was where one of the bathtubs full of ice and beer had been during Lily's wake. You could still see little paw prints in the wood, like the tub had only been taken away recently. This was where I'd noticed a giant man drinking vodka from the bottle, and a skeletal woman dancing on her own. Over by the stairs was where I'd seen the man with the nose piercing, and the man with vivid red hair who stuck his chest out when he walked. On the windowsill at the first flight of stairs I'd seen people cutting lines of white powder with gym-membership cards, and on the first landing I'd followed the red-haired man and listened to how Lily was late for their wedding because she couldn't find appropriate underwear.

One of the stairs on the way up to the top floor was loose now, and I nearly tripped on it. I peeked into rooms where revellers had been huddled, dancing, all those nights ago, and bathrooms where people had passed out or been kissing. I found my way up towards the top of the hotel and the door marked "private", which was swinging open in the breeze from a broken window. The air smelt of seawater.

The bicycle and Rollerblades were gone from the hallway of Richard and Lily's flat, as were the lampshades and carpets and kitchen table. I felt sick as I opened her bedroom door and saw its gutted walls. No suspender belt caught under the chair leg or mink scarf curled like roadkill on the floor next to the bed. There was no bed. No dresses and shoes flung over burgundy carpets, no overflowing ashtrays or spilt perfume. There was no gilt-framed mirror reflecting an image of me looking out of place in her world. All this emptiness, this sea air and dust, was my world.

If I could draw a map of my memories, a few years now after inheriting the Pink Hotel, I'd be careful to label things that used to be there. I'd label the erasures of my memories with as much precision as the ones that lasted. My mental map would be a lattice of tunnels leading nowhere, like to where particular kinds of now-dissolved hatred and nervousness and self-harm used to be, or to where memories of David linger, morphing continually, depending on my mood and on his. I'd insist on carefully labelling every shift in my feelings for David, from sitting beside him in that little Long Beach garden to the letters we wrote each other while he was in prison, to all the stupid arguments and reconciliations after that. I'd try to label the exact feeling, the terror and relief when we met up again after he got out. There would be bulldozed pleasure catalogued on my map, multi-layered incarnations of love. I'd collect my memories like he photographed the Pink Hotel as we worked on it when he came back. I'd insist on holding on to how I used to feel about Dad, too, all that vitriol and disappointment and sadness, even if we're friends again now. There would be contours on my mental cartography for Daphne, for Mary, for Sam, for Laurence and, of course, for the shifting existence of Lily. Even now I can imagine her walking around the rooms of the Pink Hotel wearing that fuchsia sundress and knee-high black boots. Sometimes I still blink, and see her smiling at me from a doorway.